CN00956579

Blue Murder

To command the International and Organised Crime branch at the heart of the CID's London operation is the dream of every Scotland Yard detective. When offered to Tommy Fox, however, it is the Met's last chance of reining in its most brilliant, single-minded and tempestuous detective before his unorthodox investigative practices overstep the mark once and for all.

But only a matter of seconds into his new job a case is handed to Commander Fox that is too inviting to leave to his subordinates. In a yacht moored off the Cyprus coast a British businessman, Michael Leighton, and his two female 'companions' have been found murdered, the victims of twenty-seven rounds from an assault rifle. With a cache of cocaine on board, it seems just another drug-smuggling murder enquiry is about to get under way – but Fox, taking personal charge of the investigation in Cyprus and London, is on the scent of something infinitely more revealing . . .

When sexually explicit videos and photographs are discovered at the dead man's company premises in Fulham, Fox and his team realise they have stumbled upon Leighton Leisure Services' profitable sideline in pornographic movies – with in-house production techniques and a Europe-wide distribution network. The star of these masterpieces? None other than the late, and apparently rather energetic, Mr Michael Leighton himself. And the recent death of a young woman in suspicious circumstances raises the heat of the investigation further, particularly as enquiries show she was the daughter of one of Fox's oldest and most slippery adversaries in the criminal underworld.

Despite uncovering a plethora of suspects, the vice trade is proving a difficult nut for Fox to crack in the hunt for a triple-murderer, who may be covering his tracks by killing again; but as its co-ordinator and chief investigator, there is no better man than Tommy Fox in getting to the bottom of this case's decidedly murky depths . . .

By the same author

THE COLD LIGHT OF DAWN
CONFIRM OR DENY
THE HOME SECRETARY WILL SEE YOU NOW
A DAMNED SERIOUS BUSINESS
LEAD ME TO THE SLAUGHTER
THE LAUNDRY MAN
TOMFOOLERY
SNOWDROP
THE TAMING OF TANGO HARRIS
UNDERNEATH THE ARCHES
ROUGH DIAMONDS

BLUE MURDER

GRAHAM ISON

LITTLE, BROWN AND COMPANY

A *Little, Brown* Book

First published in Great Britain in 1996
by Little, Brown and Company

A CIP catalogue record for this book
is available from the British Library.

ISBN 0 316 87624 0

Typeset by Palimpsest Book Production Limited,
Polmont, Stirlingshire
Printed and bound in Great Britain by
Hartnolls Limited, Bodmin, Cornwall

Little, Brown and Company (UK)
Brettenham House
Lancaster Place
London WC2E 7EN

Blue Murder

ONE

THE WHITE-HULLED YACHT LAY at anchor, rising and falling in the gentle swell like a breathing thing. The fierce Mediterranean sun glinted on its brass deck fittings and on the glass in its scuttles, and its Red Ensign hung listlessly at the after jack-staff.

The pilot of the RAF fighter had noticed it on his way out from the base at Akrotiri in Cyprus and now noticed it again on his way back. He made a few circuits but could see no sign of life. He jotted a note on the pad at his knee, shrugged and turned for home. At the routine debriefing, the pilot mentioned the yacht and gave its position in technical navigational terms. Put simply, the vessel was lying some 50 miles west-south-west of Ktima, about 100 miles south of the nearest point in Turkey and a good 250 miles north of Baltim on the coast of Egypt.

In central London, the temperature had soared until it was only about three degrees cooler than it was in Cyprus and a pollution haze hung over the capital. Men abandoned their ties and carried their jackets, and women were wearing the lightest of clothing, in an attempt to combat the oppressive heat. Diesel fumes dominated the air and everything felt dirty and sticky.

At New Scotland Yard, the flag on top of the Victoria Block also hung listlessly. It was not every day that the Metropolitan Police flew the Union Flag from its headquarters, but today was the first of July, the birthday of the Princess of Wales.

On the fifth floor of that building, Detective Chief Superintendent Thomas Fox of the Flying Squad was waiting impatiently to see the Assistant Commissioner.

Immaculately dressed as always, Fox fidgeted at the delay, but Peter Frobisher was as noted for his lack of punctuality as Fox was renowned for his sartorial elegance, and his toughness; the story of the award of his Queen's Gallantry Medal for disarming a dangerous criminal who had threatened him with a firearm was well known at the Yard. And of late it seemed that Fox was beginning to make a habit of such behaviour.

A buzzer sounded and the senior of Frobisher's two secretaries looked up. 'The Assistant Commissioner will see you now, Mr Fox,' she said and turned to pour herself a cup of coffee from the machine that stood on the housing of the air-conditioning unit.

''Bout time,' muttered Fox and strode the two paces to the door of Frobisher's office. Tapping lightly and not waiting for a reply, he entered.

'Ah, Mr Fox, so sorry to have kept you waiting.' With a beaming smile on his face, the Assistant Commissioner skirted his desk and shook hands. 'Do sit down.'

'Thank you, sir.' Fox waited until Frobisher had seated himself in one of the two armchairs and then sat in the other, gently easing the cloth of his Hackett suit over his knees.

'Well now, Mr Fox . . .' The AC rubbed his hands together vigorously. 'Two items of good news. Very good news, in fact. The first is that you are to be awarded a bar to your Queen's Gallantry Medal for your disarming of that man down at Barnes recently.' He paused, briefly. 'That was the night you got shot, of course.'

'Yes, I do remember that, sir,' said Fox, not bothering too much to keep the sarcasm from his voice. It had been a well-publicised siege that had resulted not only in Fox receiving a bullet in the shoulder but in the death of the man who had fired it.

'Many, many congratulations, Mr Fox. And well done.'

'And the second item, sir?'

'The second item is that you are to be promoted to commander. Forthwith.' Frobisher sat back in his chair and gazed steadily at the head of the Flying Squad.

Fox had received hints about the bar to his QGM, and the announcement of its award came as no great surprise to him. But the AC's second statement was a shock. Since the reorganisation of the Metropolitan Police and the consequent abolition of the ranks of deputy assistant commissioner and chief superintendent, Fox had expected to be made redundant. Deep down he had thought that the hierarchy of the service would be unable to resist the opportunity to get rid of him; he knew that for years he had been regarded in certain quarters as somewhat of a maverick who no longer fitted the approved pattern of how the modern detective should go about his duties. But now this. 'Where am I going, sir?' Fox had visions of being moved out of the Yard and worse, out of the Criminal Investigation Department, perhaps to a uniformed job in some backwater there to spend all day playing with paper.

'I am giving you command of SO1 Branch, Mr Fox.'

'I see.' Fox spoke calmly, but he could not believe his luck. SO1 Branch – the International and Organised Crime Branch – was in Fox's view, the most important. At the very hub of CID operations in London, its command was the goal of every ambitious detective. Although officially styled Commander SO1, Fox would also be in charge of several other branches, including the Crime Operations Group and Firearms Branch. And the Flying Squad.

Frobisher was ahead of him, and sighed. He somehow knew he was making a mistake. 'Yes, Mr Fox, it means that you'll still have overall charge of your beloved Flying Squad, but Detective Superintendent Brace will take over its operational command. However, there is one thing that must be clearly understood, and that is that your days of active investigation are over. There'll be no more running about London clearing up crimes. That will be a matter for your subordinates. Under your direction of course. Your task will be to remain here, at Scotland Yard, fulfilling your administrative and supervisory responsibilities. I do hope that you understand that, very clearly.' Frobisher smiled owlishly.

'Of course, sir,' said Fox, who had no intention of changing the working practices of twenty-five years.

'The pen, Mr Fox,' continued Frobisher airily, 'is mightier than the sword, as they say.' He stood up and shook hands once more. 'And how is Lady Jane?'

'She's very well, sir,' said Fox tersely. His relationship with Lady Jane Sims had begun a year and a half previously when he had investigated the murder of Jane's sister, Lady Dawn Sims, but he resented his colleagues' interest in the girl whom they called, to her delight and Fox's irritation, 'Lady Guv'.

'Good, good,' said Frobisher, and taking advantage of his rank, added, 'time you made an honest woman of her, you know.' But sensing immediately that he might have offended his newest commander, hurried on. 'Well, Mr Fox, I mustn't take up any more of your time. You'll be wanting to get to work in your new appointment straightaway. You probably don't know, but Alec Myers was discharged this morning on ill-health grounds.'

'I'm sorry to hear that, sir,' said Fox. Myers, the previous Commander SO1 had been Fox's immediate boss, but he had been troubled with angina for some time now.

As Fox stood up and turned to leave, Frobisher spoke again. 'Oh, I almost forgot . . .' He picked up a file from his desk. 'There has been a triple murder on a British-registered yacht off Cyprus. The Foreign and Commonwealth Office have asked us to investigate.'

Fox took the file. 'Why us, sir?' he asked. 'What's wrong with the Cyprus Police?'

Frobisher smiled patronisingly. 'It was in international waters, Mr Fox. And as the yacht and the victims are British, they declined to take it on. It's all a question of money, you see. Everything seems to be ruled by budgets these days.'

'Yes, I'd noticed,' said Fox drily. As operational head of the Flying Squad, he had frequently been reminded that its overtime bill was exceeding budgetary limits. Fox had responded by saying that so was crime.

Fox's new office was only a few doors down from the Assistant Commissioner's, on the opposite side of the corridor. And that did not please him one little bit; he didn't like being too close to the hierarchy. In a row along one wall of the office hung a gallery of framed photographs of his predecessors. Fox made a sour face and determined to have them all removed at the earliest opportunity. But now there were more pressing things that required his attention.

Going down to the Murder Room, three floors below his own office, Fox flung open the door. The detective inspector on duty was standing by a filing cabinet. 'Good morning, sir.'

'Good morning.' Fox nodded a brief acknowledgement and glanced around the office. Its walls were hung with shields presented by visiting detectives, and framed certificates of commendation and achievement bestowed by such wide-ranging dignitaries as the Director of the FBI and the Chief of Police of the Turks and Caicos Islands. Fox sniffed; that sort of corporate machismo did not appeal to him. 'Who's next on the list?' he asked.

The DI knew exactly what Fox meant and stepped across to a grid on the wall. 'Next in the frame is Detective Superintendent Craven-Foster, sir,' he said.

'Get hold of him and ask him to see me. Now.'

'Yes, sir,' said the DI, and looked slightly puzzled that the request should have come from an officer he believed still to be the Chief Superintendent of the Flying Squad.

One of the advantages stemming from the abolition of the post of DACSO – as the Deputy Assistant Commissioner Specialist Operations had been known – was that Fox, as the new commander of SO1 Branch, inherited Dick Campbell's secretary, Brenda. As in most large organisations, secretaries were as useful for their information-gathering as for their office skills. Brenda was no exception; in the time it had taken

Fox to visit the Murder Room, Peter Frobisher's secretary had been on the phone to her, advising her who her new boss was. The result was that the secretaries knew of Fox's appointment before the detectives who were to work for him.

'I thought you might like a cup of coffee, Mr Fox.' Brenda placed a mug on Fox's desk.

Fox frowned at it. 'Is that instant coffee?' he asked.

'Yes, it is.' Brenda sounded defensive.

'Well from today there's a new rule in this branch, Brenda. The commander drinks only ground coffee, prepared in a *cafetière,* and served in a bone china cup.' And just so that there would be no misunderstanding, he added, 'And saucer.'

Brenda looked distressed. 'But we don't have a *cafetière,* Mr Fox,' she said.

Fox took his silver bill-clip from his pocket and handed his new secretary a fifty-pound note. 'Perhaps you'd pop over to the Army and Navy Stores and get us equipped then,' he said and smiled at the girl. 'Mr Campbell may not have had any style,' he continued, 'but I do.'

Brenda smiled, picked up the offending mug of instant coffee and left the office. She had a feeling that she and the new commander were going to get on.

'Is Mr Fox in there, Brenda?' The tall figure of Detective Superintendent Craven-Foster had been searching the Yard for Fox, going first to the Flying Squad office on the second floor. Eventually he learned that he was in the commander's office on the fifth.

'Yes, he is,' said Brenda.

Craven-Foster tapped lightly at Fox's door and entered. 'Morning, sir. I understand you wanted to see me. I'm next on the list.' He was as puzzled as the DI in the Murder Room had been, as to why Fox had assumed the duties of the Commander SO1 Branch.

'There's a job in Cyprus,' said Fox without preamble, and pushed the file across the desk. 'Three murders on a yacht somewhere in the middle of the Mediterranean. Apparently it's in international waters and the Cyprus Police can't be bothered to investigate it. Probably too difficult for them,' he added.

'You want me to take it on, sir?'

'That's the general idea, Mr Foster,' said Fox. 'Does that present you with a problem?'

Craven-Foster looked slightly pained at the foreshortening of his name. 'No, sir, but I just wondered why the Flying Squad should have got it in the first place.'

'What makes you think that the Flying Squad got it in the first place?' Fox inclined his head in an expression of patient expectation.

'Well, as you're the DCS in charge of the Squad, sir, I thought—'

'Wrong!' said Fox. 'I am the Commander SO1. As of now. Next question?' He grinned at the expression on the detective superintendent's face.

Craven-Foster gulped slightly as he grasped the full implications of Fox's statement. He knew of Tommy Fox's reputation, knew that he was a hard and often irascible taskmaster, and not above interfering in every aspect of an investigation. The only advantage of the case that he had just been assigned, he thought, was that it was likely to be too far away from Scotland Yard for Fox to interfere. But he didn't know Fox that well.

'I shall telephone the Chief Constable of the Sovereign Base Areas of Cyprus,' Fox continued, 'and ask for you to be given all possible assistance, but I would be inclined not to use local scientific support. It creates the problem of getting witnesses over here when eventually we go to court.'

'If we go to court,' said Craven-Foster unwisely.

'Oh, we'll go to court,' said Fox. 'Be under no illusions about that. Any questions?'

'No, sir.'

'Well, I have,' said Fox. 'Is your name really Craven Foster?'

'It's John Craven-Foster, sir.'

'Really?'

'It's hyphenated, sir.'

'Amazing,' said Fox.

'What is, sir?' asked Craven-Foster.

'That you're not in Special Branch,' said Fox. It was a standing joke at the Yard that officers with hyphenated or double-barrelled names automatically joined Special Branch.

Brenda entered Fox's office silently and placed a cup and saucer on his desk. 'A cup of *ground* coffee, Mr Fox,' she said. 'In a bone china cup and saucer.'

'Splendid,' said Fox. 'Er, did I give you enough money?'

'No, Mr Fox, you owe me another five pounds,' said Brenda. 'Plus the cost of the coffee itself, of course.'

The discussions about Fox's future which had taken place between Peter Frobisher, the Assistant Commissioner Specialist Operations, and Sir James Gilmore, the Commissioner, had raged for some time. Despite his pomposity, and his carefully cultivated accent, Frobisher was a detective, and had been a good one in his younger days. Gilmore, however, had risen through the ranks of the Uniform Branch and always regarded CID officers with a measure of suspicion. Particularly CID officers of Fox's calibre. But Frobisher knew Fox's worth and knew also that the Metropolitan Police, particularly at this time in its history, could not afford to lose men of his experience and expertise. Frobisher had recommended Fox for promotion to commander on the grounds that it would have the effect of retaining his services while curbing his personal involvement in criminal investigation. The Commissioner certainly agreed that the latter would be beneficial; he firmly believed that it was unseemly for so senior an officer to be marauding around the capital mixing with villains. But then Sir James Gilmore had curious ideas about the status of senior police officers. He mistakenly believed that their elevation to high rank automatically turned them into gentlemen and, if he thought he could have got away with it, would have introduced an officers' mess at the Yard.

At the end of the discussion, Frobisher had won the day and Gilmore agreed, albeit reluctantly, to recommend Fox's promotion to the Home Secretary.

On the day after Fox's appointment as commander – and on the day after SO1 Branch had been assigned the triple murder in Cyprus – the Assistant Commissioner flicked down the switch of his office intercom. 'Ask Commander Fox to see me,' he said to his secretary.

Minutes later, the girl called back. 'Commander Fox's secretary says that he left for Cyprus earlier today, sir.'

TWO

FOX HAD FRETTED FOR THE rest of the afternoon. Three bodies, his first murders since taking command of SO1 Branch, rested in a mortuary in Cyprus; and he was about to send a detective superintendent whom he didn't really know, two thousand miles to enquire into their deaths. He had heard of Craven-Foster, naturally – the senior officers of the CID, even in London, were a fairly close-knit band – but he had no personal experience of the man's skills. Eventually, Fox had convinced himself that, in the circumstances, he should take personal charge of the investigation. Although he should have sought the Assistant Commissioner's permission to go abroad, he decided, now he was a commander, that he could give himself the necessary authority. Sworn to secrecy, at least until he had gone, Brenda was instructed to make the necessary reservations on the first flight out.

The following morning, Fox had appeared briefly at the Yard and then he, Craven-Foster and Detective Inspector Charles Morgan, had been driven to Gatwick Airport where they boarded the 1345 flight for Paphos International. With the two hours' time difference they had arrived at 8.15 p.m. local time.

The Chief Constable of the Sovereign Base Areas Police, Geoffrey Harding, was there to meet them. A former detective superintendent in a county force in England, Harding had personally driven them the forty-odd miles to the RAF base at Akrotiri where he had made arrangements for them to be accommodated.

'An RAF pilot spotted the yacht, Commander,' said

Harding as he drove, 'and we imposed on the Cyprus Navy to investigate. When they found that it contained three dead bodies, they brought it into the harbour at Paphos where the Cyprus Police have it under guard. The bodies have been taken to the Princess Mary Military Hospital.' He glanced sideways at Fox. 'In this heat it was essential to move them immediately but, apart from that, we have preserved the scene.'

'Thanks very much,' said Fox. It was the best he could hope for. The main reason he had decided to come to Cyprus himself was his concern for the scientific evidence, and he didn't want amateurs crawling all over the vessel in which the victims had been discovered. At least Harding was a professional and that was a great comfort.

Early the next day, Fox and the two other members of the team began their enquiries by paying a visit to the mortuary.

'Clearly been shot, sir,' said Detective Superintendent Craven-Foster, gazing down at the body of a young woman, one of the three victims.

'An extraordinarily astute observation, John,' said Fox, wondering whether his detective superintendent was being sarcastic, 'on account of the number of holes in her.' In Fox's estimation, the woman's body had been struck by at least five rounds, but he knew better than to speculate further. The most pressing decision he now had to make was whether to ship the bodies back to the United Kingdom or to have them examined locally. But Fox did not intend to have what he scathingly described as 'local GPs' carrying out autopsies. Even the highly-qualified RAF doctors at the Princess Mary hospital were unlikely to count a skilled forensic pathologist among their number.

Having afforded the other two bodies – a man and an older woman – a cursory glance, and having come to the conclusion that they too had been shot, Fox returned to the headquarters of the Sovereign Base Areas Police at Episkopi and telephoned the Murder Room at Scotland Yard. His message was terse and to the point. 'Get a Home Office pathologist out here on the next available flight,' he said. 'Preferably Pamela Hatcher.'

'Very good, sir,' said the duty DI. 'By the way, sir, the Assistant Commissioner would like a word with you. I gather he's a bit upset.'

Fox shook the receiver vigorously before putting it to his ear again. 'Hallo, hallo,' he said, 'I seem to have been cut off.' He replaced the receiver on its base. 'Line to London's terrible,' he added, turning to Craven-Foster. 'Now then, I suggest we go and take a look at the yacht.'

The arrival of three Scotland Yard officers to investigate a triple murder had been a big event in the daily routine of the Sovereign Base Areas Police, and the Chief Constable had unhesitatingly offered Fox and his colleagues all the assistance they might need. First on Fox's list of requirements had been a car and driver, and Geoffrey Harding had charitably assigned his own. Then he had telephoned the local police and arranged for a launch to meet the three officers and take them to the yacht.

'Good job Swann can't see that,' said Fox, nodding at the flag on the bonnet, 'he'd want one too.' The lugubrious Swann, who had been Fox's driver on the Flying Squad, thought that he had escaped when Fox was promoted, but had found the very next morning that nothing had changed when he was required to drive Fox and the other two to Gatwick. But there had been no need to take Swann to Cyprus, and Fox merely cautioned him not to lose too much at cards during his absence.

The promised police launch was waiting at the quayside and ferried Fox – now sporting a panama hat – Craven-Foster and Morgan out to the yacht, guarded by a Cypriot policeman, that lay at anchor in the centre of the small harbour at Paphos. The Cyprus Police had moored it offshore to prevent interested locals – and tourists, who were there in profusion – from getting close to it.

On the door of the hatchway leading below was a small red sign: a circle around a drawing of a bikini with a diagonal line through it. Fox glanced around the saloon. In the centre of the spacious accommodation was a long table. A chair lay on its side and there were several heavy bloodstains on the carpet. But the thing that interested Fox was the expensive wood panelling on the bulkhead of the cabin, much of which was splintered and torn.

'At a rough guess,' said Fox, fanning himself with his hat, 'I'd say that the maniac who committed these murders was armed with a machine-gun of some sort.'

'There appear to be one or two rounds in the deckhead, too, sir,' said Craven-Foster, glancing upwards. 'Bloody shame, really, ruining a vessel like this. Must be worth all of a hundred grand.' He looked around admiringly. 'Deep "V" type,' he added. 'Capable of cruising at about twenty knots, I should think.'

Fox shot a suspicious glance at the detective superintendent. 'You know about these things, do you, John?' he asked.

Craven-Foster smiled smugly, the sort of smile that amateur yachtsmen reserve for those they regard as 'landlubbers'. 'I've done a bit, sir, but nothing breath-taking. I've got a Corribee down at Emsworth. When I manage to get away,' he added.

'Have you really?' Firmly convinced that anything connected with boats was highly expensive, Fox briefly wondered how Craven-Foster could afford such luxuries on his pay. 'You've just got yourself a job then,' he said. 'As you're so well-versed in this nautical business, you can find out where this yacht came from, where it was going and who it belongs to.'

'Do we have a look round, sir?' asked Morgan.

'No, Charles, we do not have a look round,' said Fox. 'Not until a scientific team from the Yard has been over this thing with a fine-tooth comb.' He turned to Craven-Foster. 'When we get back to Akrotiri,' he added, 'get on the phone to the Murder Room and arrange for a team to be flown out. Might be a good idea to have a word with the bloke in charge of the air force here and see if he can arrange for them to be put on one of his flights. Save buggering about with that Cyprus Airlines lot.' Fox had been unimpressed by the Cypriot national airline which had flown him and his team out from London, but in all fairness they could hardly have been expected to rearrange their flight schedules just to suit a Scotland Yard commander. 'And if the DI on duty says that the Assistant Commissioner wants to talk to me, tell him you don't know where I am.'

By some miracle of administration, the team from the Metropolitan Police Forensic Science Laboratory and Pamela Hatcher, the Home Office pathologist, arrived in Cyprus late on the Saturday afternoon, within twenty-four hours of Fox having given his instructions.

Despite the lateness of the hour, Pamela Hatcher, her long grey hair braided into a pigtail as usual, was taken straight to the Princess Mary Military Hospital at Akrotiri and started work immediately. 'There's not a great deal I can tell you about time of death,' she said when she had finished her post-mortem examination of two of the bodies. 'The heat, the confined space of the yacht, the effect of salt water in the atmosphere, then the changes when the cadavers were brought ashore . . .' She laid down the instrument she had been using on the third body and shrugged. 'Anybody's guess really.'

'I'm not sure that it matters a great deal,' said Fox. 'We know that the bodies were discovered on the thirtieth of June and once we find the date of its last port of call, we can assume that the murders took place between those two dates.'

Pamela Hatcher grinned at him. 'You sound like a detective, Tommy,' she said. 'Incidentally, congratulations on your promotion.'

'Thanks,' said Fox. 'But I'd rather have stayed where I was.'

Pamela Hatcher extracted yet another round from the body of the woman on which she was working. 'That makes seventeen in all,' she said, dropping the round into a kidney-shaped dish, 'and I think that's probably the lot.'

'So what's the tally?' Fox glanced at DI Morgan.

'Seven taken from the man, six from his wife—'

'Do we know she's his wife?' asked Fox sharply, thinking that he had not been told a piece of vital information.

'Well, I assumed—'

'When you're working with me, Charles, don't assume anything,' said Fox. 'So, six from the older woman . . .'

'Yes, sir,' said Morgan, slightly abashed. 'And four from the younger woman.' He pointed at the body on the table which Pamela Hatcher was roughly sewing together.

Fox nodded. 'How many did the lab team find in the yacht?'

'A further ten, sir.'

'Extravagant bugger, this murderer of ours,' said Fox. 'Twenty-seven rounds altogether. Calibre?'

'At a guess, sir,' said Morgan cautiously, 'I'd say 7.62 millimetre.' And even more cautiously, added, 'Could have been a Kalashnikov AK 47, I suppose, sir.'

'Yes, it could,' said Fox. 'Or any one of half a dozen other automatic weapons. Ship the rounds back to the lab. We'll let Hugh Donovan take a look.' Dismissing the three dead bodies as of no further interest, he turned to Craven-Foster. 'How are the SOCOs getting on, John?'

'They'll finish tomorrow, I gather, sir.'

At five o'clock the following evening, the senior scenes-of-crime officer, accompanied by Craven-Foster and DI Morgan, came to see Fox in his room at the RAF officers' mess.

'Well, Frank, what have you to tell me?' Fox, jacket abandoned and shirt-sleeves rolled up, was sitting on his bed.

Frank Dobson, the senior SOCO, was a small man with a ginger goatee beard and a nervous cough. 'Fingermarks all over the place, Mr Fox, but until we can get them back to London, we shan't know whose they are.' And forestalling Fox's next question, hurried on. 'We've done a quick comparison with the fingerprints taken from the three bodies and most of them appear to match with the deceased.' He coughed and peered at Fox through his wire-framed spectacles. 'There are others, of course.'

'Of course,' murmured Fox. 'Anything else of great moment?'

'You know about the rounds taken from the deckhead and the bulkhead . . . ?' Dobson raised a querying eyebrow.

'Yes. Ten, I believe.'

'Yes indeed.' Dobson nodded gravely. 'There was also evidence of an attempt to start a fire on the deck of the galley, but as all the scuttles and the door were closed it looked as though it was defeated by lack of oxygen before it took a hold. But apart from that, nothing else of consequence. One or two of the lads are just doing a last round-up and I'll confirm later that we're all clear.'

'Disappointing,' said Fox who, despite his unorthodox approach to criminal investigation, still relied heavily on scientific evidence. He swung round to face Craven-Foster. 'Identities, John?'

'Frank's team found these in a drawer, sir,' said Craven-Foster, taking three passports from his briefcase and tossing them casually on to the occasional table. 'The man is Michael Leighton, aged fifty-four, the older woman is Patricia Tilley—'

'Not his wife then,' said Fox pointedly.

'No, sir, not as far as we know,' said Craven-Foster and shot a sympathetic glance at Morgan. 'She's aged forty, and the younger woman is Karen Nash, aged . . .' He paused and leaning forward flicked open one of the passports, mentally calculating as he did so. 'Thirty, sir.'

'Well, well,' said Fox, standing up. 'I suggest we go across to the mess and have a drink while we think about what to do next,' he said. He glanced at Dobson. 'Frank?'

'No, I won't, thank you, Mr Fox. Got a lot of paperwork to do if we're to get our stuff off to the lab promptly.'

'Of course,' said Fox. He put on his jacket and, donning his panama hat, led the way out of the building through the stifling heat and the all-pervading smell of kerosene to the mess.

There were one or two RAF officers at the bar when Fox and his colleagues entered, but beyond nodding and bidding them a good evening, they left the detectives to their own devices.

'What now, sir?' asked Craven-Foster when the three of them were settled at a table.

'A large Scotch, I think,' said Fox and beckoned to the steward. 'So, we have the bodies of three people, apparently unrelated one to the other. What d'you make of that?'

'Do we know that for sure, sir?' asked Morgan and wished he hadn't.

Fox cast a benevolent gaze at the detective inspector. 'Well, for a start, given that Patricia Tilley is only ten years older than Karen Nash, they're clearly not mother and daughter, but they could be sisters, I suppose. We can't tell from the passports any more, because they don't include maiden names. They don't even show marital status.' Fox frowned at what he regarded as slovenliness on the part of the Home Office. 'Furthermore, either one of the women could be married to Leighton, I suppose, now that some women decline to adopt their husband's name.'

'Perhaps it was a *ménage à trois*,' said Morgan quietly.

Fox grinned and took a sip of his whisky. 'These days, Charles,' he said, 'nothing would surprise me. However, you can take that little enquiry on, once we get back to London. Get someone to do a bit of research at St Catherine's House.' Despite the fact that the three detectives were chatting over a drink, Fox had no intention of allowing them to relax. 'What have you found out about the yacht's movements, John?' he asked, switching his gaze to Craven-Foster.

Craven-Foster pulled out a pocket book and thumbed through it. 'The yacht was refuelled in Paphos early on the morning of the thirtieth of June—'

'How early?'

'Six a.m., sir.'

Fox nodded. 'Yes, go on.'

'And having checked that the cruising speed is, as I suggested, twenty knots, we can assume that the yacht could have reached the point where it was found in just over two hours. Say two and a half to be on the safe side.'

'That's an awful lot of assuming, John,' said Fox. 'It could have called somewhere else along the Cyprus coastline before putting to sea, or it could have anchored somewhere for breakfast before going on.' He shrugged. 'But what difference does it make? It's fairly certain, I think, that we don't have a double murder followed by a suicide. Therefore, someone came aboard on the thirtieth of June – or was aboard already – and left after committing the murders.' A thought crossed his mind. 'You're the sailor, John. Was anything missing from that yacht?'

'Like what, sir?'

'Like a dinghy, or an inflatable? Something that our murderer could have used to escape.'

Craven-Foster shook his head. 'It doesn't look like it,' he said. 'There's no housing for a dinghy and the inflatable was still inboard.'

Fox glanced at the steward and signalled for another round of drinks. 'So we have someone who came aboard, committed the murders, and left again. In his own vessel.'

'Or a strong swimmer, sir,' said Morgan thoughtfully.

'One who can swim at least fifty miles,' said Fox crushingly.

'Oh,' said Morgan, 'I hadn't thought of that.'

Fox glanced across the ante-room as Frank Dobson appeared in the doorway, standing on tiptoe and nervously rubbing his hands together. 'Ah!' he said, 'Frank's decided to come for a drink after all.' And, as Dobson approached, asked, 'What'll you have, Frank?'

'Nothing, thanks, Mr Fox.'

'Well, what—?'

'I thought I'd better let you know straightaway. One of the lads found a package secreted behind the panelling on one of the bulkheads.'

'What sort of package?' Fox leaned forward and took a cigarette from the open case on the table.

'I shan't know for sure until the lab confirms it,' said Dobson, 'but I'd say it contained cocaine. About two kilos of it.'

THREE

FOX DECIDED THAT HE HAD done all he could in Cyprus. Leaving Detective Superintendent Craven-Foster and Detective Inspector Charles Morgan to make such further enquiries as were necessary on the island, Fox flew back to London. Straight into a row with the Assistant Commissioner.

'Mr Fox,' said Peter Frobisher at his icy best, 'I thought that I had made it perfectly clear that your function, as Commander SO1 was to oversee and supervise the operations of that branch. And yet, within twenty-four hours, I find that you have gone to Cyprus, actively to involve yourself in a murder investigation.'

But Fox was not to be easily browbeaten. 'I don't see how I can possibly supervise a detective superintendent whose qualities I am unfamiliar with, sir, if he is two thousand miles away from me.'

'Mr Fox,' said Frobisher patiently, 'one has to trust one's subordinates to get on with the job.'

'Exactly so, sir,' said Fox. 'And as you have given me command of SO1 I expect to be accorded that same trust.' He could be as icy as Frobisher. 'However,' he went on as the Assistant Commissioner was about to interrupt, 'we have a triple murder on our hands, assigned to us by the Foreign and Commonwealth Office. I think you would agree, sir, that we can't afford to make a bloody great balls-up of it.'

Frobisher wrinkled his nose slightly at Fox's coarseness. Since his appointment as Assistant Commissioner he had assumed an air of gentility that he thought accorded with his high office. It was a view not shared by Fox who firmly believed that a copper was a copper, no matter what. 'Exactly so, Mr Fox. But I think you should be aware that your branch deals with a great deal more than straightforward murder enquiries, and you must be here to make decisions as and when they are required to be made.'

'If you want my resignation, sir, you have only to ask,' said Fox. He had decided, early in his service, that it was of greater value to his career to have informants inside Scotland Yard than outside it, and he had quickly learned of the Commissioner's reservations about his promotion to commander.

'My dear Mr Fox, let's not be too hasty.' Frobisher could not bear the thought of the Commissioner saying 'I told you so' and, as he had undertaken to keep Fox on the straight and narrow, it would look like failure on his part if Fox were to leave the force so soon after his appointment. 'It's just that you need to be aware of your global responsibilities.'

It was unfortunate that Frobisher had selected a Police College expression to make his point. 'Overseeing my global responsibilities is exactly what I was doing, sir,' said Fox smoothly.

'Quite so,' said Frobisher and, secretly admitting defeat, asked, 'how is the enquiry going?'

'We have identified the three victims, sir, and we have established that they were almost certainly murdered with an automatic weapon of some description. We also found about two kilos of white powder that I'm fairly sure will prove to be cocaine. Incidentally, the PM showed traces of cocaine in all three bodies.'

'So we're dealing with international drug-runners, would you say?' asked Frobisher speculatively.

'No, I wouldn't, sir. Until further enquiries are made, that is an assumption I would not be prepared to make.'

'Very well, Mr Fox,' said Frobisher in a tired voice and stood up. He was fast discovering what a lot of other senior officers had discovered. That when Tommy Fox decided on a course of action, it was nigh-on impossible to persuade him otherwise. And he could hardly discipline an officer of commander rank for doing what he was paid to do, namely to investigate crime. 'Perhaps you'd keep me posted on progress.' And, as Fox reached the door, added, 'And if you intend going abroad again, perhaps you'd be so good as to advise me in advance. As a matter of courtesy.'

'Gavin, how are you getting on with the finest crime-fighting force in the world?' Fox stood nonchalantly in the doorway of the office which, until a few days ago, had been his own and glanced at the pile of files in the in-tray. 'You want to get rid of that lot,' he added.

Detective Superintendent Gavin Brace, who had been appointed to head the Flying Squad without the promotion and the money that hitherto would have gone with it, gazed sourly at his chief. 'Good morning, sir.'

'Gavin,' said Fox, advancing into the office and dropping into an armchair, 'I wonder if I can seek a favour . . .'

Brace regarded Fox suspiciously. 'You want something, sir,' he said. 'I can tell.'

Fox grinned. 'John Craven-Foster and his bag-carrier, Morgan, are still in Cyprus, but there are pressing enquiries to be undertaken here.'

'Yes, sir?' Brace felt cornered.

'I was wondering if you could lend me DI Evans and DC Ebdon for a week.' Fox paused. 'I appreciate that you are now responsible for the operations of the Flying Squad, but . . .'

'Just a week, sir?' said Brace, knowing that if Fox kept the two officers for so short a period, it would be nothing less than a miracle. In fact, it would be a miracle if he got them back at all, knowing Tommy Fox. But Fox was his commander and he had no real option but to accede to his request. 'All right, sir,' he said in resigned tones. 'A week then.'

'I owe you one, Gavin,' said Fox and with a reassuring smile wandered out of the office.

Fox glanced up as Detective Inspector Denzil Evans and Detective Constable Kate Ebdon entered his office. 'Ah!' he said, 'welcome to the Murder Squad.' And he shook hands with the two as if he had not seen them in ages.

'Mr Brace said that we'd been assigned to you for a week, sir,' said Evans, who had given up all hopes of ever escaping Fox's clutches.

'Probably be more than a week, Denzil,' said Fox. 'Incidentally, congratulations on getting through the board.'

'Thank you, sir.' Evans had recently been advised that he had been selected for promotion to detective chief inspector and now had an awful foreboding that the implementation of that promotion would be accompanied by a transfer to SO1 Branch. Not that it made a great deal of difference: even if he stayed where he was, Fox would still be his commander.

'I want you to set up an incident room, Denzil, and deal with the London end of the enquiries that Mr Craven-Foster is, at this moment, conducting in Cyprus.' And he gave the two officers a résumé of what had happened so far. 'The most important thing is to find out as much as possible about Michael Leighton, and the two women who were found with him, Patricia Tilley and Karen Nash.'

Evans was no longer surprised at Fox's ability to recall names without reference to any notes. He just nodded. 'Yes, sir,' he said. 'Is there a docket?'

'Of course there's a docket, Denzil. It's in the Murder Room.'

'Well, Tommy,' said Hugh Donovan, the senior ballistics officer at the Metropolitan Police Laboratory, 'your DI Morgan was certainly right about the rounds found in the bodies and in the panelling of the yacht. They were 7.62 millimetre.' He moved two Webley pistols from a chair. 'Have a seat.'

'From a Kalashnikov AK 47?'

'Possibly. There are a couple of other Russian-made assault rifles that take that calibre, and even a couple of Chinese jobs, but until you find the actual weapon, we shan't know. But the ammunition appeared to be quite old. But then, so is the AK 47.'

'Thanks a lot,' said Fox drily. 'So we're no further forward.'

Donovan grinned. 'The impossible we do at once, Tommy—' he began.

'Yes, I know,' said Fox. 'Miracles take a little longer.'

Detective Constable Kate Ebdon was Australian. She had flame-red hair, usually tied back in a pony-tail, and normally wore tight-fitting jeans and a white shirt. And she terrified villains. Now with six or so years' service in the Metropolitan Police, she had learned the trade of thief-taking on Leman Street Division in the East End of London. Then she had come to Tommy Fox's notice and he had engineered her transfer to the Flying Squad.

Sitting now at the Police National Computer in a fully-staffed incident room, she fed in the three victims' names and dates of birth, which had been recorded on the passports found on the yacht, only to discover that they were neither known to the police nor wanted by them. Mouthing a peculiarly Australian obscenity, she turned next to that handy book of reference, the London telephone directory. But there were so many people called M. Leighton, P. Tilley and K. Nash that she knew there had to be an easier way. 'Guv, have we got details of the boat that these bodies were found in?' she asked, turning to DI Evans.

'All in the docket,' said Evans, tossing a file on to Kate's desk. 'Why?'

'I'm sure I've read somewhere about a register of yachts, or some damned thing. Thought it might be a good place to start tracking this Leighton finger.' Kate was an impatient woman and although urgent enquiries were being made at the Passport Office to find out where the victims had lived, those enquiries had yet to produce a result. And even when they did, the addresses might no longer be current.

Evans dropped his pen on the desk and looked up. 'There are two registers,' he said. 'It could be listed either with the Registrar of British Ships at whichever port Leighton chose, or it could be on the Small Ships Register. I think the Royal Yachting Association runs that.'

'Right,' said Kate.

'On the other hand, it might not be registered at all.'

'Oh, terrific.'

'But as it's gone foreign, it's almost bound to be,' said Evans with a grin.

A few telephone calls later and Kate Ebdon had an answer. The yacht was, in fact, registered in Michael Leighton's name, with an address in Chelsea.

'Good,' said Evans. And tiring of his paperwork, added, 'We'll go and see if there's anyone there.'

The address that the Small Ships Register had recorded for Leighton was a block of luxury flats not far from the Kings Road. The woman who answered the door was about fifty, and had straight shoulder-length blonde hair that, over the years, had clearly been prey to both the sun and a bleaching agent. She wore hardly any make-up and her skin was lined and tanned as a result of countless hours of exposure to ultraviolet rays, on both beaches and sun-beds. She was clothed in a shapeless calf-length beige linen dress. 'Yes?' she said, peering closely at her two callers. Kate reckoned she was too vain to wear glasses.

'We're police officers, madam,' said Evans. 'Does Mr Leighton live here?'

'Yes.' The woman made no attempt to open the door wider.

'Are you Mrs Leighton?' asked Evans patiently.

'Yes.'

'I see.' Evans produced his warrant card in an attempt to allay the woman's obvious doubts about their identity. 'D'you think we could come in, Mrs Leighton?'

'What's it about?'

'It's about his yacht,' said Evans, not wishing to discuss her husband's death on the doorstep.

'Oh, that. Yes, all right.' Mrs Leighton turned away from the door and led the way into the flat, leaving Kate to close the front door. The sitting room, of which Fox would whole-heartedly have approved, was dominated by a large Chinese rug and opulently furnished with genuine antiques.

'You'd better sit down.' Mrs Leighton spoke grudgingly as though wondering whether the sort of clothing that police persons wore might sully her furniture. 'What about the yacht?'

'Do you know where Mr Leighton is?' asked Evans, avoiding the woman's question.

'Yes, of course I do.' Mrs Leighton looked from Evans to Kate Ebdon and back again, all the time her face wearing a supercilious expression. 'He's up north on business.'

'Do you happen to know a Patricia Tilley or a Karen Nash?'

'No, I've never heard of them.' At that moment, the telephone rang and Mrs Leighton rose quickly to her feet. 'Excuse me,' she said and walked out into the hall to answer it.

Kate Ebdon had looked carefully around the room the moment that she had entered it, and had spotted a pile of letters on a writing table. Now she was out of her chair in a flash and across the room. Quickly riffling through the letters, she let out a subdued expression of disappointment. 'Nothing there of interest,' she said, and promptly sat down again just as Mrs Leighton re-entered the room.

'So you've not heard of either of these two women then?' Kate now took up the questioning.

Mrs Leighton looked askance at Kate Ebdon's Australian accent. 'That's what I said.' She spoke disdainfully as if implying that the police were either doubting her word or were rather stupid.

Evans was puzzled. The triple murder on a yacht off Cyprus had been headline news, and he concluded that Mrs Leighton was one of those rare people who neither watched the television nor read newspapers. Not that the names of the victims had been released, but he thought that she might just have wondered if the yacht was her husband's.

'What exactly is this all about?' Slowly Mrs Leighton's curiosity was getting the better of her.

'A yacht registered in the name of Michael Leighton was found off Cyprus a few days ago—' began Evans tentatively.

'Found? Found? What d'you mean, found?' For the first time there was an element of uncertainty, concern even, in the woman's voice.

'Exactly what I say, Mrs Leighton. The yacht was found off Cyprus. There were three dead bodies on board. I'm afraid Mr Leighton was one of them and Patricia Tilley and Karen Nash were the other two. They had all been murdered.'

Mrs Leighton gave a little gasp and rolled gracefully off her chair to the floor.

''Struth, she's bloody fainted,' said Kate, desperately trying to recall her first-aid training. She knelt down and put a cushion under the woman's head before loosening her clothing and dashing into the kitchen to get a glass of water.

Mrs Leighton recovered consciousness quickly and stared briefly at Kate. 'What happened?' she asked.

'Nothing to worry about, Mrs Leighton,' said Kate. 'You fainted, that's all. Here, let me help you up.' She assisted Mrs Leighton back into her chair.

Kate was all for pursuing her questioning, but the wiser counsels of Denzil Evans prevailed. He knew all about complaints from witnesses – and, at the moment, that is all Mrs Leighton was – who claimed to have been harried by the police. And right now, Leighton's widow was in no fit state to be questioned.

'I think we'd better come back another time,' said Evans, 'when you're feeling a little better. Are you going to be all right, or would you like me to get a neighbour in?'

'Certainly not.' Mrs Leighton spoke sharply, her self-assurance immediately returning. 'I'm quite recovered, thank you. I rather think perhaps it's a little too hot in here.'

'We'll come back and see you tomorrow then, if we may,' said Evans.

FOUR

'IT SEEMS STRANGE THAT SHE asked no questions about her husband's death,' said Fox. 'How it happened or what the circumstances were.' He was seated behind his desk playing with a paper-clip on the end of his letter-opener. 'She just fainted and then recovered almost immediately, you say?'

'Yes, sir,' said Denzil Evans. He and Kate Ebdon were briefing Fox on their interview with Mrs Leighton.

'No expression of astonishment that he should have been floating round the Med with two women she'd never heard of, when she thought he was up north on business.'

'That's about the strength of it, sir,' said Kate. 'As Mr Evans said, she came back to life pretty bloody quick and was her usual arsey self again.'

Fox slid the paper-clip into a small pot of other paper-clips and put down the letter-opener. 'Go back and see her this morning, Kate,' he said, 'on your own. See if you can get alongside her. I've got a feeling that she knows more than she's telling. Turn on that Australian charm of yours and see if you can get her talking. Woman to woman.'

'She's not a woman, she's a bloody Amazon,' said Kate.

When Kate Ebdon arrived at the Leightons' flat in Chelsea, Carol Leighton was wearing a plum-coloured velvet leisure suit. And this morning, she wore make-up and had painted her finger-nails bright red so that they looked like scarlet talons.

'Oh, it's you,' said Mrs Leighton and with an obvious air of reluctance, admitted the young woman detective. With a languid gesture of her right hand, she invited Kate to sit down and then sat opposite her, composing herself in the centre of the settee and crossing her legs. After a moment's hesitation, she reached forward and took a cigarette from a box on a low occasional table and fitted it into an amber holder. Then she picked up a table-lighter and applied a flame to the end of the cigarette. She did not offer one to Kate, but sat back in the settee, crossing her legs again and cupping the elbow of the arm that held the cigarette-holder with her other hand so that she was tightly bunched.

'You said yesterday, Mrs Leighton, that you believed your husband to be up north on business.'

'Yes.'

'So it was something of a surprise to learn that he was on his yacht in the Mediterranean.'

'Obviously.'

Conscious that she was dealing with a newly-bereaved widow, Kate nonetheless had an overwhelming desire to reach across and slap this haughty woman's face. But she knew that she was unlikely to get any information from her other than by patient questioning. 'Did he tell you what he was supposed to be doing up north? Where up north, incidentally?'

'Manchester. And no, he didn't say. Michael never discussed his business with me.'

'What was his business, Mrs Leighton?' Kate was beginning to think that if she had possessed a cut-glass accent that matched Mrs Leighton's, she might get more out of her.

'I'm afraid I don't really know.'

'You don't know?' Kate sounded incredulous. She did not believe that this woman could be married to a man without knowing what he did to acquire the obvious wealth that she enjoyed.

'No.'

Kate's patience finally snapped. She leaned forward, resting her elbows on her denim-clad knees and linking her hands loosely together. 'Look, Mrs Leighton,' she said in a quietly menacing voice, 'we are trying to discover who murdered your husband. Right now, all we know is that he and two women about whom we know next to nothing, were gunned down aboard his yacht. You're the only person who knew him that we've been able to trace. We need to know a hell of a lot more about him and his way of life if we're to stand any chance of finding his killer. Or don't you care?'

Carol Leighton suddenly dissolved into tears, her whole body shaking with emotion. Cigarette ash fell on to her trousers, but she seemed not to notice. And her mascara began to run. Within seconds she looked very old.

'Here, hold up, for Christ's sake,' said Kate, leaning across and taking the cigarette-holder from the woman. 'You'll bloody set fire to yourself.'

Carol Leighton pulled a handful of tissues from her pocket and began to dab her eyes. 'I'm sorry,' she said, her voice muffled.

Kate was not sure whether it had been her own sudden aggressiveness, or Mrs Leighton's delayed reaction to her husband's death, that had caused the woman to break down, but she knew how to handle it. Standing up, she looked around the room until she saw the drinks cabinet. She found a bottle of brandy and poured a stiff measure into a tumbler. 'Here, drink this,' she said, handing the glass to the distraught woman.

'Thank you.' Mrs Leighton gulped down the fiery spirit, put the empty glass on the table and picked up the cigarette-holder that Kate had laid in the ashtray. 'It's not what you think, you know.'

'I don't know what I think,' said Kate. 'But you tell me what you think I think.' She grinned at Carol Leighton, trying to make her remark sound like a joke.

'I haven't seen Michael for about three months now. He walked out on me in April. We'd had a row – another row – and that was that.'

It seemed to Kate that Carol Leighton's earlier hauteur had been a defence against prying questions, including those from the police. 'What was the row about?' she asked.

'Women.' Mrs Leighton leaned forward and carefully

removed the half-smoked cigarette from its holder and stubbed it out in the ashtray.

'Were Patricia Tilley and Karen Nash two of them?'

'Probably.' Carol Leighton sounded resigned. 'I said yesterday that I'd never heard of them and I haven't. They were probably just two more in the long line of his fancy women.' She laughed, a short humourless laugh. 'Looks as though the poor bitches paid a high price for his company,' she said.

'So there was no truth in your statement that he was up north on business, Mrs Leighton.'

Carol Leighton shot the detective a sharp glance as though she was about to resume her previous arrogance. But then she relented. 'I had to say something, didn't I?' she said. 'Are you married?'

'No,' said Kate.

'Wise girl. Well, it's a very private thing, marriage, or it ought to be. At least in my book. I hate having to admit that ours was a disaster. I don't know why but people always seem to blame the wife, as though a man running off with another woman is a result of his wife's inadequacy in some way.' Carol held a tissue to her nose and sniffed. 'It's a damned unfair world,' she said.

'D'you still maintain that you knew nothing of his business?' asked Kate.

'He was the managing director of a company that marketed fruit machines and juke-boxes. That kind of thing.' Carol Leighton glanced up at the young Australian, as though willing her to understand what she was to say next. 'It's not the sort of business you can be proud of,' she said. 'Not the sort of thing you can boast to your friends about.'

That sort of pretentiousness was completely alien to Kate Ebdon, but she confined herself to asking where the firm had its offices.

'You'll find a business card over there.' Carol Leighton pointed to the writing table.

'D'you know the names of any of the others?' asked Kate as she sat down again.

'The others?' Leighton's widow appeared mystified by the question.

'Yeah, the other women in your husband's life.'

'Oh, I see. No, I'm sorry, I don't.'

'How did you know of their existence then?'

Carol Leighton smiled condescendingly. 'When one is married to a philanderer,' she said, 'one knows instinctively when he's seeing other women. Surely I don't have to spell it out to you, do I?'

'No, I guess not,' said Kate.

'He was a cruel man, too.' Leighton's widow looked into the middle distance, recalling the agony of their life together. 'He would beat me, quite savagely at times, and tell me that I wasn't as good in bed as some of his other conquests. But it was the mental cruelty more than the physical that really got me down. I even heard that he'd been kerb-crawling in King's Cross once.'

'Oh? How did you know that? Was he arrested?' Kate immediately thought back to her search of police records. But these days, he would probably have been cautioned, and that was likely to be recorded only at the police station which dealt with him. But she made a mental note to check with King's Cross. If Michael Leighton had been looking for prostitutes once, it was likely that he'd done it before. And since.

'I shouldn't think so. He was far too clever for that.'

'How did you know then?'

'A friend rang me and told me. She and her husband were driving through the area late one night and they saw our car. There was some awful woman in a mini-skirt leaning through the window, talking to Michael.'

Kate stood up. She had decided that she was not going to get any more out of Carol Leighton for the time being. 'I might have to come back and see you again, Mrs Leighton,' she said and paused. 'There'll be the question of the funeral, too, once the coroner has released the bodies. If I can be of any help, give me a ring.' She took a card from her pocket and quickly amending the telephone extension to that of the incident room at the Yard, laid it on the table. 'Are you going to be all right?'

Carol Leighton held out a hand and grasped Kate's arm. 'Thank you, my dear,' she said. 'You've been very kind.'

'We've got details of the two women,' said DI Evans when Kate Ebdon arrived back at Scotland Yard.

''Bout time,' said Kate. 'The Passport Office finally got the files out, did they?'

Evans nodded and handed Kate a page of rough notes. 'Yes,' he said. 'Both live in the London area.'

'Toms are they, sir?' asked Kate.

'I don't know,' said Evans. 'You ran them through the computer, didn't you? What makes you think they might have been prostitutes?'

'Just something that Mrs Leighton mentioned,' said Kate, perching on the edge of Evans's desk, and she told him about the kerb-crawling incident in King's Cross.

Evans shrugged. 'Might be as well to check with the local nick,' he said. 'Did you find out what he did for a living?'

'Yeah.' Kate slid off Evans's desk and sat down behind her own. 'In a pretty big way of business, I should think. There's a few quid in that flat of theirs, that's for sure. Fruit machines and juke-boxes apparently, but I'll need to check at Companies House, just to see what he was worth.'

'I'll get someone else to do that, Kate,' said Evans. 'In the meantime, we'll go and see if we can find any relatives of the two women.'

'Why don't we visit the firm first, guv?' said Kate. 'Might kill two birds with one stone.' She paused and grinned. 'In a manner of speaking.'

It did not appear to be a prosperous company, but appearances, as any detective will tell you, can be deceptive. Situated in one of the back streets of Fulham, the offices of Leighton Leisure Services occupied a large converted house. The paint on the door and the windows was peeling and the concrete facing on the lower part of the house had fallen away in places to reveal the brickwork beneath. There was a driveway at the side leading to what had once been the garden but was now a tarmacadam area where a couple of plain vans were parked.

Evans and Kate mounted the steps, strode in through the front door and looked around. A secretary-cum-receptionist sat behind a chipboard desk. A computer screen stood to one side, but it was switched off.

'Help you?' The receptionist looked as though that was the last thing she wanted to do.

'Police,' said Evans tersely. 'I want to see whoever's in charge.'

'That'll be Mr Webb,' said the girl. 'Hang on.' She picked up the handset of a telephone and pressed down a button. 'Ray? There's a copper here to see you.' She grunted an acknowledgement and pointed at a door. 'Go through there and up the stairs. First door on the right.' And she resumed her reading of *The Sun* newspaper.

'Raymond Webb. How d'you do?' The man who stood up behind his desk had greasy black hair and a small moustache, and was dressed in a grey suit that seemed a couple of sizes too big for him, but Evans imagined that this may have been the man's idea of prevailing fashion.

'I'm Detective Inspector Evans of Scotland Yard, and this is DC Ebdon.'

Webb sat down again after waving Evans and Kate to sit down too. 'So, what can I do for you?' He spoke nervously as though the police could have called about any one of a dozen infractions of the law. It was a reaction that Evans had seen often in shady businessmen.

'Mr Michael Leighton was the managing director of this company, I believe?'

'Was?' Webb raised his eyebrows. 'He still is.'

'Mr Leighton's body was found on board his yacht, about fifty miles off Cyprus,' said Evans calmly. 'He had been murdered.'

'Good God Almighty!' Webb's mouth opened and he stared at the detective inspector. 'But he, I mean, oh, surely not.'

'I'm afraid so, Mr Webb.'

'Christ! What a tragedy. What a bloody tragedy.' Webb shook his head. 'What can I say?' he asked, opening his hands in a gesture of hopelessness. 'Who would do such a thing? I read about that yacht in the papers, but I never thought for one moment that it could be Mike's.'

'When did Mr Leighton leave here?' asked Evans.

Webb glanced at a calendar on the wall. 'About the eighth of June, I suppose. That's when he flew down to Cannes to pick up the yacht.' He spoke slowly, obviously still stunned by the news.

'Holiday, was it?' asked Evans.

Webb dragged his gaze away from Kate's figure. 'Er, yes, sort of.'

'What d'you mean, sort of?'

'Well, Mike was always on the lookout for a bit of business. He said something about dropping in on Cyprus, now you mention it, to see if he could interest the locals. And the air force base there. Do quite a bit of business with service canteens and that, you know.' Webb suddenly remembered what else he had read in the papers. 'Weren't there two women with him? It didn't give any names, of course, otherwise I'd've known about Mike.'

'Yes, two women were found with him, but we don't release the names until we've advised relatives,' said Evans. 'But the two women were Patricia Tilley and Karen Nash. I wonder if—'

'No! I don't believe it.' Webb looked genuinely shocked. 'Not her too.'

'I see you do know them.'

'I know Tricia Tilley, Inspector. She used to work here.'

'Used to? D'you mean she'd left?'

'Yes, she resigned the same day that Mike left for his holiday.'

'Did she tell you she was going with him, Mr Webb?'

'No, she didn't.' Webb looked shifty. 'I can't say I'm surprised though.'

'Oh? Why not?'

Webb lowered his voice, even though only the three of them were in his office. 'Mike and Tricia had something going,' he said. 'Common knowledge here, of course. She felt sorry for him, I think. His wife had left him, you know. Went off with some other bloke apparently.'

'Is that what Leighton told you?' Kate spoke for the first time and her strong Australian accent surprised Webb.

'Er, yes, love. He did.'

'Don't call me love,' said Kate, a quiet menace in her voice. 'It's Miss Ebdon.' She had already taken a dislike to Raymond Webb, mainly because he kept undressing her with his eyes.

'Oh, sorry.' Webb was taken aback by Kate's forthrightness and stared at her for a moment or two before going on. 'He reckoned his missus was a bit flighty and eventually he got fed up with it and told her to hoof it. Reckoned he found her in bed with some guy when he came home unexpectedly.'

'What about Karen Nash, Mr Webb?' asked Evans. 'That name mean anything to you?'

Webb considered the question for a moment as though trying genuinely to assist the police. 'No,' he said eventually. 'Might have been a friend of Tricia's, I suppose.'

'How long had Patricia Tilley worked here?'

'Six or seven months, I think.' Webb reached out for his telephone. 'I can check.'

'Don't bother,' said Evans. 'Not at the moment. Was she married?'

Webb paused and looked distinctly uncomfortable as though concerned for Patricia Tilley's reputation, even though she was dead. 'Yes, but she wasn't living with her husband. He was a right bastard—' He broke off and glanced at Kate. 'Oh, sorry,' he said, only just preventing himself from calling her 'love' again. He looked back at Evans. 'Her husband came round here one day, demanding to see her and creating merry hell. I had to threaten to call the police eventually.'

'Have you got an address for Mrs Tilley?' asked Evans. Although he had been given an address by the Passport

Office, it was possible that Patricia Tilley had moved since taking out her passport five years previously.

'Yes, of course.' And once again, Webb's hand moved towards the telephone.

FIVE

'THE BODIES OF THE THREE victims have arrived in the United Kingdom, sir,' said Detective Superintendent Craven-Foster. He and Detective Inspector Charles Morgan had returned from Cyprus on an early morning flight and were now in Fox's office along with DI Evans and DC Ebdon. 'The inquest will be convened at Uxbridge, probably tomorrow.'

'Good,' said Fox. 'You can look after that, Charles.' He nodded towards DI Morgan and then fingered a sheet of paper across his desk. 'It's been confirmed,' he went on, 'that the white powder found aboard Leighton's yacht was cocaine.' He glanced at Evans. 'How does that fit in with your visit to Leighton Leisure Services, Denzil? Bit "iffy", are they?'

'This character Webb, who now runs the show, has got form, sir,' said Evans. 'Previous for fraud, only a minor job, but he got nine months back in the seventies. Since then, he appears to have gone straight.'

Fox snorted; he could never bring himself to believe that anyone ever went straight. 'Worth spinning, is it, this Leighton Leisure Services?'

Evans considered the possible value of executing a search warrant on the seedy premises in Fulham and then nodded. 'Might turn something up, I suppose, sir,' he said. But he sounded doubtful.

'And the two women?' asked Fox.

'Webb gave us an up-to-date address for Patricia Tilley, sir, but we haven't checked it out, or the address for Karen Nash that we got from the Passport Office.'

'I think that's a priority then,' said Fox. 'Webb and his dodgy operation can wait. They're not going anywhere in a hurry. I hope,' he added. 'But in view of the fact that cocaine was found on the yacht, we have to ask ourselves whether this fruit-machine set-up is a cover for a drug-smuggling operation.'

'Possible, I suppose,' said Evans mournfully. He had never been an expert on drugs and always regarded any case involving them with a measure of apprehension.

'Right.' Fox stood up. 'You and Kate chase up the two women's addresses, Denzil, and then we'll take it from there.' He switched his gaze to Craven-Foster. 'And you, John, do some digging on this Leighton Leisure lot. Beat on the ground and see what comes up.' The brief conference was over.

Patricia Tilley had shared a flat near Clapham Common in south London with a divorcee called Helen Crabtree who worked as a computer operator for a firm of bookmakers.

'I can't believe it,' said Mrs Crabtree, her face blanching as she sunk into an armchair. 'I knew she was knocking about with her boss – he was loaded apparently – but she never said anything about going on holiday with him. I mean, she said she was going to France for a fortnight, but nothing about a yacht.' She shook her head slowly. 'Murdered. My God! What a world we're living in.' She glanced up at Evans and Kate. 'I mean, you read about these things in the paper, but you never think it's going to happen to anyone you know. I saw about the yacht, but it didn't say who was on it. I never thought about Tricia. Well, you wouldn't would you?'

'Did she tell you that she was leaving her job, Mrs Crabtree?'

'No.' Helen Crabtree looked up at the detective as if realising that there was a lot that her flatmate hadn't told her.

'And was she married?' asked Evans, seeking to confirm what Webb had told him.

'Yes, but she said it was over.'

'D'you know if she was actually divorced?'

'Isn't everyone these days?' Helen gave a despairing shrug. 'I don't know really. She moved in with me about six or seven months ago. That's when she got the job at Leighton's. Said she was making a fresh start all round.'

'Did she ever mention her husband, or say where he lived?'

'Twickenham, I think. I'm sure that's where she said.'

'Did she ever say anything about having had children?' put in Kate. The pathologist's report had mentioned that Patricia Tilley had borne at least one child.

'No, she didn't. As a matter of fact, she never said very much about her life at all.'

'We'll need to look through her things,' said Evans. 'I presume she had a room of her own?'

Helen Crabtree, still obviously stunned by the news of her flatmate's death, nodded slowly. 'We each had a room of our own,' she said, 'but shared this room and the kitchen and bathroom. It was the usual sort of arrangement.'

The search of Patricia Tilley's room yielded very little that would help the police to find her killer. It was clean and tidy, and the bed was made up. A tattered teddy bear sat in the centre of it. The drawers of the dressing table contained the usual proliferation of underclothes and cosmetics, and there was a pile of correspondence. Kate went through it and found a letter from a solicitor, addressed to Patricia Tilley care of Leighton Leisure Services, about her separation from Keith Tilley; and another from her mother with an address in Manchester. Evans recalled that Carol Leighton had told them initially that Michael Leighton had gone to Manchester on business, but as that had turned out to be a downright lie, he discounted it as a coincidence.

'Did you know of, or did Mrs Tilley mention, a woman called Karen Nash, Mrs Crabtree?' asked Evans when they returned to the sitting room.

'No, I don't think so.' Helen Crabtree appeared to be giving the question careful thought. Eventually, she shook her head. 'No, I'm sure I've never heard the name. Was that the other girl on the yacht?' Newspaper reports, some of them inaccurately describing the triple murders as 'The Mary Celeste Mystery', had mentioned that the victims were a man and two women.

'It's just a name that's come up in our enquiries,' said Evans casually.

Keith Tilley, whose address in Twickenham the police had obtained from the solicitor who had written to Patricia, was utterly distraught at the news of his wife's death. Two children, a boy and a girl, had been playing in the sitting room when Evans and Kate Ebdon arrived, but were quickly ushered away to another part of the house by an attractive young woman whom Tilley described as his housekeeper. Cynically, Kate kept an open mind about the girl's precise status in the household.

Keith Tilley was seated in an armchair, his head bowed, as he answered Evans's questions. 'She walked out on us about six or seven months ago.'

'Are you sure of that, Mr Tilley?' Evans was aware that both Patricia Tilley's employers and her erstwhile flatmate had told them that, but he was a great seeker after what the police called collateral.

'Absolutely. It was not long after she got the job at Leighton's. She did it to help out with the mortgage after I lost my job. Then one day, she upped and left.'

'Did she say why?'

'She didn't say anything.' Tilley paused as one of the children upstairs laughed, and then began to scream defiantly. 'One day she was here, the next day she was gone. I tried phoning Leighton's, but she refused to speak to me. Eventually I got my solicitor to write to her.'

'What happened?' asked Evans.

'I got a reply saying that she didn't want to know. He said that she wouldn't let him give me her new address. I went round to Leighton's once, to see if I could see her, but I got into a ruck with some bastard there who threatened to call the police. So I thought, well, that's that. If she doesn't want to see me, so be it. I wrote to the solicitor and asked him to start proceedings.'

'So you never saw her from the day she left you, Mr Tilley?'

Tilley looked up, a tired expression on his face. 'No. I always hoped that she'd see sense and come back, but she never did.'

'How long has your housekeeper been with you, Mr Tilley?' asked Kate quietly.

Tilley looked up sharply. 'About five months,' he said. 'I had to have someone to help with the kids.' He paused and ran his hands through his hair. 'What puzzles me is what Tricia was doing on a yacht in the middle of the Mediterranean.'

'She was with her boss, Michael Leighton, and another woman,' said Evans.

'The bitch,' said Tilley. 'So that's what it was all about. She was having it off with him, I suppose.'

Evans shrugged. 'I don't know, Mr Tilley,' he said. 'It was suggested at Leighton's that it was a business trip, but all three of them were naked when they were found.'

'Huh! Some business trip,' said Tilley angrily.

'Right,' said Fox, rubbing his hands together, 'let's get this bloody enquiry moving. Denzil, you get a search warrant for Leighton's. And while you're about it, one for Raymond Webb's private address, wherever that is. Kate, you check this Nash woman's last known address, see what you can find out.'

'Are we going to do Webb's private address straightaway, sir?' asked Evans.

Fox grinned. 'Only if we find something interesting at the Fulham office, Denzil.'

'But I was wondering what were our grounds for doing either, sir.' Evans was still unhappy.

'Simple.' Fox regarded the DI patiently. 'Cocaine was found on Leighton's yacht. Leighton was the managing director of Leighton Leisure Services. Therefore, Denzil, dear boy, there is reasonable suspicion that further quantities of the said substance may be found at his place of work. And if that proves to be the case, we are entitled to conclude that quantities of it may be found at the home address of Raymond Webb who now runs the show. How's that?'

'I suppose it's all right, sir,' said Evans with a reluctance born of knowing that he was, after all, the one who was going to have to satisfy the magistrate.

'Of course it is,' said Fox, dismissing his DI's concerns.

Karen Nash's last known address was a flat in a modern block to the west of Ealing Common. Not surprisingly, there was no answer when DC Kate Ebdon rang the bell, but fortunately she had thought to bring with her the bunch of keys which had been found in the dead woman's handbag on Leighton's yacht. She let herself in and closed the front door.

It was a small flat – one-bedroomed – with a fresh, clean smell and it had obviously been tidied before its occupant left for the last time. Kate sat down in one of the armchairs and let her gaze travel around the clearly feminine sitting room, comparing its luxury with her own meagre flat in Dulwich. Karen Nash had obviously gone to a great deal of trouble furnishing her home: a peach-coloured carpet that blended with the curtains and upholstery, a small bookcase containing mainly paperback novels, a low coffee table, and a writing table on which were a telephone and an answering machine. Kate saw that the answerphone had recorded three messages, and she switched it to play-back. The first two messages were from women, neither of whom had identified herself, presumably because she knew that Karen Nash would recognise her voice. But the third call was from a man who introduced himself as Harry Pritchard. He left a brief message telling Karen that he had a job for her and asking her to contact him as soon as possible. But he did not leave a telephone number.

Kate opened one of the drawers of the writing table and found Karen Nash's personal book of telephone numbers. Skimming quickly through it, she found Harry Pritchard's number which, as far as she could tell from the dialling code, belonged to an address in the West End of London. She dialled the number of the incident room at the Yard and waited while one of the DCs did a subscriber check.

'Yeah, you were right, Kate,' said the DC. 'The number goes out to a place in Soho.' And he read out the address.

Putting Karen Nash's book of telephone numbers in her handbag, Kate wandered into the dead woman's bedroom. There was a double bed, made up, with a black satin coverlet. Inside a fitted wardrobe that ran the length of one wall, Kate found a stunning array of good quality clothing, and considerably more shoes than her own wardrobe contained. On a shelf at the top were two thick loose-leaf display books of photographs.

Kate took the books back to the sitting room and sat down, opening the first volume and riffling through the glossy plates. The photographs, each one of which was contained in a clear plastic envelope, showed an elegantly-dressed Karen Nash striking a pose. Some of them had been taken in the open air, others in a studio. In some she was displaying well known products, mainly cosmetics and perfume, but the remainder were obviously intent on showing off the clothes she was wearing.

But just as Kate had come to the conclusion that Karen Nash had been a professional model, she picked up the second book and opened it. The photographs in that book were also of Karen Nash, but these consisted wholly of the racy poses popular in the sort of men's magazines usually found on the top shelves of seedier newsagents. And Karen Nash was naked in each one of them.

'Well, well, well,' said Kate to herself, and closed the book. She spent the next ten minutes searching the rest of the flat but discovered nothing else of immediate interest. There was certainly no evidence of either hypodermics or any of the other paraphernalia that would indicate habitual drug abuse.

Taking the two books of photographs with her, Kate closed the front door behind her and double-locked it again. Then she rang the bell of the other flat that shared the small landing. After a moment or two, the door was opened by a man of about thirty. He was wearing jeans and a tee-shirt with a meaningless message on it. He was muscular, had blond hair that Kate suspected may have been dyed, and wore the inevitable gold chain around his neck.

'Hi!' The man openly appraised Kate's figure and placed a hand high on the door jamb, supporting himself.

'D'you know Karen Nash?' asked Kate.

'Sure. You a friend of hers?'

'No, I'm a police officer.'

The man took his hand away from the jamb and folded his arms. 'You've got to be joking,' he said, staring at Kate's red hair and the neat hips clothed in blue denim.

'It's no joke, mister,' said Kate, well versed in dealing with men who thought they were God's gift to women. 'She's dead.' She decided that there was no point in concealing that fact from this macho male. If he was the murderer, he would know it already. And if he wasn't, it would certainly remove the smirk from his face.

It did. 'Christ! When? What happened?' The man was clearly shocked by what Kate had told him.

'She was murdered,' said Kate in matter-of-fact tones. 'Can I come in, or d'you want to carry on this conversation out here in the entrance hall?' she asked.

'Er, no, come on in.' The man shook his head and showed her into a sitting room identical in size and shape to the one that Kate had just left. 'Sit down. Can I get you a drink?'

Kate shook her head. 'No thanks, Mr—?'

'Chapple. Kevin Chapple.' Chapple sat down opposite the Australian girl. 'What happened then?' The bravado that he had first displayed had clearly been deflated by the news that his neighbour was dead.

'She was murdered on a yacht in the Mediterranean, about four or five days ago, Mr Chapple. Along with a man and another woman.'

Chapple's eyes opened wide. 'D'you mean the one they found with three bodies on it?'

'That's the only one I know about,' said Kate drily.

'Good God!' Chapple shook his head once more in disbelief. 'Well, I'm going to have a drink. Are you sure you won't have one?'

'Perfectly,' said Kate. 'How well did you know Karen Nash?'

'Just as a neighbour,' said Chapple. He went into the kitchen and returned a few moments later with what looked like a large Scotch in his hand. 'I did think about dating her when she first moved in, but to be perfectly honest, I never really fancied her. And there's always the old saying about not doing it on your own doorstep. In this case, literally. It makes it much more difficult to shake them off when you get tired of them.' He grinned at Kate, his earlier vanity having returned. 'Anyhow, I'm not short of girl-friends. It's more a case of fighting them off.' He grinned again and stared insolently at Kate's breasts.

'That's nice,' said Kate sarcastically. 'What did she do for a living, Mr Chapple? Any idea?' Kate thought she knew, at least from a study of Karen Nash's book of photographs.

'She called herself an exotic dancer, whatever that is,' said Chapple without hesitation. 'Topless, I suppose. You don't need any talent to flash your boobs around in a night-club, do you?'

'I wouldn't know,' said Kate. 'Did she ever mention where she performed these exotic routines?'

'No idea, I'm afraid. She was sometimes out every evening, often weeks at a time, which seems to imply that she was working then, but other times she was what they call resting, I suppose.'

'As a matter of interest, Mr Chapple, what d'you do for a living?'

'I'm a ballet dancer,' said Chapple.

'Really? Well, that knocks one theory on the head,' said Kate, determined not to let this chauvinistic pig have the last word.

Chapple got the implication immediately and grinned. 'Want proof?' he asked.

Kate ignored Chapple's comment and stood up, fishing in her handbag for a card. 'I'm Detective Constable Ebdon of Scotland Yard,' she said, and scribbling her new extension on the card handed it to Chapple. 'If you think of anything else, perhaps you'd give me a ring, but I'll probably have to come and see you again, anyway.'

'It'd be a pleasure,' said Chapple and paused. 'Are you doing anything this evening, by any chance?'

'Yes, I'm looking for a maniac who machine-gunned three people to death on a yacht in the Med.'

SIX

FOX SWIVELLED HIS CHAIR SO that he was facing Detective Superintendent Craven-Foster. 'Did you turn up anything interesting about Leighton Leisure Services, John?'

'I got DS Stone to give them a run through at Companies House, sir,' said Craven-Foster. 'As I expected, there was very little there except for the names of the two directors.'

'Leighton and Webb?'

'Yes, sir,' said Craven-Foster. 'Leighton held ninety-eight per cent of the shares and Webb the other two. Patricia Tilley was shown as company secretary, but that, I suspect, was a mere formality to comply with company law. I think,' he added. Craven-Foster was not too well versed in company law.

'Sounds like bribery to me,' said Fox cynically. 'I wonder why he didn't just pay her for her favours.'

'Perhaps she wasn't doing him any, sir. From what Kate was saying, I think the favours came from Karen Nash.'

'Really? Then what was Tilley doing on Leighton's yacht, stark naked?'

'Perhaps it was hot, sir,' said Craven-Foster with a grin.

'Yes, well, talking of heat, I think it's time we turned some on Mister Webb. Did you get the warrants, Denzil?'

'Yes, sir. For the business premises and for Webb's home address.' Evans laid two search warrants on Fox's desk.

'You hang on to them, Denzil. You're coming with us.'

'But what about this Harry Pritchard character that Kate mentioned, sir?' asked Craven-Foster.

'He'll keep,' said Fox. 'Probably just some sort of pimp. First we'll do Leighton's.'

'Did you say "we", sir?' asked Craven-Foster, unused to Fox's interference in matters that a commander ought not to be interfering in.

'Indeed, John. It's time I got involved.'

Denzil Evans shot an insolent smirk at the detective superintendent. Mr Craven-Foster was about to discover what it meant to have Tommy Fox as a governor.

The two unmarked police cars swept into the forecourt of Leighton Leisure Services' offices and stopped, blocking the entrance. Telling his driver, Swann, to remain where he was, Fox alighted from his Ford Scorpio and waited until the others had joined him.

The same disinterested receptionist who had been there when Evans and Kate had called, was sitting behind her desk, once again reading a copy of *The Sun.* 'Yes?' she said.

'We've come to see Mr Webb.' Fox gave the girl a comforting smile.

'I'll see if he's available. Who shall I say it is?' The receptionist had obviously not recognised either Denzil Evans or Kate Ebdon from their previous visit.

'We are the police,' said Fox, gazing around the office and frowning at its disordered state.

Moving languidly, the girl picked up the handset of her telephone and pressed down a switch, idly tapping the edge of the desk with a ball-point pen while she waited for an answer. 'Ray, there's some more coppers to see you.' She laughed at Webb's response – a response that Fox was unable to hear – and replaced the receiver. Pointing at the door leading to the stairs, she said, 'You can go up.'

'How kind,' murmured Fox and led the way.

Raymond Webb was standing at the top of the staircase and looked surprised – and not a little apprehensive – to see five police officers coming towards him. He laughed nervously. 'What's this?' he asked. 'A raid?'

'Exactly so,' said Fox, and ignoring Webb's outstretched hand, moved past him into the office.

'Er, what seems to be the problem?' asked Webb, hurriedly following Fox.

For several seconds, Fox surveyed Webb, making him feel even more anxious than he was already, but said nothing. Then he spoke. 'I am Commander Thomas Fox . . . of Scotland Yard. And the problem is that someone murdered one Michael Leighton and two women aboard a yacht in the Mediterranean, Mr Webb.' Uninvited, Fox sat down. 'But then you'll know about that because my Detective Inspector Evans had a conversation with you about it, didn't he?'

'Yes, but I don't see what—'

'I have therefore caused to be obtained a search warrant for these premises and I now propose to execute it.' Fox had no intention of telling Webb that he also had a warrant for his home address. At least, not yet.

Webb sat down behind his desk and scowled at Fox. 'I suppose this is all because I did a bit of time back in the seventies,' he said.

'Did you really?' Fox affected surprise. 'I didn't know that.' He turned towards Evans. 'Did you know that, Denzil?'

Confronted, yet again, by one of Fox's sarcastically ambiguous questions, Evans found himself in the usual position of being unsure what his chief wanted him to say and merely confined himself to a shrug.

'What was that for?' Fox turned back to Webb.

'They reckoned it was fraud,' said Webb sullenly, 'but it was all a mistake.'

Fox nodded. 'Alas, life is full of little injustices,' he said. 'Tell me, Mr Webb, what is your precise status in this company?'

'I'm a director,' said Webb. 'The only director now that Mike's dead. And I'm the accountant.'

'Are you really? How interesting.' The fact that Leighton had employed an accountant with a previous conviction for fraud fascinated Fox. And merely caused his suspicions to deepen. 'Now then, perhaps you can point my officers in the direction of the late Mr Leighton's office.'

'Perhaps I ought to see your warrant first,' said Webb. He did not intend to give in easily.

'Of course.' Fox smiled disarmingly. 'Denzil, show Mr Webb the documentation, there's a good chap.'

Evans withdrew the search warrant and laid it on Webb's desk. But he kept one hand firmly on it; he had seen warrants torn up before.

Webb leaned forward and pretended to study it closely. In fact, it was the first time he had seen a search warrant and had no idea whether it was genuine or not. 'Yes, well, that all seems to be in order,' he said grudgingly. 'Mike's office is next door. It's not been touched since he left.'

Originally a bedroom, Leighton's office was on the front of the house. A large desk stood across one corner of the carpeted room and there were two armchairs, a side table, a cabinet and a floor-mounted safe. Fox walked first to the cabinet, but it was locked.

'That's only got booze in it,' said Webb.

'D'you have a key?' asked Fox, 'and while you're about it, one for the safe?'

Webb leaned against a wall, his hands in his pockets. 'Sorry, no. I haven't got any keys.' He was determined to be as obstructive as possible.

'Pity,' said Fox and turned to Kate Ebdon. 'Kate, pop down to the car and get a case-opener, will you. I'm afraid that we're going to have to do some damage here, Mr Webb,' he added, turning back to the sole remaining director of Leighton Leisure Services. Then he addressed Evans. 'Denzil, get on the radio to the Yard, will you, and arrange for someone to come along and open that safe. Might try Wormwood Scrubs for a start. Sure to find a few expert locksmiths in there. Was that your experience, Raymond?' He smiled at the luckless Webb.

'Look, hang on a mo,' said Webb hurriedly. 'It's just possible that there's some keys somewhere. I'll see what I can find.'

'Most helpful,' murmured Fox. 'It would save an inordinate amount of time,' he added.

Minutes later, Webb returned and slapped a bunch of keys on the late managing director's desk. 'Try those,' he said.

Fox winced. 'You'll damage the leather top if you do that,' he remarked in an offhanded way. He picked up the keys and handed them to DI Morgan. 'See what you can do with those, Charles,' he said.

Webb was right: the cabinet that Fox had tried contained a huge amount of alcohol. There were bottles of whisky, gin, vodka, rum, brandy and sherry, and a range of 'mixers'.

Fox nodded approvingly. 'Expecting a siege?' he asked. He glanced at Evans. 'Try the safe, Denzil.'

Evans found the appropriate key and swung the heavy door wide. Inside were several bundles of papers and files, all of which were brought out and placed on the desk. Behind them was a video cassette and a thick envelope. Evans opened it and took out a number of large glossy photographs and spread them across the desk. Each photograph depicted Michael Leighton engaging in an astonishing variation of the sexual act with a female partner.

'Good gracious me,' said Fox, casting a cursory eye over the lurid prints. 'Interesting exposures, one might say.'

'I didn't know anything about those,' said Webb, instantly on the defensive.

Fox ignored Webb's comment and studied the photographs more closely. 'Quite an athlete, your MD,' he said. He glanced sideways at Kate Ebdon. 'How old was this bloke?'

'Fifty-four, sir,' said Kate promptly, without taking her eyes off the photographs.

'Not bad,' said Fox, a hint of admiration in his voice.

'This looks like Karen Nash, sir.' Kate jabbed a forefinger at one of the photographs. 'I reckon she must have been a bloody contortionist before she took this up. A miracle she didn't break her back.'

'And this is almost certainly Patricia Tilley,' said Craven-Foster, handing another print to Fox. 'In fact there are several prints here featuring both women.'

'Now I know what's meant by exotic dancing,' said Kate quietly.

'What's that supposed to mean?' Fox asked.

'Karen Nash's next-door neighbour, a muscle-bound ballet dancer called Kevin Chapple, said that Karen had told him she was an exotic dancer.'

'D'you know any of these other women, Raymond?' asked Fox, turning to Webb.

Webb examined the photographs more closely than was necessary to make an identification. 'Apart from Tricia, only that one,' he said finally, pointing to a picture of a girl in a G-string and knee-high boots who was holding a whip and smiling at the camera.

'How d'you know her?'

'I met Mike in a dive one night and she was with him. He introduced her, said her name was Gail Thompson. I don't know if it was. She looked more like some tart he'd picked up in the West End.'

'Any idea where she lives?' asked Fox. He knew there was no chance that Webb would know, but he had to ask the question.

'No. I only met her the once. Mike tended to keep his private life to himself.'

'To himself and whoever took these photographs,' said Fox acidly. 'Incidentally, d'you recognise where they might have been taken?'

Webb took the question as an invitation to study the photographs once more. 'No, don't recognise it,' he said eventually. 'Could be anywhere.'

'That,' said Fox, 'is what they call a truism.'

They searched the rest of the office without much success, but it was Kate Ebdon who came up with the link. 'This is his private phone book, sir,' she said, flourishing a small leather-bound book. 'And I've just found an interesting name. Harry Pritchard.'

'Who the hell's Harry Pritchard?' asked Fox, for once at a loss to recall a name that had come up in the enquiry.

'He's the guy who left a message on Karen Nash's

answerphone saying that he'd got a job for her, sir,' said Kate and placed the phone book into one of the exhibits bags that the police had brought with them.

Back at New Scotland Yard, Fox viewed the video cassette tape that had been seized from Leighton's office. Fox told the operator to fast-forward it until a female face was in close-up. But none of the detectives was able to identify any of the five women who featured in Leighton's home movies. But there was another man. In his late twenties or early thirties, with long brown hair gathered into a pony-tail, he proved to be a sexual athlete who surpassed even Leighton's creditable performances. But then, as Fox said, he was that much younger.

Lady Jane Sims lived in a block of mansion flats behind Harrods of Knightsbridge. Her face lit up when she answered the door to Fox and, flicking a loose lock of hair out of her eyes, she led him into her sitting room and poured him a large Scotch.

'Where have you been, Tommy?' she asked when Fox was settled in an armchair. 'I haven't seen you for ages.'

'Cyprus,' said Fox. He offered Jane a cigarette, which she refused, and lit one for himself.

'What on earth were you doing there?'

Briefly, Fox outlined the reason for his sudden departure and then said, 'Oh, by the way, I've been promoted.'

'Tommy, that's wonderful. We must celebrate. But why on earth didn't you tell me?'

'It's not important,' said Fox. 'Anyway, I've been too busy chasing sex-mad company directors.'

'Oh?' Jane looked suddenly interested.

Fox laughed. 'You should have seen the video we took from his office,' he said. 'Enough to make your eyes water.'

'Why didn't you bring it with you?' asked Jane teasingly. 'I've got a video-recorder.'

'Not suitable for chaste young ladies like you,' said Fox. 'Apart from which it mustn't leave the property store.'

'You never know, I might learn something,' said Jane with a laugh. 'Anyway, Tommy Fox, are you going to take me out to dinner to celebrate? Incidentally, what do they call you now?'

'Commander,' said Fox. 'To my face, anyway. What they call me behind my back is another thing.' In fact, Fox's immaculate appearance had many years ago earned him the nickname of the Beau Brummell of Scotland Yard.

The telephone call came early the next morning, from Geoffrey Harding, the Chief Constable of the Sovereign Base Areas Police in Cyprus.

'I don't know if there's anything in it, Tommy,' said Harding, 'but the Provost Marshal at Akrotiri – he's a Royal Air Force wing commander – passed me some information he got from a Second Lieutenant West who's in the army here. Apparently he overheard a conversation between two soldiers in his platoon.'

'What about, Geoff?' asked Fox.

'Seems they met up with a man who was making enquiries about hiring a speedboat, and was also asking questions regarding the whereabouts of Leighton's yacht.'

'Interesting,' said Fox, and aware of the dangers of relying on hearsay, even when it was unlikely to be put in evidence, said, 'can you get this Second Lieutenant West to ring me?'

'No problem, Tommy,' said Harding.

By some miracle of modern communications, the call came through exactly fifteen minutes later.

'Is that Commander Fox?' asked a confident, youthful voice.

'Yes,' said Fox.

'It's Jeremy West, sir. I'm a second lieutenant in the—'

'Yes, I know who you are, Mr West,' said Fox.

'Well, what I heard, sir, from these two lads of mine, was that—'

'Mr West.'

'Yes, sir?'

'Perhaps you would be so good as to arrange for these two soldiers to be sent to London in order that I can question them.'

'Oh! I thought that you'd have come out here, sir.'

'Certainly not, Mr West,' said Fox. 'You see it's much cheaper to send two soldiers from Cyprus to London, than to send a commander from London to Cyprus. But if there's a problem, I'll speak to Charles about it.'

'Charles, sir?'

'He's the Chief of the General Staff,' said Fox. He had never met the CGS, but he knew how to deploy a good 'verbal'.

Even two thousand miles could not conceal the gulp that came from Second Lieutenant West. 'I'll arrange it immediately, sir,' he said.

'Jolly good,' said Fox.

SEVEN

'MR C-F SAID YOU WANTED to see me, guv. DS Stone. Wally Stone.' The detective who appeared in Fox's office was of medium height and had the distinct advantage, for one of his profession, of not looking like the popular image of a detective at all. He wore a sharply-cut suit with a flamboyant tie, overflowing top-pocket handkerchief, and had a pencil-thin moustache and hair that was slightly longer than Fox regarded as proper. However, Detective Superintendent Craven-Foster had told Fox that Stone was the man for the job.

'I thought you were supposed to be a plain-clothes officer,' said Fox, carefully examining Stone who was now standing in front of his desk. 'Where on earth did you get that suit?'

Stone glanced down at his one-button-show-two creation of navy blue wool-and-polyester mix, and then looked back at Fox. 'A little *schneider* I know down the East End, guv. I can introduce you if you're interested.'

'I wouldn't be seen dead in a suit like that,' said Fox mildly.

DS Stone looked pained. 'Why's that, guv? Something wrong with it, is there?'

'Let's just say that if you continue to use this East End tailor of yours, your chances of making DI are somewhere between extremely remote and non-existent,' said Fox. 'However, I haven't sent for you to discuss your sartorial inadequacies. Mr Craven-Foster tells me that you know the West End like the back of your hand.'

Stone grinned. 'I've got a few snouts out and about, guv, yes,' he said.

'Good,' said Fox. 'Time to call in a few favours.' Walking across his office, he opened his safe and took out the photographs and video-tape that had been taken from Leighton's office. 'Have a good look at these,' he said, 'and see if you can ID any of the participating women. But in particular, I want you to find a bird called Gail Thompson. She's probably a tom, but she features in two or three of the photographs and on the tape. If you find her, just let me know where she lives and where she operates. Don't talk to her about the murders. Just get out and beat on the ground. See what comes up.'

'Right, guv.' Stone picked up the envelope of prints and the video-tape.

'And, Wally . . .'

'Yes, guv?'

'I do not want to find, in the months to come, that copies of either the photographs or the video-tape are circulating at New Scotland Yard.'

Stone looked offended by the implications of Fox's comment. 'Would I do a thing like that, guv?' he asked.

'Probably,' said Fox.

The two soldiers who were ushered into Fox's office by Denzil Evans looked apprehensive. Bundled on to a flight at Akrotiri early that morning, they had been met at Northolt and brought straight to Scotland Yard by one of the detective sergeants of SO1 Branch. The soldiers' platoon commander had, on Fox's instructions, told them only that police wished to interview them in connection with the triple murder that had occurred on a yacht some fifty miles west of Cyprus.

'Thank you for coming, gentlemen,' said Fox, beaming at the two soldiers, attired now in civilian clothes.

'S'all right, sir,' said one of the men. It was a pointless exchange. Neither had had any choice in the matter.

'Now then, your Mr West tells me that you know something about a man who was in Cyprus some time before the discovery of three bodies on a yacht.' Fox paused. 'You have heard about that, I suppose?'

'Oh yes, sir,' the two men chorused.

'Good, well perhaps we can start with your names.' Fox looked at them expectantly.

'I'm Corporal Higgins, sir,' said one of the men, 'and this here's Private Farmer.'

'Tell me the tale then,' said Fox.

'Well, it's not much, sir,' said Higgins, 'but we was out in Limassol one evening—'

'When was that?'

Higgins looked thoughtful. 'Round about the middle of June, I s'pose.'

'Can you be more specific?'

Higgins considered the question further and then took a diary from his pocket. He spent a few moments thumbing through it and then looked up. 'Yeah, it'd be the twentieth, I think. In fact, I'd say definitely.' He glanced at his companion. 'What d'you reckon, Taff?'

'That was the night we met up with them English birds down Pedro's, Corp, weren't it?' Private Farmer normally called his companion Wayne, but the presence of a commander, albeit a policeman, imposed a military formality upon him.

'And who were these English women?' asked Fox.

Higgins grinned. 'Couple of birds what was on holiday over there, sir, looking for a bit of the night life, like.'

'I see. And were they privy to this conversation?'

'Was they what, sir?' Higgins looked puzzled.

'Did they overhear you talking to this mystery man?'

'Oh, no, sir. We didn't pick them up . . . I mean, we never met them till later on, like.'

'Go on then.'

'Well, we was sitting having a quiet drink, Taff and me, sort of looking over the talent' – Higgins grinned – 'when this geezer come up and asked if he could join us. The place was beginning to jump a bit by then, and there weren't much room. So we says, yes, like. Anyhow, he bought us both a drink, on account of old times, he said—'

'What did he mean by that?'

'Well, he said as how he'd been in the Kate hisself, but that he'd chucked it in after five years. Reckoned he'd been in some Scottish mob.'

'Did he have a Scots accent?' asked Fox.

'Nah! Spoke like me, without no accent.'

Fox smiled. 'You mean he was a Londoner?'

'Reckon so, sir.' Higgins wrinkled his brow, failing to follow Fox's argument. 'Anyhow, he said he was in Cyprus on holiday. Well, that never meant much. You get a lot of punters over there on packages. Don't know why they waste their money. They can have my share. I'm sick of the bleeding place.'

'Can we get to the point, Corporal Higgins?' said Fox.

'Oh, yes, sir, sorry, sir. Well, after we'd had a couple of wets at his expense, he asked us if we knew where he could hire a speedboat. Something fast, he said.'

'I presume he hadn't been stationed in Cyprus during his military service.'

'He never said as how he had, sir.'

'Well, he wouldn't have had to ask you about hiring a boat if he'd known the place, would he?'

'Oh no, I never thought of that.' Higgins glanced at Farmer. 'Never thought of that, did we, Taff?'

'No,' said Farmer.

'Did he say why he wanted this boat?'

'Nah! I s'pose he wanted to do a bit of diving, snorkelling, p'raps. Anyhow, we didn't know, so we told him to have a go down the harbour. Then he asked if we'd seen this yacht . . .' Higgins spoke hesitantly, as though that part of the conversation was of no interest.

'And which yacht was that?'

'Well, it was the one what them bodies was found on.'

'Did he actually know the name of the yacht?'

'Yeah, well it was in all the papers and I remembered it the minute I saw it, so we thought we'd better mention it to our officer. But just as we was talking about it, Taff and me, he come in the room and heard what we was talking about.' Higgins grinned. 'So here we are, like, sir.'

'Did this man tell you his name, Corporal Higgins?'

'Not really, no. He just said to call him Jock, like everyone else did on account of him having been in this Scottish mob what I was telling you about.'

'Then what happened?' asked Fox.

'Well nothing. He just bought us another beer and then he sheered off, like.'

'And did you see him again?'

'No, sir, we never.' Higgins glanced at his companion. 'Did we, Taff?'

'Nah, never,' echoed Farmer.

'Right,' said Fox. 'What I'd like you to do now is to go next door with this officer' – he waved a hand towards Evans – 'and make a statement, giving as full a description of the man as you can.'

'Right, sir.' The two soldiers stood up.

'And thanks for coming over.'

'S'all right, sir,' said Higgins. 'We got a few days Blighty leave out of it, what we wouldn't never have had otherwise.'

'By the way, did you score?' asked Fox, grinning.

'Beg pardon, sir?' Higgins frowned.

'Did you score? With the two birds you picked up?'

Higgins's eyes opened wide. The detective who had met them at Northolt had told them who they were going to see and, in reply to their query, explained that a commander in the Metropolitan Police equated roughly with a brigadier in the army. But Higgins had never been asked a question like that by a brigadier. 'Yes, sir, thank you, sir,' he said, and grinned broadly.

The scant information on a Londoner who claimed to have been in a Scottish regiment for five years was too vague a basis upon which to initiate a search with the Ministry of Defence. And the description furnished by the two soldiers could have fitted a thousand men. Geoffrey Harding, the Chief Constable of the Sovereign Base Areas Police, told Fox that immigration formalities were a bit lax in Cyprus, but he promised to see what he could find out. He also undertook to get the Provost Marshal of Cyprus to circulate details of the man 'Jock' to see if any other serviceman remembered having met him. Finally, Fox rang the Cyprus Chief of Police and asked him to make enquiries about any hirings of speedboats between the twentieth and thirtieth of June. There was a stunned silence at this request, and the Chief of Police pointed out that it was in the tourist season and that boats were being hired all the time. Nevertheless, he promised to do what he could. But it was all a bit of a vain hope.

Fox glanced at the clock and then walked down the corridor to the lift lobby. Riding down to the second floor, he opened the door of the incident room. 'Kate.'

'Yes, sir?'

'Tell Swann to get the car on the front. We're going to see this Harry Pritchard.'

Harry Pritchard's studio, if it could be dignified with such a description, consisted of two large rooms over a shop in the depths of Soho. The man who answered the door wore a pair of faded jeans and was stripped to the waist. His brown hair was tied back in a pony-tail and both Fox and Kate recognised him immediately as the man who appeared in the video seized from Leighton's office.

'Good afternoon,' said Fox affably, and held up his warrant card. 'Thomas Fox . . . of Scotland Yard.'

'Oh!' Pritchard turned in the doorway. 'Carrie,' he yelled up the narrow staircase, 'we've got visitors. It's the fuzz.' He turned back to face Fox. 'Doing a session,' he explained.

'How fascinating,' said Fox.

'Er, you'd better come up,' said Pritchard and led the way upstairs and into a large room. Black screens covered the windows and although the room was carpeted, its only furniture comprised a huge bed and a couple of director chairs. There was an abundance of lighting 'floods' on stands of varying heights, and suspended from gantries across the room. Against one wall was a bench laden with camera equipment.

Sitting in one of the chairs was a young blonde girl of about twenty-three. She was attired in a peach-coloured satin wrap, worn in such a way as to expose one bare shoulder, and her legs were crossed to display a provocative amount of thigh. And she was wearing too much make-up. Kate came to the conclusion that she had donned the wrap only seconds previously.

'This is Carrie,' said Pritchard. 'She's a model.'

'How interesting,' said Fox. He glanced at the sour-faced blonde who appeared set to stay where she was.

'What can I do for you?' asked Pritchard. He appeared quite unconcerned by the arrival of the police and made no attempt to find a shirt, presumably believing that Kate Ebdon was an admirer of the sun-tanned male form.

'You'll have heard about the death of Michael Leighton, I suppose,' began Fox. The identities of the yacht victims had now been released to the Press.

'Yes, indeed. Bloody terrible, that. But how does that—?'

'It's about a set of photographs we found in his office yesterday.'

'Oh!' Pritchard picked up a tee-shirt and slipped it on. 'Er, Carrie, love, I think we'll call it a day,' he said to the languid blonde. 'Same time tomorrow suit you?'

Carrie stood up, seemingly disappointed that she was going to miss what she was sure were the juicy bits of the exchange. 'If you say so, Harry.' She pouted.

'Be a good girl and get dressed next door, will you?'

'Anything you say, Harry.' Carrie gathered a bundle of clothing from the other chair that stood in the corner of the room and flounced out.

Pritchard closed the door behind the girl and turned to face Fox and Kate. 'Won't you sit down,' he said, pointing at the chair just vacated by Carrie. He moved the other chair alongside it and then sat on the edge of the bed.

'What exactly is your business here, Mr Pritchard?' asked Fox.

'I'm a photographer,' said Pritchard.

'Yes, I'd rather gathered that,' said Fox drily, 'but what sort of photography do you specialise in?'

Pritchard laughed. 'When you're as hard up as I am,' he said, 'you take anything that comes along.'

'Including porn?'

'Look . . .' Pritchard spread his hands. 'I'm not into kinky stuff. I mean I wouldn't touch paedophilia.'

'Pleased to hear it.'

'In fact, a guy came to see me about three or four years ago. Wanted me to take some of that stuff.'

'Oh? What did you do about it?'

'Shopped him to the law, didn't I? Porn's one thing, but that sort of pervert makes me bloody sick. No, I admit that I do quite a few explicits. Sell a lot of my stuff to well-known mags. You've probably seen them in high street newsagents.'

'I doubt it,' said Fox, 'but tell me, how did you get involved with Leighton?'

'Dunno, really. It's not a secret, this sort of stuff . . .' Pritchard waved a hand round his studio. 'I mean, it's not against the law, is it? Not any more.'

'What d'you mean, you don't know how you got involved with Leighton?'

'I got a phone call from him one day, out of the blue, and he asked me if I could take some private shots. He said that someone had given him my number.'

'And you did, just like that?' Fox gazed at the photographer with a cynical expression.

Pritchard grinned. 'He made me an offer I couldn't refuse. I reckon the bloke must have been loaded as well as kinky. But it was all straight stuff. Only him and some chicks.'

'Did you know any of these women?' asked Fox.

'No. He said they were all friends of his.' Pritchard laughed. 'They certainly seemed friendly enough.'

'What about Karen Nash?' asked Kate suddenly.

Pritchard switched his gaze to the woman detective, surprised by her Australian accent. 'Wasn't that one of the women who was killed along with Leighton?' he asked.

'That's right, Mr Pritchard,' said Kate. 'You've got a good memory for names. Did you ever meet her?'

'I don't think so.' For the first time, Pritchard looked shifty.

'She appeared in some of the photographs that you took,' said Kate.

'Oh, well, in that case, I suppose I must have—'

'And you left a message on her answering machine, telling her that you'd got a job for her.'

Pritchard looked away, breaking the firm gaze with which Kate had fixed him. 'Oh, you know about that, do you?' he said, looking down at the floor. He looked up again. 'I was doing a series for a soft porn mag and I was going to offer her the part.'

'The part?' Kate looked askance at the photographer.

'Yeah, well, although she was basically a straight model, she wasn't averse to doing "skin", and I thought she might be interested. But I didn't hear from her.'

'That's probably because she was lying dead on a yacht in the Mediterranean,' said Fox caustically.

Pritchard shrugged. 'Yeah, well I know that now,' he said.

'And you and Karen Nash appeared on a video-tape we found, Mr Pritchard,' asked Fox.

'On a tape?' Pritchard appeared stunned by the fact that the police had seen it.

'You and she were performing some quite astounding gymnastics,' said Kate, relishing both the moment and Pritchard's obvious discomfort.

'I suppose one of the others must have been videoing us,' said the photographer lamely. 'I certainly got involved in some of the action.' He spread his hands and grinned at Kate. 'But then, given the offer, who wouldn't?'

'Me for one,' said Kate sarcastically.

'D'you know a Gail Thompson?' asked Fox.

'Name doesn't mean anything,' said Pritchard.

Kate produced the photograph of the girl wearing a G-string and boots, and wielding a whip. 'This is her,' she said.

Pritchard glanced briefly at the print. 'I took that,' he said. 'But that's not whoever you said. That's Carrie, the girl who just left.'

'Doesn't look like her,' said Fox, annoyed that the girl had escaped.

'That's because she was wearing a wig in that picture,' said Pritchard.

'And precious little else,' said Kate.

EIGHT

'WHAT D'YOU THINK, KATE?' ASKED Fox, once they were back at Scotland Yard.

'I think that Pritchard didn't tell us the whole story, sir. D'you remember him saying that he was going to offer Karen Nash a part? Well, you don't talk about offering someone a part when you're taking stills for a soft porn mag. I reckon he's into making porn videos.'

Fox nodded. 'You're probably right, but so what? It's a big jump from that to murdering three people on a yacht in the Med, isn't it?'

'Depends, sir. There's a lot of money involved, and if someone was cheating, that someone might just have been taken out.'

'Like Leighton, you mean?'

'Yes, sir, like Leighton.'

'Maybe,' said Fox thoughtfully. 'However, have you done a check on that telephone number we got from Pritchard? The one he had for Carrie, alias Gail Thompson.'

'Goes out to an address in Battersea, sir.'

'Good.' Fox glanced at the clock. 'In that case, I think we'll pay her a visit, before she sees Pritchard again tomorrow.'

'He's bound to have rung her, sir,' said Kate.

Fox shrugged. 'I don't doubt it.'

Fox had held out little hope of finding Carrie at home at eight o'clock in the evening, given that she was probably a prostitute in addition to her other pursuits, but to his surprise, she was in.

'Oh, I thought I'd be seeing you again,' said the girl when she opened the door of her tiny terraced house. 'You'd better come in.' She was wearing a pair of old jeans and a baggy sweater, and the toe-nails of her bare feet were varnished a vivid red.

'Is your name Gail Thompson?' asked Fox.

'No, not really. It's a name I use for—'

'A name you use for what?'

The girl sighed. 'For making porn movies,' she said resignedly.

'What's your real name then?' asked Fox.

'Carrie Grant,' said the girl. 'It was my old man's idea of a joke.'

'You knew Michael Leighton,' said Fox. It was not so much a question as an accusation.

'Well, he screwed me regularly for his skin flicks, if that's what you mean,' said Carrie. She showed neither embarrassment nor remorse at revealing the way in which she earned a living.

Fox reflected on how much more open with the police the young were now, compared with when he was first a copper. 'Was he into porn movies in a big way then?' he asked.

Carrie laughed scornfully. 'And some,' she said. 'Although I think it was more for his own pleasure than for the profit. He wasn't short of money, you know.' She reached over and took a cigarette from an open packet, lit it and leaned back in her chair, draping one denim-clad leg over the arm. 'He had about six or seven of us at some of his sessions. Group sex with a vengeance, that was. Frankly, I don't know where he got his energy from.'

'Was he the only man involved?'

Carrie hesitated, drew deeply on her cigarette, but said nothing.

'Look,' said Kate, 'we know Harry Pritchard featured in at least one of those films. We've seen him on video doing it with Karen Nash, one of the women who was found murdered with Leighton on his yacht.'

'Yeah, I know.' Carrie's indifference to the world in which

she operated made her seem much older than her years. 'But he wasn't the only one. There was another bloke called Ray Webb, but he wasn't much cop. I think he was a mate of Mike's.' She yawned and looked at the clock on the mantelshelf. 'But Harry was the best for mixing business with pleasure.' She laughed cynically. 'Mike was all right, but he was the wrong side of fifty I should think, and Ray wasn't a lot younger. But he hadn't got Mike's stamina. One trick and he was knackered. I think they only let him play to give the rest of us a giggle.'

'When did you last see Michael Leighton, Carrie?'

'About nine months ago,' said the girl promptly. 'That's when I decided to have no more to do with him.'

'Oh? Why was that?'

'Drugs,' said Carrie laconically.

'What about drugs?' asked Fox.

Carrie stubbed out her half-smoked cigarette and crossed her legs. 'He took us out on his yacht one weekend. Said it was a treat for being good girls.' She laughed scornfully. 'That's rich when you think about it. Anyway, we thought that it was a weekend off, but when we got down to somewhere near Southampton – that's where the yacht was – we found Harry Pritchard on board with his damned video camera, and we knew it was another working weekend.' She sighed at the thought. 'Anyhow, we put to sea, well out of sight of land, and it started. "Water-Porn Games", Mike said he was going to call it, silly bastard. It was bloody freezing, romping around on deck without any clothes on. It was then that Mike suggested that we should take a little something so that we wouldn't feel the cold. And he said it would get rid of our inhibitions.' She laughed, a throaty, cynical laugh. 'As if we had any by then. But that was it, as far as I was concerned. I said no way was I getting into drugs, particularly coke—'

'Was it cocaine that he offered you?' asked Fox.

'Yeah. At least, that's what he said it was.'

'Who else was on this trip?' asked Fox with unconscious humour. 'Apart from Harry Pritchard.'

For a moment, Carrie looked as though she wasn't going

to answer the question, but then she shrugged as if knowing that the police would find out anyway. 'Tricia Tilley and Karen Nash.'

'When was this?'

'September last year. Like I said, it was bloody freezing.' Carrie glanced at Kate. 'If you ever think of taking up the profession, don't do it in September on a bloody yacht,' she added.

'I'll remember that,' said Kate.

'Presumably Tricia Tilley and Karen Nash accepted his offer of drugs then?'

'I think so. I don't know what they did up on deck, apart from the obvious, of course.' Carrie grinned at the two detectives. 'But I made up my mind there and then that I'd had enough of the whole damned business. I went down and put my clothes on, and had a stiff brandy.'

'And Leighton let you go, did he? Didn't make a fuss?'

'Oh, sure he did, but Harry and I had a thing going then, still have in fact, and Harry told him to lay off. I think he threatened to do his legs for him.' Carrie grinned at the thought. 'Anyway, he laid off.'

'Do you happen to know the names of any of the other girls that Leighton employed to make these movies?' asked Fox.

Carrie shook her head. 'Only their first names, but they weren't their real names anyway. None of us used our proper names. Just to be on the safe side.'

'How did you know the names of Tricia Tilley and Karen Nash then, Carrie?' asked Fox.

'I didn't, not until Harry Pritchard told me that they were the two who'd been found on Mike's yacht.'

'When did he tell you that?'

'A couple of days ago, after their names were in the paper,' said Carrie.

'Do you know if drugs were used at any other time? For instance in the sessions held at Pritchard's studio?' That was a guess, but Fox knew that Carrie would correct him if he was wrong.

'Oh, they weren't held at Harry's studio. Mike had a place near Waterloo Station, off Baylis Road.'

'But were drugs used?' persisted Fox.

'I don't know. How d'you tell? I never saw anyone taking them, but if Mike's performance was anything to go by, I reckon he must have been on something.'

'And are you still making porn videos?' Fox looked searchingly at the girl.

'Yeah,' she said defiantly. 'But only for Harry. There's a lot of money in it. And you don't last forever, not in that game. Not unless your name's Tricia Tilley.'

'Meaning?' asked Fox.

'Well, she was forty last birthday, but Mike reckoned that being that much older, she had some sort of special appeal. Sounded kinky to me, but she did have a good body.'

—

There were thirty detectives packed into the small incident room, along with the liaison officer from the laboratory, and the civilian support staff.

'For those of you who think that this bloody enquiry is starting to run away from us,' said Fox, 'I'll just run over the salient points. To begin with, there were three dead bodies and two kilos of cocaine on a yacht off the coast of Cyprus. Unfortunately, too far off the coast to interest the Cyprus police,' he growled in an aside and received a muffled laugh from those who knew him well. 'Furthermore, Leighton Leisure Services now appears to be a cover for the making and distribution of porn videos. A photographer called Harry Pritchard is involved, as is Webb, Leighton's erstwhile partner, and a nudist who operates under the professional name of Gail Thompson.'

'I've traced Gail Thompson, sir,' said Detective Sergeant Stone from the front row.

'So have I,' said Fox. 'She's called Carrie Grant and she lives in Battersea.'

'Oh!' said Stone. 'You know then.'

Fox nodded. 'Yes, Wally, we had a bit of luck.' He addressed his audience again. 'According to Carrie Grant who, no doubt, describes herself as an actress, Leighton has, or had, a studio near Waterloo which will be subject to our intense scrutiny. As I said, Raymond Webb, Leighton's partner, who until now has been a model of injured innocence, was an active participant in these films, along with Leighton. And that is confirmed by the said Carrie Grant, alias Gail Thompson.' Fox sniffed. 'I can only presume they were cheap budget productions,' he added and received another laugh.

'I've taken the precaution of getting a search warrant for the Waterloo premises, sir,' said Craven-Foster.

Fox looked surprised. 'Very foresighted of you, John,' he said. 'But I do not intend to turn the place over just yet.' His gaze swept his audience once more. 'However,' he continued, 'we are in danger of losing sight of the main problem here, and that's finding the killer, or killers, of Leighton, Tilley and Nash.'

'Was there any evidence of this porn video business being conducted from the Fulham offices of Leighton Leisure Services, sir?' asked a detective sergeant.

'No,' said Fox. 'It had all the appearance of a legitimate business retailing fruit machines and the suchlike. However, a further in-depth study of the enterprise won't go amiss, and we'll deal with that in due course.'

As Carrie Grant had said, Michael Leighton's centre of operations was in a back street off Baylis Road in the Waterloo area. But far from being what most people visualised as a film studio, it proved to be a small, disused warehouse set back some eight or nine feet from the roadway. There was a pair of large double doors facing the street, with a smaller door set into one of them. The paint, once green, was faded and dirty.

Altogether some twenty officers were engaged in keeping observation on the premises. Some were on foot, a couple on the roof of a nearby building, and the remainder in a variety of nondescript vehicles, none of which was immediately obvious as being connected with the police. All the officers were complaining about the heat and the diesel fumes which affected their eyes and throats and left their clothes with a foul odour.

For the first few days nothing happened, and Fox began to wonder if the warehouse-cum-studio had been abandoned in view of the police interest in both Webb and Pritchard. But on the fourth day of the observation, between ten and ten-fifteen in the morning, three girls arrived, followed by Pritchard.

Detective Sergeant Douglas Croft, attired in jeans and a tee-shirt, and sweltering in an observation van, noted this occurrence in the log. 'I'd say that shooting was about to start,' he said, 'in a manner of speaking.'

Information about the renewed activity was relayed to Fox at Scotland Yard. He ordered that the so-far-unknown women should be 'housed', a police term for discovering where they lived, and by four that afternoon, Fox's surveillance team had identified all three.

The three women had been named by the officers who had followed them as Babs Stocker, Anna Coombs and Kirsty Newman. The first lived in a studio flat off the Edgware Road and the other two at Wandsworth and Gipsy Hill respectively. Because Babs Stocker lived nearer to Scotland Yard than Anna Coombs or Kirsty Newman, Fox decided to interview her first. It proved to be a lucky choice.

On Fox's instructions, Babs Stocker's Edgware Road address had been kept under observation for no better reason than Fox's desire to know that the woman would be there when he and Kate Ebdon called on her. A quick trawl of the records at central London police stations had indicated that the Stocker woman had been cautioned for prostitution some eighteen months previously by officers at Marylebone. Fox assumed that, following that mild confrontation with the police, she had either decided to give up 'the game' or had become a call-girl, a marginally safer way of attracting clients; his long experience told him that the latter was the more likely.

Babs Stocker was about twenty-six, tall and slender with long dark hair, almond eyes and high cheekbones. When she opened the door, she was wearing a black leotard and leg-warmers, and was perspiring freely. She dabbed at her face with a towel and looked at the two detectives. 'Whatever it is you're selling,' she said sharply, 'I've either got it or I don't want it.'

'Miss Babs Stocker?' asked Fox.

The girl stopped mopping at her face and held the towel against her chest. 'Yes. Who are you?'

'We're police officers,' said Fox and produced his warrant card. 'We'd like to have a word with you.'

'What about?' The girl looked apprehensive.

'The murder of Michael Leighton, among other things,' said Fox mildly. 'May we come in?'

By way of a reply, the girl swung the door wide and led the way into her small living room. 'I was just working out,' she said, stooping to gather up a couple of soft aerobic weights and a portable step-up board. She put the equipment in a corner and slipped into a towelling robe that had been over the back of a chair. 'You'd better sit down,' she added, indicating a sofa-bed and sitting down on an upright chair that she pulled from beneath a small table. 'What's this all about?' She still looked nervous.

'We're investigating the deaths of Michael Leighton, Patricia Tilley and Karen Nash,' began Fox.

'I don't know anything about that,' said Babs Stocker.

'But you knew them, didn't you?'

After a moment's hesitation, the girl nodded. 'Yes.'

'And you were actively engaged with them in the making of pornographic videos.'

'Look, I don't think I ought to be talking to you without a lawyer,' said Babs.

'Miss Stocker, there is nothing for you to get worried about,' put in Kate Ebdon, thinking that reassurance from another woman would allay the girl's fears more readily.

'I'll be quite frank with you,' said Fox. 'The stuff which is produced at Michael Leighton's Waterloo studios may or may not contravene some obscenity law, but I'm not really interested in that. All I'm concerned about is finding the killers of Leighton and the two women.'

Babs Stocker looked slightly relieved, but was obviously still on edge. 'How d'you know all this?' she asked.

'Did Leighton ever offer you drugs?' asked Fox suddenly.

'No, never.'

'We need to know,' said Kate. 'It's important.'

Fox gazed at Babs Stocker, a cynical expression on his face. 'I don't care whether you accepted or not,' he said.

'Well, once or twice. But, look, I don't want to get involved—'

'I'm not interested in you, or what you do for a living, Miss Stocker,' said Fox patiently. 'I'm asking these questions for a reason. I'm not looking to prosecute you.'

Babs relaxed slightly, leaning back in her chair and folding her hands in her lap. 'It was always on offer,' she said. 'I wouldn't touch it though. Not after what happened to Beverley.'

'Who is Beverley?' Fox leaned forward.

'She was one of the girls. Mike used to call us his stable of fillies.'

'She's involved in the making of these films, is she?'

'Not any more,' said Babs. 'The poor little bitch's dead.'

'How?' asked Fox.

'From a drugs overdose,' said Babs listlessly and then looked, first at Kate and then back at Fox. 'And you can blame Mike for that.'

'You mean he supplied her?'

'Yes, but that was only incidental. He took her over. Mike Leighton was a bastard. He lavished everything on that girl. He was very rich, you know.' Babs blurted out her accusations disjointedly, but Fox knew better than to interrupt. 'Right from when he recruited her, she was given everything. They used to go away for weekends on his yacht, and he bought her a car . . .'

'What did the rest of you think of that?'

'Not much,' said Babs. 'It caused a lot of discontent. One

or two of the girls wanted to pack it in. But it wasn't easy. Mike used to threaten us that if we left him, he'd make sure we never worked again. But I don't think they knew the price Beverley was paying.'

'What d'you mean by that, Miss Stocker?' asked Kate.

'There were two of the girls, I think, but Beverley was certainly one, who he picked out for what he called his special films.'

'What sort of special films?'

Babs Stocker hesitated for a moment before explaining. 'He'd chain them up and whip them, and sometimes he and Pritchard would rape them, quite brutally. And it'd all be filmed. It was sickening because they weren't at all willing, believe me, but by then he was paying them so much and giving them gifts – like I said, he gave Beverley a car – that they couldn't afford to quit. He asked me if I was interested once, but I told him I wasn't into that sort of thing. Straight sex is all right, but that . . .' She shuddered at the thought.

'Does the name Gail Thompson mean anything to you?' asked Fox. 'Apparently she quit.'

'Did she?' Babs Stocker shook her head. 'Doesn't ring any bells.'

'And he was supplying this Beverley with drugs, regularly, was he?'

Babs nodded. 'He said that any of us could have the stuff if we wanted it. He reckoned that it would improve our performance.' She stared at Fox and then, wanting to make sure that he fully understood, added, 'I'm talking about our sexual performance. For the cameras. Beverley's trouble was that she became hooked. That's why she put up with it, poor little cow. She knew that if she went, her supply'd be cut off, and she couldn't afford to finance the habit herself.'

'Were there any other men involved in these films, apart from Leighton, Webb and Pritchard, Miss Stocker?' asked Kate.

Babs Stocker switched her gaze to the Australian girl. 'There was one bloke, a real stud he was, who turned up once, but I've no idea who he was. I think they called him

Gary. But this is all a load of crap, you know. Mike Leighton was running this so-called film business mainly for his own pleasure. He got some sexual gratification out of doing it with a whole group of us and putting it on film. Oh yes, sure, he sold what he made, but that wasn't the main reason.' It was exactly what Carrie Grant had said about him. 'But, like I said, he was loaded and he paid us well for our services.' She laughed scornfully. 'Huh! Services. That's rich when you think about Beverley.'

'What was this Beverley's surname, Miss Stocker?' asked Kate.

Babs shook her head. 'I've no idea,' she said. 'We don't go in for last names much in this game.'

'And when and where did she die?'

'I don't know where.' Babs shrugged. 'But Harry Pritchard told us that it was about last August some time. Nearly a year ago now,' she added, and shook her head slowly. 'Poor little bitch.'

NINE

THE SMALL TEAM OF DETECTIVES that Fox had sent to the General Register Office at St Catherine's House in Kingsway turned up four women named Beverley whose deaths had been reported during August of the previous year. One in Swansea at the age of sixty-one, and a second in Axminster as the result of a road accident. Of the other two, both of whom had died in London, a thirty-seven-year-old had not survived giving birth, but the remaining one, a Beverley Watson, had yielded to a drugs overdose at the age of twenty-four, shortly after being brought to a central London hospital by ambulance.

'And what have you found out about this Beverley Watson, Bob?' asked Fox.

The detective sergeant who had led the team was called Robert Hurley. 'The ambulance service got a call from a male anon, sir,' he said. 'Apparently, he'd found Beverley Watson in a comatose state slumped on a bench outside a block of flats in Westminster. She died within seventeen minutes of admission. The PM showed signs of habitual drug abuse, but the specific cause was a lethal cocktail of amphetamines and alcohol.'

'How was she identified?' asked Fox. 'What did she have on her?'

'The only ID was a credit card, sir. That's where they got her name from. But enquiries of the credit card company showed that the card-holder, and the one who settled the bills was . . .' Hurley paused. 'One Michael Leighton, sir.' The DS grinned.

'So we don't have an address for this woman, other than Leighton's presumably. Incidentally, what address did the credit card company hold for him? Was it the Chelsea one?'

'No, sir,' said Hurley. 'Leighton Leisure Services of Fulham.'

Fox opened his cigarette case and offered it to the detective sergeant. 'That reckons,' he said. 'I'll bet Leighton didn't know she'd still got that on her. Do a birth search on this Beverley Watson, Bob—'

'Done it, sir,' said Hurley. He laid a sheet of paper on Fox's desk. 'Details are there. She's the daughter of Bernard Watson and Lee Watson, née Frith.'

'Bernie Watson?' Fox pondered the name. 'Not the Bernie Watson who—?'

Hurley nodded and laid a file on the desk. 'That's the one, sir. This is a printout of his microfiche. He's got about twenty-three previous for anything ranging from robbery to GBH, but he's fifty-seven now and he's gone straight for the last ten years.'

'You mean he hasn't been caught for the last ten years,' growled Fox.

'You could say that, sir, yes.'

'I just did,' said Fox, and picked up the file containing Watson's criminal record.

Fox, accompanied by Denzil Evans, hammered on the door of the large detached house on the outskirts of Welling in Kent and waited.

The man who eventually answered the door, and who had shouted, 'All right, all right, I'm coming,' before opening it, was short and stocky. The shirt he was wearing failed to disguise the muscular build that he had developed during his youth when he had done a variety of jobs ranging from fairground boxer to Canadian lumberjack. But he had always ended up on the wrong side of the law. In the 1960s, he had been on the fringe of one of the gangs that had plagued south London but, with their demise, he had gone into business for himself. But again, always in the twilight world between illegality and legitimacy. The file held by the National Criminal Intelligence Service suggested that he had interests in prostitution, gaming – legal and illegal – strip-joints, massage parlours, and even dog-fighting, still a popular pastime in the seedier parts of Kent and Essex. However, that information had never been strong enough to bring about proceedings for the further crimes that the police were convinced he had committed. But the Rolls-Royce languishing in his driveway was, in Fox's view, a good enough indication of a south London villain who just couldn't resist showing off his power. And his success.

'Well, well, well, if it ain't Superintendent Tommy Fox.' Watson grinned broadly and insolently.

'Commander Fox,' said Fox mildly.

'Really? Well, congratulations . . . Commander.' Watson pulled the door open. 'You'd better come in and have a celebratory drink, Mr Fox. And this, I take it, is a colleague of yours.'

'Detective Inspector Evans,' said Fox.

The room – Watson described it as his lounge – was huge but, in Fox's view, quite tasteless. The carpet had what, in some quarters, would be called a bold pattern, and seemed to stretch for miles. Two settees and five armchairs, all upholstered in black leather, were lost in the large room, one corner of which was filled by the biggest television set presently on the market. In another corner there was a state-of-the-art sound system flanked by several tall racks of compact discs. Hanging from the centre of the ceiling was the most grotesque crystal chandelier Fox had ever seen, much too big even for this room.

'Nice, ain't it?' said Watson, noticing Fox's close examination.

'It has all the aesthetic charm of a municipal mausoleum,' said Fox pensively.

'I knew you'd like it,' said Watson. 'All legit an' all. Nothing in here fell off the back of a lorry, Mr Fox, so you needn't go worrying on that score.'

'If it had fallen off the back of a lorry,' said Fox, 'I doubt that the driver would have bothered to stop.'

Watson roared with laughter. 'You always was a wag, Mr Fox. By the way, this here's the wife. I don't think you've ever met her, have you?'

'No,' said Fox. 'I'm sure I would have remembered.' The blonde, frizzy-haired woman who had entered the room was slightly taller than her husband and her monstrous figure was contained in a tight-fitting one-piece polyester garment in a leopard-skin design. The trouser legs stopped inches below her knees and the outfit did nothing to restore her bulges to their rightful place. In fact, her high-heeled mule sandals caused her bottom to stick out, accentuating its size.

'Geraldine, meet Mr Fox. He's an old friend of mine.'

'Charmed, I'm sure,' said Geraldine Watson, holding out a limp hand rather like a hostess receiving a debutante.

'I thought your wife's name was Lee,' said Fox.

Watson grinned. 'That was the first wife,' he said. 'We got divorced. Geraldine and me's been married for three years now.' He put an arm as far round his wife's figure as he could reach and gave her a squeeze.

'I see.' Fox could not believe that Geraldine Watson had deteriorated to her present gross state in so short a period as three years. The only conclusion at which he could arrive was that Watson must have married her when she looked much as she did today. 'Congratulations,' he said drily.

''Ere, what am I thinking of?' said Watson. 'Talking of congratulations, Gerry,' he said in an aside to his wife, 'Mr Fox was just telling me he's a commander now. Sit down, sit down, both of you, and let me get you a drink.' He approached a large cabinet on the far side of the room. It seemed to take him ages to reach it. 'You was always a Scotch drinker, as I recall, Mr Fox,' he said.

'Thank you,' said Fox. 'Water, no ice.'

'You an' all, Mr Evans?'

'Just a small one, please,' said Evans, unhappy, as always, about accepting hospitality from known criminals.

'No sooner said than done,' said Watson and opened the

front flap of the cabinet. Immediately, a fluorescent light began to flicker inside and some hidden speaker gave vent to an inferior recording of a German drinking song. 'Nice, ain't it?' he said. It seemed to be one of his favourite phrases.

'I had a cousin in the Navy,' said Mrs Watson, a vacant expression on her face.

'Really?' said Fox, at a loss to understand this sudden turn in the conversation.

'He was a chief petty officer,' said Mrs Watson proudly. 'His name was Nelson, Charlie Nelson. Good name for a sailor, isn't it? I wonder if you knew him at all.'

'Why should I know him?' asked Fox, totally bemused by Mrs Watson's babblings.

'Well, what with you being in the Navy an' all.'

Watson turned from the drinks cabinet, a glass in each hand. 'Mr Fox is a commander in the police, Gerry, not the Navy,' he said.

'Do what, dear?' asked Watson's wife.

Watson came nearer. 'I said Mr Fox is in the police, not the Navy.' He handed a glass of whisky to Fox. 'She's a bit Mutt-and-Jeff,' he explained. 'If you catch her on the wrong side, like. Well, cheers.'

'You had a daughter, Beverley, I believe,' said Fox.

'Ah, I wondered why you was here, Mr Fox,' said Watson. He became suddenly serious and set his glass down on a table. 'I mean, it's always nice to see old friends, but I knew there had to be something. Have you found her?'

That took Fox by surprise. 'Found her?' he said.

'Yeah, didn't you know? She's been missing for two years now. Ain't seen hair nor hide of her in all that time. I thought she might have gone off to Lee's. Like I said, she was my first wife, Bev's ma. But she ain't heard nothing neither.'

Fox took a sip of whisky. 'I'm afraid I've got some bad news for you, Bernie,' he said.

'You don't mean—?'

'I'm afraid she's dead,' said Fox. 'She died last August in a London hospital.'

Bernie Watson's jaw fell and he sat down suddenly in one

of the armchairs. 'But what happened?' he asked. 'She get run over or something?'

'No, she died from a drugs overdose.'

'Drugs? The silly little cow,' said Watson angrily. 'I always told her to stay away from drugs. Have a few vodkas by all means, girl, I used to say. Even smoke if you has to, but for Gawd's sake stay away from drugs.' He picked up his Scotch and drained the glass, even though it was half full. 'But there you are, you see,' he said. 'You can't watch 'em forever, can you?' He stared into his glass and remained silent for some seconds. 'Where's she buried, Mr Fox?' he asked.

'I don't know,' said Fox, 'but I'll get someone to ring you with that information.'

Watson looked up. 'There's more to this, ain't there, Mr Fox?' he said. 'More 'an what you're telling me. I mean a commander don't come all the way down to Welling just to tell someone that their daughter'd died nearly a year ago. What's going on?'

'We have reason to believe that she was associated with a man called Michael Leighton for some time immediately prior to her death—'

'Leighton, Leighton?' Watson savoured the name. 'That rings a bell. 'Ere, that's the geezer what got topped on his yacht out in the Med somewhere, ain't it? With a couple of birds. You on that, Mr Fox?'

'Yes, Bernie, I'm dealing with that.'

'The bastard. Was it him what introduced my Bev to drugs then?'

'It seems likely, yes.'

'Well, if there's anything I can do, Mr Fox,' said Watson, 'you just say the word.' He stood up, angrily gripping his empty glass. 'I know I haven't always played it straight, and I've done a bit of bird in me time, but drugs, well, that's something else, ain't it? I've still got contacts, see, Mr Fox. There's still a few favours I can call in from certain faces what I can lean on, if you take my drift. You just say the word.' He pointed at Fox's empty glass. 'One for the road, Mr Fox?'

* * *

'You ever met him before, Denzil?' asked Fox when the two detectives were travelling back to the Yard in Fox's Scorpio.

'No, sir. Heard of him, of course,' said Evans, 'but I've never had dealings with him. Confident sort of bastard, isn't he?'

'Too confident for my liking,' said Fox, 'but he's always been the same. Even when we had him bang to rights, he'd pop up at the Bailey, chirpy as you like, convinced that he was going to walk away. I remember once, back in the late seventies, he went down for a seven-stretch – that was for that wages job at Heathrow – and he just laughed. Shrugged it off.'

'D'you really think that he knew nothing about his daughter being dead, sir?' asked Evans.

'If he didn't, he's a bloody good actor,' said Fox, 'but then I always knew that. The point is that he's got a lot of contacts. He's also into porn in a big way, although we've never been able to prove it, and he must have come across Leighton long before his death. There's no way that anything happens in London that Bernie Watson doesn't know about. Nothing vaguely criminal, that is.'

'What d'you reckon then, sir?' asked Evans.

'We shall examine him closely, Denzil,' said Fox. 'Very closely indeed.'

In the first instance, the close examination of Bernie Watson's nefarious activities was entrusted to Detective Sergeant Wally Stone. Fox told him that he was interested to know all there was to know about the south London villain who now lived in Welling, and that he should make no secret of the sudden police interest. In short, Stone was told to get out and beat on the ground. Just to see what came up.

Stone sallied forth into the hinterland of London's criminal world and began, enthusiastically, to ask questions. His wide-ranging coterie of informants was interrogated about Watson's business activities, his life-style, his money and his friends and acquaintances.

Stone's frequent allusions to Fox's interest in Watson sent a frisson of apprehension through the villainry; they knew that when Tommy Fox started to involve himself in one particular individual's business, others were likely to become casualties. That was all part of Fox's plan, and although he was no nearer finding the killers of Leighton and the two women, he had developed an instinctive feeling about his old adversary. DS Stone had been asking questions in the haunts of the unrighteous for only a day when word got back to Bernie Watson that the heat was on. And that disconcerted him.

In the meantime, Fox decided that Raymond Webb, the late Michael Leighton's partner, was overdue for an interview. Webb's close association with Leighton, and his participation in the making of the pornographic videos, had convinced Fox that he knew more than he was telling but, in all fairness, Fox had not posed any questions about the seamier side of the activities of Leighton Leisure Services. Now he intended to find out a lot more about it and its sole surviving director. As Fox put it to Evans, 'I think it's time we rattled his bars for him, Denzil.'

TEN

FOX DECIDED TO POSTPONE HIS renewed harassment of Raymond Webb, the acting head of Leighton Leisure Services, for another day. Instead, he resolved to mount a raid on the studio near Baylis Road where, despite police interest, the porn videos were still being made; Fox tended to regard this as a personal affront. And he decided to do it as soon as his watchers told him that the film director had shouted 'Action' for the first time. It was not that Fox had the slightest interest in the live performance that he knew he and his officers would encounter, but it was an opportunity to identify more of the participants, either on tape or in the flesh. Literally.

Just for good measure, Fox had arranged for the presence of a few 'feet' as he called the Uniform Branch, and the attendance of two officers from the Obscene Publications Squad to give their professional opinion and maintain continuity of evidence.

Swann, Fox's driver, who was also an expert at picking locks, made short work of the small door that was used as a main entrance to the warehouse and, led by Fox, the team of eight detectives entered. The centre of the warehouse, bathed now in floodlights, was carpeted, and several pieces of tawdry furniture stood against a background of drapes. On a large bed in the centre of this makeshift set, a naked man was being well and truly ministered to by three naked girls. Two other men in dressing gowns and three other girls, each attired in the sort of micro-underwear favoured by whores, stood behind the cameras watching with bored expressions on their faces.

'Ah!' said Fox. 'Six of one and half a dozen of the other.'

One of the girls screamed as she sighted the CID officers, but when the 'cast' saw a couple of uniformed police officers trooping in behind them, they dissolved into laughter. One of them shouted, 'We've been busted, folks,' in a mock-American accent. The quartet on the bed got unhurriedly to their feet and went in search of some clothing with which to cover their nudity.

The cameraman was Harry Pritchard. 'Oh, it's you,' he said offhandedly when he sighted Fox. 'Now what?'

'Making a film?' asked Fox innocently.

'You know bloody well we are,' said Pritchard. 'Here,' he said to a naked girl who sauntered past him. 'Cover yourself up, for Christ's sake, it's the fuzz.' He turned back to Fox. 'Well, what d'you want now?'

'For a start,' said Fox, 'are you in charge of this little enterprise?'

'Yeah.' Pritchard stepped away from his camera and faced Fox. 'This is all kosher, you know,' he said, playing with the light meter that hung on a cord around his neck. 'There's nothing bent about this lot.' He waved a hand towards the actors and actresses, some of whom were grouped in a corner while others were seated on the bed. They had all covered themselves now and were watching the proceedings with interest. 'It's just blokes screwing birds. Happens all the time.' He grinned. 'All we're doing is putting it on tape.'

'And what d'you propose doing with these Oscar-winning productions when you've finished?' asked Fox.

'All for export, squire,' said Pritchard. 'We sell them to the Scandinavian countries and to Europe. The Prime Minister encourages trade with the Community, you know,' he added with heavy sarcasm.

'Bit like taking coals to Newcastle,' said Fox laconically. 'And where's your star performer this morning?'

'Who's that?'

'Raymond Webb, Esquire.'

Pritchard laughed outright. 'You must be joking,' he said.

'The only reason he ever got involved with this was because Leighton let him come and play. In lieu of wages, probably. But he was a piss-poor performer, I can tell you that. One stunt and he was blown out. When Leighton died, I told him his services were no longer required.'

'Why did you make videos of him in the first place then?'

'For laughs,' said Pritchard. 'We used to show them to the girls after he'd gone. Used to fall about in hysterics, they did.' He glanced across at the group of girls sitting on the bed. 'This copper reckons that Ray Webb was our star stud,' he shouted.

There was a burst of laughter, and one of the girls mouthed a rude comment on Webb's performance and made an obscene gesture.

'Well, we'll just have a few names and addresses,' said Fox, 'and then we'll be on our way.'

'Sure,' said Pritchard. 'And don't forget to give these horny coppers your phone numbers as well, girls,' he shouted.

It was a pointless exercise – Fox knew that the names would be false – but he was deliberately wasting time. He had told DI Charles Morgan to seize as many tapes as he could find. And while Fox had been engaged in his bantering conversation with Pritchard, Morgan had done exactly that. A van had been backed up to the rear entrance of the warehouse and some four hundred tapes had been loaded into it.

When Morgan approached and nodded, Fox turned, once more, to Pritchard. 'By the way,' he said, 'we've seized all your video tapes. This officer will give you a receipt.'

'What?' Pritchard showed the first signs of losing his composure. 'You can't do that. What entitles you to do that?'

'Oh dear!' said Fox, shaking his head sagely. 'There are several sections of the various Obscene Publications Acts which give police power of seizure on the grounds that you have an obscene article for publication or gain. There's a lot more to it, but doubtless your solicitor will explain the finer points.'

'But I told you,' said Pritchard, 'they're all for export.'

'Unfortunately for you, the aforementioned Acts of Parliament don't make allowances for the export trade,' said Fox and smiled benignly.

That afternoon a start was made on viewing a small selection of the video tapes. Most of them consisted of the sort of poor quality, tacky filth that is to be found in shady shops throughout the larger cities of the country, and in the suitcases of innocents returning through British airports where they are relieved of their expensive purchases by Her Majesty's Customs.

Several of the tapes featured Raymond Webb. As Pritchard had said, his performance was little short of ludicrous and at one stage, Kate Ebdon, overcome with hysterics, had to leave the room. In general though, there was little to lead Fox and his team any closer to finding the murderer of Leighton and his two female companions.

Fox and his murder squad had time to look at only a few of the video-cassettes; the job of analysing the entire four hundred would be the unenviable task of the Obscene Publications Squad. Fox was determined that Pritchard and Webb, and anyone else who came into the frame, would be prosecuted at least for the obscenity offences, if for nothing else.

Just in case he needed it, Fox took another search warrant with him for the premises of Leighton Leisure Services in Fulham. He also took Detective Constable Kate Ebdon, knowing that she had the ability to terrify a male witness when the occasion demanded. Or, to put it another way, Kate would take liberties that no one else would get away with.

'Oh, not again,' said Raymond Webb. 'I'm trying to run a business here.'

'That's exactly what interests me, Raymond, old dear,' said Fox as, uninvited, he and Kate sat down in Webb's office. 'I am greatly interested in your film-making enterprise. As a matter of fact, I was only saying to Miss Ebdon on the way here, how much I deprecate the demise of the British film industry.' He assumed a wistful expression. 'All those marvellous Ealing comedies . . .' He smiled at Webb. 'It's good to know that someone's doing something about it.'

'I haven't the faintest idea what you're talking about,' said Webb, a hint of exasperation in his reply.

'Really?' Fox sounded surprised. 'Now I would have thought that a fellow like you, Raymond, old fruit, would have been on top of your wide-ranging business empire. D'you mean to say that you are unaware of the film-producing side of this set-up?' He waved a hand around the office.

'I don't know what you're talking about,' said Webb again.

'Well now . . .' began Fox patiently. 'Let me explain. I have recently interviewed a horde of young ladies' – Fox had no intention of revealing that, so far, he had spoken to only two – 'who claim to have taken part in your latest productions. Young ladies who, it seems, readily shed their clothes, and their inhibitions, and indulge in riotous sexual congress with Mr Harry Pritchard, well-known society photographer, and your good self. They also claimed to have done it with Mr Michael Leighton before his untimely demise.'

'That's a bloody lie.' Webb gave a derisive laugh. 'Do I look like a porn movie star, for Christ's sake?'

'I have to admit that I found it a little surprising,' said Fox mildly. 'I just put it down to the fact that there is always a market for depraved variations. Have you heard that, Kate?' He switched his gaze to the woman detective.

'So I've heard, sir.' Kate grinned at Webb disconcertingly.

'Look, I don't have to put up with this,' said Webb furiously. 'You can't just come into the office of a respectable businessman and make these wild and, I have to say, quite ludicrous accusations. I'll sue you for slander, that's what I'll do.'

'Couple of problems there, Raymond, old sport,' said Fox. 'Firstly . . .' He made a point of peering around the office. 'Firstly, you don't appear to have any witnesses – although I do – and secondly, I happen to know that what I've just said is true. Yesterday morning, my officers and I searched the warehouse at the back of Waterloo Station that you and your late partner had the temerity to describe as a studio. You will be pleased to learn that we found ample cinematographic evidence there of your athletic prowess.' He paused. 'Although, in all fairness, I must say that several of the young ladies I interviewed were singularly unimpressed by your performance.' Fox shook his head. 'Chaps of our age need to learn when to pack it in, you know, Raymond,' he added.

Webb, who until now had been seated behind his desk, leaped to his feet. 'I'm not having this,' he said angrily, his fists clenching and unclenching rhythmically. 'Just because Mike gets murdered thousands of miles away from here doesn't mean you can come in here and walk all over me.'

'Funny you should say that,' said Kate mildly. 'One of the videos we found shows a naked young lady doing exactly that. Walking all over you, I mean. And you weren't wearing any clothes either. At the same time, another young lady was . . .' She broke off. 'Well, you know what she was doing, don't you?' She grinned insolently at the hapless director. 'Taking dictation, was she? But quite frankly the sight of your bare arse on those videos was too much for me. Last time I saw anything going up and down like that it was the first violinist's elbow at the Sydney Opera House.' Kate had been primed by Fox, prior to their arrival at the Fulham offices, to goad Webb. Fox was convinced that he had something to hide, and possibly to tell, but he also knew that to arrest Webb and take him to a police station there to interview him under formal conditions would be a waste of time. Within minutes, the place would be swarming with solicitors. But, as things stood, Fox had no intention of prosecuting Webb at present. He saw him possibly as a useful witness. At least, that's what he hoped.

Webb collapsed into his chair, an expression of resignation on his face. 'I don't know what that video was doing there,' he said. 'It was taken for purely private amusement.'

'How splendid,' said Fox. 'Who were the young ladies?'

'Girl-friends of mine,' said Webb. He had leaned forward in his chair, his head resting between his hands, elbows on his desk.

'Names?' demanded Fox.

For a moment, Webb looked as though he was going to refuse to identify his carnal companions, but then he surrendered. 'They're called Anna and Kirsty,' he said.

'Anna Coombs and Kirsty Newman, I presume,' said Fox, grateful that the surveillance team at the studio near Waterloo had succeeded in identifying those two girls for him.

Webb looked up sharply. 'How did you know that?' he asked.

'Because, Mr Webb, I made it my business to find out,' said Fox, assuming a sudden formality that disconcerted the wretched man opposite him. 'I am investigating a triple murder and quite frankly, I get bloody annoyed when people try to obstruct me in those enquiries. So annoyed, in fact, that I am sorely tempted to arrest such persons and charge them.'

'I still don't see what this has to do with Mike's murder,' said Webb. 'All right, so we were making porn videos. That's not a crime, is it? Not any more?'

'That depends,' said Fox seriously. Secretly, he had never understood why so much smug anger was directed against filming the sexual act, provided it was straightforward and didn't involve children or any other perversions. But it still contravened the law and that was good enough for Fox. 'I have evidence that Leighton was administering drugs to some of these girls. It is said by witnesses that he did so in order to heighten their abandonment and to reduce them to a state where they were unable to resist being tortured. Just so that you and Leighton could profit from your filthy trade.' He paused and fixed Webb with a malevolent stare that made the man squirm. 'What d'you know about Beverley Watson?'

The question came like a whiplash and its suddenness clearly shocked Webb. 'I, er, I—'

'Don't pussyfoot about,' said Fox. 'You know perfectly well what I'm talking about.'

'She was Mike's girl-friend . . .'

'Come off it,' said Fox. 'She was one of the girls who took part in your dirty movies. We have her on film doing it with Leighton. And with you. And, incidentally, with Pritchard.'

Webb shrugged. 'So what? You seem to know all the answers, so why ask me?'

'She died of a drugs overdose last August, Mr Webb, having been abandoned in a London street, almost certainly by Leighton. And I want to know where she got the drugs from.' Fox knew that Leighton had been the supplier, but he wanted to hear it from Webb. He was also anxious to know if Webb had played any part in their supply.

'It wasn't me,' said Webb quietly.

'Who then?'

'Mike. He used to hand them out to any of the girls who wanted them. Some took them, some didn't.'

'Why? Why did he give them drugs?'

'It was like you said.' Webb still avoided meeting Fox's gaze. 'The girls used to perform much better when they were high.'

'Scum like you disgust me.' Fox spoke quietly but menacingly. 'And if I get even the sniff of any evidence that you were actively involved in drug-dealing, I shall make sure you go down for a very long time.'

'I tell you, I had nothing to do with it. It was all down to Mike. He was into drugs in a big way.' Webb spoke desperately. He had been in prison for only six of his nine-months sentence, and that was nearly twenty years ago, but he still recalled what happened to those perverts incarcerated for sex crimes, and he shuddered at the recollection.

'Very convenient,' said Fox as he stood up. 'Incidentally, I suppose you know who Beverley Watson was.'

'Who she was?' Webb made a pretence of not understanding the question.

'She was Bernie Watson's daughter.'

Webb had been in the act of standing up also. But now

he sank down into his chair again, gripping its arms as his face paled. 'Who?' he asked lamely.

Fox grinned. 'I see you know who Bernie Watson is,' he said.

'Well, yes,' said Webb, recovering a little of his composure. 'Mike used to have dealings with him. Business dealings.'

'What sort of business dealings?' Fox also sat down again.

'Fruit machines and juke-boxes. That sort of thing.' Webb was clearly panicking now. The mention of Bernie Watson's name had frightened the life out of him, and it was obvious to Fox that Webb was, at best, little more than a pander, a pimp who had been drawn into Leighton's shady activities. And, as Pritchard had said, Webb's reward had been free sex with any of what Leighton called his stable of fillies. But Fox thought that Webb, despite being described as a director, was probably no more than the accountant he had admitted to being. And that Leighton had brought him in to indulge in some creative bookkeeping that would disguise the income that came from the less desirable side of his business. Doubtless, Webb's previous conviction for fraud, albeit a minor one, was seen by Leighton as insurance against his co-director opening his mouth.

'Fair enough,' said Fox, standing up again. 'Well that seems to let you off the hook, Raymond, old love. I doubt that we shall have to bother you again.' He held out his hand and Webb seized it like a drowning man and shook it vigorously. It was only later that he found out that it was very dangerous to underestimate the well-dressed commander from Scotland Yard.

'Did you mean what you said, sir?' asked a bewildered Kate Ebdon as she and Fox rode back to Scotland Yard.

'I rarely mean anything I say, Kate,' said Fox. 'What, in particular, did you have in mind?'

'About not bothering with Webb any more.'

'Good heavens no.' Fox grinned. 'But it suddenly dawned on me that a close examination of the books of Leighton Leisure Services might just reveal all sorts of interesting facts.

And a few lies as well. And I didn't want him destroying all the evidence before I can get an expert to look at the books. And I'm not an expert at everything,' he added. That statement, when repeated by Kate to the staff of the incident room, brought forth ironical laughter.

Fox said nothing more until they arrived at the Yard. He gestured to Kate to sit down and then tapped out an internal number on his telephone. 'Ray? Tommy Fox.'

There was an audible groan from the other end of the phone as Commander Ray Probert, head of the Metropolitan and City Police Company Fraud Department, better known to the Press as the Fraud Squad, realised that he should have let his secretary answer the call. 'What d'you want, Tommy?' he asked guardedly.

'A favour, Ray. Have you got an officer you can spare for a day to go through the books of a shady enterprise called Leighton Leisure Services down at Fulham?'

'Well,' said Probert reluctantly, 'I suppose I could. But just for a day. What's it all about?'

Briefly, Fox outlined what he wanted. 'And I'd like my DC Ebdon to go with your officer,' he said. 'She's fully conversant with the case.'

'Yeah, all right then,' said Probert. 'What will my man be looking for? In particular, I mean.'

'Nothing,' said Fox, 'in particular.'

ELEVEN

DETECTIVE SERGEANT IRVING MAYNARD WAS a portly individual. His rimless spectacles should have lent him the sort of clerkly appearance that befitted his role as a member of the Fraud Squad, but they merely served to create a rather sinister impression. Few people would have mistaken him for anything but a policeman, and he would have been a gift to any television producer looking for an archetypal Flying Squad officer.

'Are you Ebdon?' Maynard appeared in the doorway of the incident room, his gaze settling on the flame-haired Australian.

'Yeah! Who are you?'

'DS Maynard, Fraud Squad. My guv'nor says your guv'nor wants us to turn over some sleaze-merchant in Fulham.'

'Oh, right, sarge,' said Kate. She stood up and grabbed her bag, carefully placing the strap over her right shoulder.

'Got a brief, have you?'

'Too right, sarge,' said Kate, grinning. She produced the search warrant from her bag and handed it to the Fraud Squad DS.

'Don't want to see it,' said Maynard. 'Just wanted to make sure you'd got one, that's all. Shall we hit this guy, then?'

They took the Underground to Parsons Green and walked the rest of the way. For the whole journey, Maynard talked incessantly about fly-fishing, a hobby to which, it seemed, he devoted most of his spare time. As they reached the offices of Leighton Leisure Services, he asked, 'Ever done any fishing yourself, Kate?'

Kate, who had become increasingly bored by Maynard's diatribe on angling, shrugged. 'Only for sharks off Bondi,' she lied crushingly.

Since Fox's departure the previous day, Raymond Webb had convinced himself that he was in the clear. Consequently, the arrival of DS Maynard and, yet again, Kate Ebdon, came as a complete surprise. 'Look,' he said, 'your boss said that he wouldn't have to bother me again.'

'We're not bothering *you*, Mr Webb,' said Maynard, whose monologue on fishing had been interrupted by Kate long enough for her to brief him thoroughly. 'We've come to do the books.' He grinned and perched on the edge of Webb's desk. 'It's not you we're interested in. It's Mr Leighton.'

'But—' began Webb.

'You see, Mr Webb,' began Maynard patiently, 'when someone is murdered along with two other people, all of whom are connected with the blue movie business, we in the police tend to come to the conclusion that there's a connection.'

'Someone went to a lot of trouble to take out your partner Leighton,' said Kate. 'That wasn't just a killing for the hell of it.'

'She's right, you know,' said Maynard, leaning closer to Webb in an attitude of amiable menace. 'And we in the Fraud Squad have often found that the answer lies in the books.' He smiled and flicked over a page on Webb's desk calendar. 'You're out of date,' he murmured.

'Fraud Squad?' Webb stared at the detective sergeant. 'Did you say Fraud Squad?'

'That's right, Mr Webb. You've doubtless heard of us.' Maynard gazed at Webb, an enquiring expression on his face. Kate had told him about Webb's previous conviction.

'You'll find nothing wrong with the books here,' said Webb, more in hope than certainty.

'You the accountant then?' enquired Maynard, well knowing that to be the case.

'Well, yes, among other things.'

Maynard pursed his lips and nodded. 'Well,' he said, 'we'll see.'

'Are *you* an accountant?' asked Webb. 'A qualified accountant, I mean.'

'Good heavens no,' said Maynard. 'I'm a detective. But I'm sure I'll muddle through.'

Webb looked slightly less worried, but what Maynard had not said was that accountants instinctively want the books to balance, whereas detectives instinctively want to prove that they don't.

Maynard rubbed his hands together and slid off the desk. 'Shall we make a start then?'

'Look, I'm not sure that I can allow you to come in here and just demand to see the firm's books. What authority d'you have for that?'

Kate Ebdon smiled and, opening her handbag, produced an official-looking piece of paper. 'This is a search warrant, Mr Webb,' she said. 'I know you've seen one before. And just to be on the safe side we obtained it from a Crown Court judge. Takes care of any nonsense about excluded material and all that twaddle. Okay?'

'How did you get on?' asked Fox.

'Very interesting, sir,' said DS Maynard as he and Kate Ebdon sat down opposite Fox's desk. 'I told him he was in the clear.'

Fox raised an eyebrow. 'And is he?'

'Good Lord no, sir.' Maynard looked askance at the implication that a Fraud Squad officer of his calibre and experience should have found nothing wrong with a set of books. 'There was some evidence of teeming and lading—'

'You'd better explain that for Kate's benefit,' said Fox.

Maynard glanced at the woman detective. 'In short,' he said, 'it means that monies coming in today have been used to cover that which was embezzled yesterday. Robbing Peter to pay Paul in other words.' He looked back at Fox. 'I imagine that Webb's had his hand in the till, sir. And there were one or two fanciful entries that merely showed "Royalties and Fees", whatever that means. I didn't bother to examine the supporting dockets because, in my experience, they'd've been bent too. Probably hiding the income from their porn videos. Cunning bastards didn't want to upset either the Inland Revenue or the VAT boys, I should think, but they obviously didn't expect a visit from us.'

'Worth doing anything about it?' asked Fox.

Maynard shrugged. 'Depends on the Crown Prosecution Service really, sir. It's certainly not big enough to worry the Serious Fraud Office with. But if you nick Webb for this murder, it'll all be irrelevant anyway, won't it?'

'I think we're a long way from doing that,' said Fox, 'but it might provide us with evidence that Leighton's were profiting from blue movies, if you can prove what you found.'

'Anyway, sir,' said Maynard, 'I left him with the impression that his accountancy was all kosher just so that he doesn't do anything stupid.'

'He's left it a bit late for that,' growled Fox. 'So, what else did you find?'

'Nothing really, sir,' continued Maynard. 'There's some trade in juke-boxes and fruit machines certainly, and all legitimately accounted for, but they're not making much profit. I didn't let on to Webb that I was doubtful about those dodgy entries I mentioned because he thought that I was there just to see if the books contained anything that might lead you to Leighton's killer. In fact, I told him that we weren't interested in him and he seemed quite satisfied with that, relieved almost. And it's my bet that it'll be business as usual from now on. Incidentally, sir, most of what they do sell goes for export. Some of it to service bases abroad. Germany mainly, but also to Northern Ireland. And to Cyprus, sir.'

'Thanks,' said Fox acidly. 'That's just the sort of complication I needed.' He swung round to face the woman detective. 'Any indication of consignments being despatched in the near future, Kate?' he asked.

'Yes, sir.' Kate flicked open her pocket book and thumbed through the pages before glancing up again. 'One of the things we learned from looking at Webb's books is that

Leighton's have got a warehouse in another part of Fulham where they keep their stock.' She glanced back at her pocket book. 'It would seem that there are three fruit machines going to Germany the day after tomorrow, sir. Out through Heathrow Airport. There was also an order for six fruit machines that are to be sent to a warehouse in Croydon, also the day after tomorrow. There was no company name on the despatch note, just an address.'

Fox gazed out of the window. 'I think we'll have a look at those,' he said thoughtfully.

'Only too delighted, Commander,' said the Assistant Collector of Customs and Excise at Heathrow Airport when Fox telephoned him with his request. 'Pornographic videos, you say?'

'If they're anywhere,' said Fox, 'they'll be in the fruit machines.'

'Leave it to us. If they're there, we'll find them,' said the Assistant Collector.

Having set that trap, Fox now took an interest in the consignment of six fruit machines destined for the warehouse in Croydon. Deciding, for once, to remain detached from the operation, he assigned Detective Inspector Denzil Evans and a team of ten officers to follow the consignment from Leighton Leisure Services to Croydon.

Fortunately, one of the detective sergeants on Evans's team had secured a discreet vantage point on top of a building that gave a clear view of the yard at the rear of Leighton's warehouse. At eight o'clock, a van from a lesser-known freight-carrying company pulled into the yard and three fruit machines were loaded on to it. This information was relayed to Fox at Scotland Yard, and ten minutes later, the mobile surveillance team reported that it was definitely heading for Heathrow Airport. That observation was broken off and customs at the airport alerted. At ten minutes past ten, another, larger van from the same company collected six fruit machines, each in a distinctive wooden crate, and this van was followed to Croydon by Evans's mobiles.

The warehouse to which the machines were delivered actually proved to be nearer Thornton Heath than the centre of Croydon and, on the van's arrival, the fruit machines were unloaded and moved inside on a fork-lift truck. To the observers there appeared to be nothing covert or underhand about the delivery.

But that did not satisfy Fox. He ordered Evans to continue his surveillance at the warehouse until more was found out about it and its owners.

Fox was convinced that anything connected with Leighton Leisure Services had to be bordering on the criminal at best. He sent for Detective Sergeant Wally Stone and told him to find out all about the warehouse at Thornton Heath. And he told him not to waste time because a valuable officer, in the shape of DI Evans, was sitting watching it.

That Fox's instincts proved to be accurate, yet again, was borne out by Stone's report that the warehouse was owned by one Dimitri Constantinou, a Greek gentleman whose business was, in turn, owned by a certain Mr Bernard Watson of Welling.

'Good gracious me,' said Fox. 'That makes up for the bad news.'

'What bad news is that, guv?' asked Stone.

'Customs at Heathrow took those bloody fruit machines apart. Nothing!'

Because of Watson's interest in the warehouse at Thornton Heath, Fox ordered Evans to maintain the observation. He was a little annoyed that Watson, despite the overt enquiries that DS Stone had made throughout the West End, seemed to be carrying on as normal; Fox didn't like villains who thought that they were now too big to worry about the law. He was convinced, rightly as it happened, that the fruit machines would not languish at Thornton Heath for long. And the benefit of keeping watch on the premises was proved when another, unmarked, van arrived within an hour or so of the fruit-machine delivery. A large cardboard box was unloaded from this van and wheeled into the warehouse. The second van's index number was noted and run through the Police National Computer. It was registered to Harry Pritchard at his Soho address.

'Aha!' said Fox, rubbing his hands together. 'I do believe that something is about to happen.' And he caused a message to be sent to Evans, still keeping watch, to report any movements.

Fox did not have long to wait. At four o'clock that afternoon, the same six crates were loaded on to a van which left the Thornton Heath warehouse clearly bound for Gatwick Airport.

Fox threw open the door of the incident room. 'Kate,' he said, 'get hold of Swann and tell him to get the car on the front. I'll meet you there.'

'Right, sir,' said Kate. 'Where are we going?'

'Gatwick,' said Fox. 'Once I've made a phone call.'

The telephone call that Fox made was to the Surveyor of Customs and Excise responsible for anti-smuggling operations at Gatwick Airport. Briefly, he explained his suspicions about the consignment of fruit machines and promised the officer that he would be with him as soon as possible. And in a flurry of blue lights and sirens, Fox and Kate Ebdon set off for the second-largest airport in Britain.

A few years ago, there would have been very little chance of the fruit machines passing through the airport quickly, given the plethora of documentation that accompanies such movements. But since the advent of the Citizens' Charter, cargo is normally cleared within four hours. When Fox arrived at the airport, the consignment had already been delivered and several customs officers of the élite cargo crew were sniffing around it like ambitious terriers.

'Well, Commander,' said the Surveyor, shaking hands, 'when you're ready, we'll make a start.' He nodded to a customs officer who, large case-opener in hand, was hovering enthusiastically. 'They're destined for Brussels, by the way,' he added.

One by one, the six crates were opened and the fruit machines removed. Another customs officer approached and began to dismantle the first machine.

'Does he know what he's doing?' asked Fox.

The Surveyor nodded. 'He's a fruit machine addict,' he said nonchalantly. 'I'm told he spends most of his time – and half his salary – playing the bloody things.'

Within seconds, the customs officer had found what Fox had fully expected him to find. The machine contained six video cassettes. And by the time the search had been completed, thirty-six cassettes stood in a neat pile on a table.

'Right,' said the Surveyor, 'let's have a look at them.'

'How kind,' murmured Fox.

'Not at all,' said the customs chief. 'We would have done anyway.'

'Well, I don't suppose for one moment that they're pirated copies of *Coronation Street*.' Fox grinned expectantly.

'What d'you want us to do now?' asked the Surveyor, once police and customs had satisfied themselves that the videos were indeed pornographic.

'What would you normally do?' asked Fox.

'Well, I don't want to do anything that will cock up your murder investigation,' said the Surveyor. 'After all, we're supposed to be on the same side. But usually we'd seize them and substitute blanks.'

'I was going to suggest that anyway,' said Fox, one hand resting lightly on the pile of video tapes.

The Surveyor looked crafty and immediately thought that it would be much better if the cost of the replacement blanks came from the Metropolitan Police budget rather than his own. 'You can get them in the North Terminal,' he said quickly before Fox had a chance to change his mind.

'Do you have to inform the consignors of what you've done?'

'Eventually,' said the Surveyor, looking vaguely into the middle distance.

Fox turned to the woman detective. 'Have you got a credit card with you, Kate?' he asked.

'Yes, sir.'

'Good,' said Fox. 'Pop over to . . .' He paused and glanced at the Surveyor. 'North Terminal?'

'Yes, but it's a long way from here.'

'That's all right,' said Fox. 'DC Ebdon is a fit young officer.' And addressing Kate once more, he said, 'Buy thirty-six blank cassette tapes and make sure you get a receipt.' He turned back to the Surveyor. 'If we substitute them for these' – he tapped the pile of cassettes – 'it will probably cause exactly the sort of grief and aggravation that might flush someone or something out of the woodwork when they arrive in Belgium.' And he grinned maliciously.

'Fine by me,' said the Surveyor with a shrug. 'And I can probably get you the VAT back on your blank tapes. As they're going for export,' he added.

TWELVE

THE SURVEYOR OF CUSTOMS AND Excise at Gatwick Airport had undertaken to liaise with his counterparts at Brussels National Airport, and Fox had spoken to a colonel of the Belgian gendarmerie in the city. But he did not relish leaving matters in the hands of other people, especially people over whom he had no control.

'It's a great shame, Denzil, that we can't put a tap on Webb's and Pritchard's telephones. But there's no way the Home Secretary would grant a warrant, not unless we could prove a connection between porn videos and the murder of Leighton.' Fox sighed. 'And probably even then, he'd refuse. But I'll bet the wires will be burning once the recipients of that consignment, whoever they may be, find that they've got thirty-six blank tapes.' He fingered the receipt that Kate Ebdon had obtained when she had purchased them. 'Property of the Receiver for the Metropolitan Police District,' he added gloomily.

In the absence of a telephone intercept, Fox ordered that surveillance be mounted on Webb and Pritchard. And, playing a hunch, on Watson also. It was expensive in terms of manpower, but Fox believed that it would be of short duration. He was right: only twenty-four hours elapsed before something happened.

The fruit machines were collected from Brussels Airport and officers of the gendarmerie followed them to a warehouse in the Obourg region of Mons just north of the Canal du Centre, some forty miles distant from the airport at which they had arrived.

There, unbeknown to the watching police, Karel van Hooft removed the video tapes and placed them in a locked cabinet in his office pending delivery to his more salacious customers. But van Hooft was something of a voyeur himself and after his workmen had gone home, he fed one of the tapes into his video-player and settled down, with his secretary and a bottle of his favourite sparkling Saumur, to watch the latest production from England. With mounting annoyance, he eventually tried all thirty-six tapes.

The following day, van Hooft telephoned Bernie Watson in some place called Welling.

Bernie Watson threw down the telephone, his face black with rage, and then marched about his enormous house shouting for his wife Geraldine. Getting no answer, he eventually made his way through to the back of the house and into the wood-and-glass extension which had been built to accommodate the swimming pool. Bernie Watson never used it, couldn't swim in fact, but he had succumbed to the wishes of Geraldine, upon whom he lavished every luxury.

'Gerry!' Watson gazed down at the figure of his wife, slowly ploughing up and down the pool in a travesty of the breast-stroke.

Slowly, like a tanker altering course, Geraldine changed direction, reached the steps and climbed out of the water. Her skirted swim-suit, which would have been more fashionable on a Victorian matron emerging from a nineteenth-century bathing-machine, clung to her gross body, and her hair, normally a frizzy blonde, was plastered to her head like a skull cap. Her arms and legs, exposed for too long on a sun-bed, were bright red. 'What is it, Bernie?'

'I'm going up west,' said Watson.

'What, now?' Geraldine glanced at her gold wrist-watch, careless that it was not impervious to water, and then looked at her husband. 'What for, Bernie, love?'

'Because some bleedin' toe-rag's had me over, that's what for,' said Watson, his face still suffused with anger.

'And what's more I'm going to take it out of the little bastard's hide.'

Geraldine put her leg-of-mutton arms around Watson, regardless of the fact that she was still wet, and clasped him to her immense bosom. 'Bernie, love, don't. You're in the big time now. If someone's done you down, speak to your lawyer. Let him deal with it. That's what he's paid for.'

Watson eased his wife's bulk away and pulled his wet shirt from his body. 'It's not on, Gerry. See, this particular business was just a bit dodgy, like. Know what I mean?'

'What?' Geraldine picked up a vast towel and wrapped it around herself before sitting down suddenly on a sun-lounger and staring at Watson accusingly. The chair groaned in protest and for a moment it looked as though it might collapse altogether. 'How was it dodgy?'

Watson sighed and sat down opposite his wife. 'They was some tapes what I sent to Karel van Hooft in Belgium. Only a bit of fun, like.'

'Tapes? What tapes? What are you talking about, Bernie Watson?' Geraldine fixed him with a disparaging gaze.

'Well, they was videos, like.'

'Videos?' Suddenly the truth dawned on Geraldine. ''Ere,' she said, 'you don't mean sex an' that?'

Watson laughed uneasily. 'Like I said, only a bit of fun.'

'They was blue films, wasn't they?' In her anger, Geraldine struggled to get up, but her exertions caused the sun-lounger finally to sink beneath her. For a moment, she sat in the wreckage, her fat legs stuck out ludicrously in front of her so that she looked like a great cooked lobster. Watson stood up and held out his hands, but Geraldine knew she was beyond any help that her husband could afford her. She rolled over and eased herself up on to all-fours before ponderously regaining her feet. 'What on earth are you doing getting mixed up in that sort of business, Bernie?' she asked, turning to face Watson. 'Is that what that copper come down here for the other day?'

Watson laughed dismissively. 'No, course not. You know why he was here. He come to tell me about Bev.'

'You're selling these dirty films aren't you, Bernie?' Slowly, Geraldine advanced on her husband.

'No, nothing like that. Karel van Hooft's a mate of mine and he likes them, see. So I sends him some every so often. Takes all sorts, don't it?'

Geraldine began to rub fiercely at her hair with the towel. 'I thought you was supposed to be a respectable businessman, Bernie Watson. That's what you told me when we was married.'

'Yeah, well I am, pet,' said Watson, slowly retreating in the face of his wife's obvious wrath.

'Well then, what the hell are you doing flogging blue films? You taken leave of your senses or something? How d'you expect to keep friends like that nice commander if you go about doing stupid things like that?' Geraldine dropped her towel, but appeared not to notice. 'I shouldn't think he'd be too happy if he knew what you was up to.'

'Well, he's not going to know, is he?' said Watson nervously. 'I keep telling you, Gerry, it was only a favour for a friend.' By now, he was at the edge of the pool.

'I'm warning you, Bernie, if you want to keep me, you'll pack it in.' Suddenly realising that she had lost her towel, Geraldine stooped to pick it up, her head colliding with Watson's midriff as she did so.

With a cry, Watson fell backwards into the pool. 'I can't swim,' he yelled, standing upright in the forty inches of water that was the maximum depth of the pool.

Without a thought for the possible danger she might cause in her attempt to save her beloved, and now apparently drowning, husband, Geraldine jumped in after him. 'Bernie, Bernie,' she cried as a great tidal wave lapped over the sides of the pool.

'All right, all right,' said Bernie as he waded towards the steps.

Anxiously, Geraldine followed him out of the water. 'Bernie, love, you all right?'

'Yeah, course I am,' said Watson. 'Silly cow!' he added with a grin.

'That was a daft thing to do, falling in like that,' said Geraldine. 'You might have drowned if I hadn't been here. You ought to be more careful.'

'I'll just get changed,' said Watson, beginning to strip off his wet shirt. 'Then, like I said, I'll get going.'

'Well, don't you go getting into no trouble, Bernie Watson.'

Watson glanced at the clock over the door to the changing room. 'I won't be long,' he said. 'Should be back in time for drinks, I reckon.'

Before leaving Welling, Bernie Watson had made a telephone call to a man called Eddie Hooper and arranged a 'meet'. Hooper was the longest-serving, and most trusted, of Watson's small group of 'enforcers', the men who made sure that Watson's every wish was complied with in the murky world in which he operated. Hooper was big in everything but brains, and was capable of inflicting unbelievable pain on any of his boss's enemies when the situation demanded it.

At about three o'clock in the afternoon, the pair arrived at Harry Pritchard's studio and Watson pressed the bell push.

Seconds later, Pritchard's voice, crackling through the intercom, demanded to know who his caller was. The security device was something new and its installation had been prompted by the attention the police had been paying to both him and Webb in recent days. But learning that Bernie Watson was outside, Pritchard released the lock and carried on photographing his current model.

The door to the studio flew open and Watson and Hooper moved threateningly towards the photographer. 'I want bloody words with you, mister,' said Watson angrily.

'Christ, Bernie,' said Pritchard, 'what the hell's wrong?' He looked nervously at Hooper who was standing slightly behind Watson, pointedly cracking his knuckles.

Watson glanced at the couch upon which a naked, red-headed girl was artistically draped in an explicit pose. 'You,' he said. 'Get your bloody clothes on and piss off.'

Unaware of the power wielded by Pritchard's visitor, the girl smiled but remained where she was.

But Pritchard knew when there was trouble abroad. 'Do as he says, Marilyn. See you tomorrow.'

Marilyn stood up and walked provocatively across the room to where her clothes lay on a table. 'That's all very well,' she said as she plucked a pair of briefs from the untidy pile, 'but what about my money? Can't live on fresh air, you know, Harry.'

'Here . . .' Pritchard took a roll of banknotes from his pocket, peeled off a few and handed them to the girl. 'Now get out of here, there's a love.'

The three men watched the girl dispassionately as she dressed and when they heard the street door slam after her, Watson took a menacing step closer to Pritchard. 'Now, you listen to me, you double-dealing bastard. Them latest videos what I had from you four days ago—'

'Best we've done so far,' said Pritchard, attempting a reassuring grin.

'They was all blank. The whole bleedin' lot of 'em. Now how d'you explain that away, eh?'

Pritchard laughed nervously. 'You're joking,' he said.

Watson seized the front of Pritchard's tee-shirt and twisted it in his fist. 'Would I come all the way up from my drum in Welling to make jokes?' he asked grimly.

'I don't understand—' began Pritchard.

'They was all blank—'

'Yeah, okay, okay, I understand what you're saying, but I don't understand why they were all blank, Bernie.'

'Just bloody listen,' shouted Watson. 'My whole bleedin' reputation's been put on the line and I want to know what happened.'

'It must have been Webb,' said Pritchard lamely. 'I reckon he's trying to drop me in it just because I won't let him come down to the studio and have his end away.'

'Perhaps you should think again then,' said Watson darkly. 'Let him go down there and screw himself stupid, if that's what it takes for a bit of harmony. But I'll tell you this. If he's going to bugger up the business, someone's going to pay. And it's either going to be you or him. Got it?'

'Yeah, sure, Bernie, sure,' said the now thoroughly alarmed Pritchard. He knew Bernie Watson's reputation only too well and, until now, had regarded him as something of a protector. Suddenly it had all gone wrong. 'Have you had a word with Webb?'

'No, my son, I'll leave that to you.' Still holding the front of Pritchard's tee-shirt, Watson gently slapped his face two or three times with his other hand as he spoke. 'And don't forget, you're not the only blue-video maker in London. Got the message, have you?'

'Yeah, all right, Bernie, all right,' said the terrified Pritchard.

'In the meantime, I want another thirty-six tapes, and this time they'd better be kosher.' Then, just to make the point, Watson deliberately pushed over a lighting tripod. There was a crash as it fell to the ground, followed by a small explosion as the huge floodlight bulb burst. Taking this as a signal to move into action, Hooper began knocking over all the other floodlights and, one after another, they too were smashed. He finished up by sweeping Pritchard's table clear of its expensive stock of camera equipment.

With a satisfied grin on his face, Hooper turned to Watson. 'Want me to give him a seeing-to, Mr Watson?' he enquired calmly.

Watson had watched this orgy of destruction with apparent indifference. 'Not for the time being, Eddie,' he said. He turned back to Pritchard. 'And don't think of sending me no bill for the second lot of tapes, neither,' he added.

The small team of detectives who were keeping observation on Pritchard's studio had noted the arrival and departure of Bernie Watson and an unidentified male, and duly reported these interesting facts to Fox, together with their opinion that Watson was looking none too pleased with life. A further report stated that some five minutes after Watson and his companion had left, an extremely agitated Pritchard was seen to emerge from his studio and hail a taxi.

Fox smiled when he received this intelligence, but when

the detective sergeant in charge of the team told him that during the twenty minutes that Watson had been with Pritchard, Watson's Rolls-Royce had collected a parking ticket, Fox burst out laughing.

Pritchard wasted no time in getting to Fulham, despite the inordinate cost of the cab fare. Neither did he wait for the receptionist to go through the niceties of announcing his arrival. He bounded up the stairs and pushed open the door of Webb's office.

'What the devil d'you want?' demanded Webb, surprised by Pritchard's aggressive entrance.

Pritchard slammed the office door and advanced threateningly across the room. Leaning over the desk, he grabbed hold of Webb's shirt front, pulling him close, and said, 'What the bloody hell are you playing at, sport?'

'What the hell . . . ? Have you gone stark, staring mad, Harry?' Webb tried to release himself from Pritchard's grasp.

'Listen to me, you little toad,' said Pritchard. 'I've just had an uncomfortable quarter of an hour with Bernie Watson and some hood who wrecked my bloody studio. Those sodding tapes I sent you somehow got nicked after I delivered them to you and before they got to wherever. Belgium, wasn't it?'

Webb laughed nervously. 'They couldn't possibly have done,' he said. 'Perhaps they got seized by customs. It does happen sometimes, you know.'

Switching his hold, Pritchard grabbed Webb's tie and pulled it tight around his neck, before standing upright. 'And they put blank tapes in our original covers when they do that, do they? Just so none of us'll be out of pocket. Well, Raymond, listen to this, and listen good. You're going to find out what happened to those tapes. And you're going to pay for the damage that Bernie Watson did to my studio. Because if you don't, mister, the first phone call I make when I leave here's going to be to your missus. And I'm going to invite her to a very private viewing of some of the videos in my possession. Got it?' It was an empty threat; all the videos featuring Webb were now in Fox's possession.

'Look,' said the red-faced Webb as he attempted to unknot his tie, 'it's no good going on at me. What would I switch those tapes for? There's no profit in that. This sideline operates on trust. You know that.'

'Yeah, I know that, Raymond, but the question is, do you? I'll tell you this much, though. One more slip like that and you're dead meat.' Pritchard paused at the door. 'And it won't be me who does the business. It'll be Bernie Watson. I tell you, he's one angry man.'

There was an almost beatific smile on Fox's face as he listened to the report of the detective sergeant in charge of the surveillance team. 'Let me get this straight,' he said. 'Bernie Watson and an assistant turned up at Pritchard's studio and left twenty minutes later, looking unhappy. Right?'

'Right, sir,' said the DS.

'And then our Mr Pritchard promptly hightails it down to Fulham in a growler, where presumably he interviewed Mr Raymond Webb. Finally, the aforementioned Mr Webb left for his Richmond abode looking somewhat distraught.'

'That about sums it up, sir,' said the DS, grinning.

'From which,' mused Fox, 'one might deduce that news of the missing blue videos has reached them.'

'Certainly looks that way, sir,' said the DS.

Fox nodded amiably. 'You know,' he said, 'it gives an entirely new twist to the old saying about the biggest cock-up since Mons.'

THIRTEEN

THE MORNING AFTER THE COMING together of Watson and Pritchard, and Pritchard and Webb, Fox decided to interest himself in what had been going on. It was not that he really hoped to learn anything that would take him nearer a solution to the three murders, but Fox was a great collector of snippets of information. Often in the past, he had found that among all the minor scraps of intelligence that came his way, there would eventually come a dawning. But apart from anything else, Fox was inveterately inquisitive; no bad thing in a detective.

'I see that our Mr Pritchard has acquired himself a security intercom, Denzil,' said Fox as he pressed the bell push at the door of the photographer's studio.

'Who is it?' asked a distorted voice, squawking through the metal box.

'Thomas Fox . . . of Scotland Yard. And friend.'

There was a buzzing noise as the lock was released and Fox and Evans made their way up the stairs.

'Good heavens,' said Fox as he gazed at the heap of wrecked floodlights and their stands, now piled in a corner. 'Have an accident, did you?'

'What can I do for you?' Pritchard ignored the question and lowered his camera. 'That'll do, gorgeous,' he said to a naked black girl, her hair in dreadlocks, who was performing contortions on the green satin sheet that covered the bed. 'I think we'll call it a day. Doesn't look as though we're going to get the chance to do any more, not with all these interruptions.' He shot a sour expression in Fox's direction as the black girl stood up and sauntered across to a screened area in the corner of the room.

But Fox was not to be so easily diverted. 'What happened here?' he asked, looking around.

'Had a break-in,' said Pritchard, a surly tone in his voice.

'Oh, bad luck,' said Fox. 'Particularly after you've had that expensive security device fitted to your door. How did they get in, as a matter of interest?'

'Dunno!' said Pritchard. 'Must have left a window open.'

'You've reported it to the local police, I presume?'

'What's the point? They never catch anyone.'

'Yes, I know,' said Fox sympathetically. 'It's all the minor crimes getting in the way. Tends to divert resources from the mainstream, if you take my meaning. Criminal damage, for instance.' He looked pointedly at the pile of wreckage in the corner, and at Evans who was examining it with apparent interest.

Pritchard followed the detective's gaze nervously. 'Yeah, well it happens a lot these days, doesn't it? Yobs breaking in and smashing things up, just for the sheer hell of it.'

'See you, honey,' said the black girl, now dressed in a white satin blouse, scarlet leggings and high-heeled shoes, as she emerged from behind the screen.

'Yeah, see you, honey. Be good.' Pritchard waved a hand.

The girl sashayed across the room and out of the door leading to the stairs.

'Seen Bernie Watson lately?' asked Fox suddenly.

But Pritchard was not easily caught out. 'Who?' he asked innocently.

'Bernie Watson. Thought you might know him. I understand that he's something of an entrepreneur in the blue film world.' Fox continued to gaze airily around the studio. 'I do hope you're insured, Harry, dear boy,' he said.

'Don't you worry about that,' said Pritchard earnestly. 'I'm covered.' He glanced ostentatiously at his watch. 'Look, I've got another session in a few minutes. Was there something particular you wanted to talk about, or have you just dropped in for a chat?'

'D'you remember a girl called Beverley?' asked Fox, switching back to the subject of the Watson family. 'Used to be one of your porn actresses, so I hear.'

'Beverley, Beverley?' Pritchard looked thoughtful. 'Seem to remember someone of that name,' he said.

'Died of a drugs overdose last August,' said Fox helpfully.

'Oh yeah, I did hear something about that. What's the problem then?'

'I'm told she was Michael Leighton's girl-friend.'

Pritchard laughed. 'One of many,' he said. 'To be perfectly honest the only reason he took an interest in the skin flick game was so that he could have his pick of the available talent.' He leaned against the edge of the bench that, until yesterday, had held most of his camera equipment. 'There's not a lot of money in this racket, you know. Not any more. There's so much of it on the market that the prices are rock-bottom. And for us, in this country, to try to compete with the stuff coming out of Holland, Denmark, Sweden and now the Eastern European countries, is a bit of a non-starter.'

'Why d'you do it, then?' asked Fox.

'The money,' said Pritchard, with a grin, as though that was the sole reason for doing anything.

'But you just said there wasn't any profit in it,' said Fox.

'Not for Leighton there wasn't,' said Pritchard, 'but what he was really doing was paying for his fun, and he paid me well, so I didn't complain. It was just a form of prostitution really. Leighton seemed to get some weird satisfaction out of being filmed having it off with kids young enough to be his daughters. I suppose he showed the videos to his cronies, just to prove that he was still up to it. And he paid the girls well for their services.'

'What did the girls think about it?'

Pritchard shrugged. 'You know what these girls are like,' he said. 'Once they've got used to the idea, they don't give a toss, if you'll pardon the expression. They'll take their clothes off and screw with anyone if the price is right. After all, it's a short-lived career, if you think about it. Most of them are raddled old toms by the time they're thirty. I don't think they liked it much, and they liked doing it with Webb even less. I suppose when they started they thought they'd be performing with some handsome young stud, but that's not the way Leighton worked. He'd convinced them that the market called for young girls doing all sorts of stunts with older men.'

'How did he convince them of that?' asked Fox.

Pritchard held up his hand and rubbed the thumb across the tips of his fingers. 'Pay them enough and they'll do anything,' he said.

'So this Beverley wasn't any more than another one of his videoed bed-mates then?'

'She might have believed it, but he didn't. Soon as he tired of one, he'd replace her with some other chick. So long as she had big boobs.'

'And is that what happened to Beverley?'

'Search me,' said Pritchard. 'But why are you so interested in *her*? I mean, OD-ing on drugs sends bad vibes, but it's not exactly news, not these days.' He paused. 'You're not saying she was murdered too, are you?'

'No,' said Fox mildly. 'I'm interested because she was Bernie Watson's only daughter. But as you've never heard of Bernie Watson, it doesn't matter.'

'Like I said, name means nothing to me.' If that piece of information had shocked Pritchard, he did a very good job at concealing his surprise. And that gave Fox a subject for serious consideration.

Realising that he had been neglecting Lady Jane Sims of late, Fox made a point of calling on her that evening.

'Oh, Tommy, it's you. I've only just finished drying my hair.' She was wearing a white Terry robe when she answered the door. 'A little earlier and you'd've caught me in the shower.'

'Really?' said Fox with feigned indifference as he followed

her into the living room. 'Thought I'd take you out to dinner.'

'Wonderful,' said Jane. 'Be a dear and pour us a drink while I get dressed.' She touched his arm lightly and disappeared into the bedroom on the other side of the flat's narrow hall.

Fox poured two stiff measures of whisky and walked through to the small kitchen in search of water. 'Sorry I've not been to see you lately,' he called as he returned to the living room.

Jane had left the doors open so that they could talk while she dressed. 'You could have phoned,' she shouted.

'Yes, I suppose I could, but I've been too busy searching a studio where they make blue movies.'

'What?' Jane's head appeared briefly round the bedroom door.

'I thought that'd get you going,' said Fox, smiling as he sat down in one of the armchairs. 'It was full of naked women.'

'I despair of you, Tommy,' said Jane, retreating once more into the bedroom. 'Is it connected with these Cyprus murders? Or was that just a good excuse?'

Fox laughed. 'It's supposed to be connected,' he said, 'but quite frankly, I seem to be getting further and further away from solving them.'

'Bring my drink in, there's a love,' Jane called.

When Fox entered the bedroom, Jane was attired in bra and briefs, and was sitting at her dressing-table applying her make-up. She smiled at him through the mirror. 'Sorry to disappoint you,' she said, turning to take her drink. 'But you've probably had your fill of nudity for one week.' She took a sip of her whisky and set the glass down. 'One of the chaps at that dinner you took me to at the Yard last year said that policemen on the Vice Squad often ask to be transferred because they get fed up with the sight of naked flesh. Is that true?' She paused, lipstick pointed at her face, and gazed quizzically at him, again through the mirror.

'I don't know what it is about coppers,' said Fox, 'but

whenever they get into conversation with a pretty woman, they always have to talk about sex.'

'Who said anything about sex?' said Jane and closed her lips over a tissue, blotting them.

'It's a pretty sordid world, Jane,' said Fox, for once without a trace of cynicism in his voice. 'Some of the girls in this set-up were given drugs so that they'd perform more actively.'

'And did they?' Jane was only half sure that Fox was telling her the truth. He often teased her, and the world he so rarely mentioned was completely alien to her. That her sister, Lady Dawn, had been following a life of high-class prostitution when she was murdered had come as a terrible, and even now unbelievable, shock to her. Jane stood up and put on her tights, doing her best to make the inelegant procedure as graceful as possible, before stepping into an expensive sheath dress. Since meeting Fox, some eighteen months previously, she had been persuaded by him to improve her appearance. Whereas formerly she had slopped about in old rugby shirts and jeans, and had even been prepared to go out dressed like that, she had recently bowed to his wishes and begun to take a real interest in her clothes. 'Do me up, Tommy, please,' she said.

Fox deftly did up the fastener at the back of Jane's dress and then stood back, thinking that to watch a woman getting dressed was almost as provocative as watching her disrobe. 'One of them died of a drugs overdose,' he said.

Jane turned to face him. 'That's awful, Tommy. Whatever did her parents think?'

Fox shrugged. 'It's the way of the world, I'm afraid,' he said, 'and her parents didn't know about it. Not until I told them eleven months later. Or at least, her father.'

'You mean her mother still doesn't know?'

'I've no idea,' said Fox. 'She's divorced from the father and he doesn't have anything to do with her now. As far as I know. He said that he'd last spoken to her at the time of the girl's disappearance, about two years ago.'

'Well, don't you think you should find her, just to let her

know?' Jane looked quite shocked at the thought of a mother not knowing of the death of her daughter.

'We're not running a welfare service.' Fox spoke defensively but, he thought, there might be some profit in tracing the first Mrs Watson; it could well provide him with another lead. He made a mental note to get one of his officers to start looking for her, first thing tomorrow. Then, noting Jane's sudden seriousness, he clasped her shoulders and kissed her lightly on the cheek. 'You look good,' he said.

'I suppose that's a real compliment,' said Jane, 'coming from you.' And smiling, she picked up her handbag.

'I've got a job for you, Bob,' said Fox.

'Yes, sir?' Detective Sergeant Robert Hurley stood up behind his desk in the incident room.

'When you did the death search on Beverley Watson, you also did a birth search and found that Bernie Watson was her father.'

'That's right, sir.' Hurley took a sheet of paper from among the pile in his pending-tray.

Fox waved the proffered search-form away. 'I know what's on it,' he said. 'You found that her mother was Lee Watson, née Frith.'

'Yes, sir.' In common with many of Fox's other officers, Hurley was always impressed by his commander's ability to recall minor details.

'Find her,' said Fox. 'But don't talk to her. I'll do that. And don't ask Bernie Watson where she is either. I don't want him to know that we're taking an interest in his ex-wife. Not that I think he knows where she is anyway.'

'Any idea where I might start looking, sir?' asked Hurley, knowing that Fox did not always share his fund of information with the rest of the team.

'Not a clue,' said Fox. 'But you're a trained detective. Detect!'

Hurley grinned. 'You mean beat on the ground and see what comes up, sir.' He had rapidly become conversant with the new commander's favourite catch-phrase.

Fox nodded gravely. 'You're learning, Bob,' he said.

Given the constraints he had placed upon DS Hurley, Fox had set him an almost impossible task. Hurley started, as all good detectives start, by interrogating the Police National Computer. But unless the individual had been convicted of a crime, or was wanted for one, or had been filed as a missing person, the PNC wouldn't help. And it didn't in this case. Mrs Lee Watson, née Frith, had not come to the official notice of the police.

The London telephone directory didn't help either. Discounting those subscribers whose first name had been included, there were still forty-three Watsons with the first initial 'L'. And that meant an awful lot of telephone calls. To complicate the search even more, Hurley was mindful of the fact that as Bernie Watson lived in Welling, it was also possible that Lee Watson was living in the suburbs. And given that there were a further five telephone directories that covered the areas outside the London postal district, the task assumed insurmountable proportions.

On the other hand, thought Hurley miserably, Lee Watson may have decided, at some time since her divorce, to move to Birmingham, or Cornwall, or Wales. Or even abroad.

In common with most detectives facing such an awesome task, Hurley knew, deep down, that he would finish up doing what every other detective usually finished up doing. One hell of a lot of legwork.

There were other options, of course, but they were dependent upon the co-operation of officials who sometimes claimed privilege or client-confidentiality in their dealings with the police. And unless the subject of the search was wanted for a serious crime, it was unlikely that Hurley would get any assistance from those quarters.

But there was one source left. The Driver and Vehicle Licensing Agency at Swansea. But only if Mrs Lee Watson held a driving licence.

FOURTEEN

'I'M GETTING FED UP WITH this bloody enquiry,' said Fox, glowering at the assembled detectives. 'We've been poncing about for days now, getting nowhere. All we seem to have done is get ourselves involved with naked women, and others, taking part in the blue film business.'

One of the detectives at the back of the room complained bitterly to his neighbour that he hadn't seen any of it.

'Therefore the time has come to start pulling the loose ends together,' continued Fox. 'So what have we got?' He glanced at DI Evans. 'Denzil?'

In his role as manager of the incident room, Evans was expected to be able to furnish the entire team with an up-to-date summary of what had happened so far, principally for the benefit of those officers who were not at the centre of the investigation. 'We started with the three bodies on the yacht off the coast of Cyprus,' he said. 'Michael Leighton, a wholesaler of amusement machines, Karen Nash and Patricia Tilley. All had evidence of cocaine in their bodies, and two kilos of it was found on the yacht. The two women were porn actresses in Leighton's dubious sideline of making blue films. Leighton's partner was Raymond Webb, who seems to have taken over the business, at least for the time being. Harry Pritchard was the cameraman, but now Bernie Watson, well known villain, has come into the frame. He owns the warehouse at Thornton Heath through which the latest batch of fruit machines passed on their way to Belgium. The thirty-six blue videos which were intercepted at Gatwick by the guv'nor' – he nodded towards Fox – 'went from Pritchard to Watson and were loaded into the fruit machines there. Which makes it look as if Pritchard has taken over where Leighton was forced to leave off, despite what he said when the guv'nor and I saw him yesterday, that there was no money in it and,' he added significantly, 'he claims not to know Watson. But the only real lead we have, and that doesn't amount to very much, is that two squaddies in Cyprus reported having spoken to an Englishman called Jock. This man, purporting to be an ex-soldier, was enquiring about hiring a speedboat and was asking questions about Leighton's yacht.'

'Thank you, Denzil.' Fox's gaze swept the room. 'I have spoken to the Chief Constable of the Sovereign Base Areas Police this morning who tells me that nothing has come of wider enquiries among the troops in Cyprus – he was arranging for the Provost Marshal to circulate details of Jock – and neither has the Commissioner of the Cyprus Police come up with anything about speedboats.' He paused. 'I did not expect any result from his enquiries about that, or from the immigration people in Cyprus,' he said pointedly, and with a sour expression, added, 'and I was not disappointed.' There was muted laughter from his audience. 'So now, we're going to rattle a few bars.' His gaze switched to DS Hurley. 'How are you getting on with tracing Mrs Watson the First, Bob?' he asked.

'Enquiries are proceeding, sir,' said the luckless Hurley.

'With vigour, I trust,' said Fox.

It was Fox's idea that his avowed intention of 'rattling a few bars' should take the form of renewing interest in all those people who had been interviewed to date, but from whom, Fox now believed, more might be forthcoming. Before he began on that personal task, however, he sent for Detective Superintendent John Craven-Foster.

'John, I'm not satisfied that enough has been done in Cyprus. It's all very well for Geoffrey Harding to say that the Provost Marshal's enquiries have come up with nothing and, frankly, I don't think the Cyprus Police have made too great an effort either. Take Charles Morgan and get back out there. Beat on the ground—'

'And see what comes up, sir?' said Craven-Foster wearily.

'Look on it as a bit of a holiday,' said Fox. But they both knew he didn't mean it.

Detective Sergeant Robert Hurley had struck lucky, or so he thought. According to the DVLA, Mrs Lee Watson was the holder of a current driving licence, and the address recorded for her was in Crystal Palace in south-east London.

The house, in a comparatively quiet road close to the park, was semi-detached and quite small. Hurley rang the bell.

The woman who answered the door was young, probably no more than twenty-three. She wore black and white striped leggings and a man's shirt, and her hair was in that state of regulated disorder thought by many women to be stylish. Hurley knew immediately that she could not be Lee Watson who, according to the records at Swansea, was now fifty-four.

But this younger woman might be a relative, or even a 'daily', and Hurley was prepared to spin her a yarn without disclosing his true identity, bearing in mind that Fox had told him not to 'show out'.

'Mrs Watson?'

'Don't live here no more,' said the woman.

'I'm a police officer,' said Hurley, producing his warrant card.

'Oh yeah?'

'D'you know where she's gone?'

'Moved,' said the woman.

'How long ago?'

The woman thought for a moment. 'Let me see,' she said. 'We've been here for a year now, so it was a year ago.'

'Any idea of her new address?' Hurley had somehow known that he would be unlucky on the first call.

'No. She'd been gone for a week before we moved in.'

'Did you buy the house through an estate agent?'

'Yeah.'

'Which one?' It was hard work and Hurley began to think that it would take ages to get any useful information out of this woman.

'Just a mo', I've got it written down somewhere.' The woman walked away from the door, leaving it open and not inviting Hurley in. A few moments later, she returned. 'There you are,' she said and held out a piece of paper.

'And you've no idea where she went. She hasn't been in touch since?'

'No,' said the woman.

'Thank you for your help,' said Hurley.

'Yeah,' said the woman. Curiously, she had not asked why the police were interested in the previous occupier of her house.

Fortunately, the estate agent's offices were close by. The senior negotiator who had dealt with the sale of the house was extremely helpful. He turned up a file, told Hurley that he had thought about joining the police a couple of years ago, and produced an address in Pinner, just west of Harrow in Middlesex. And that was about eighteen miles, straight across central London. As the crow flies. But not being a crow, Hurley climbed into his six-year-old Ford Fiesta, for which he was paid an inadequate mileage allowance, quietly cursed his luck, and set off for Pinner.

The observation on the studio at the back of Waterloo Station had identified three of the late Michael Leighton's 'actresses': Babs Stocker, whom Fox and Kate Ebdon had interviewed already, Anna Coombs and Kirsty Newman. Oddly enough, none of these girls had been present when the studio was raided. And Fox now decided that Kate Ebdon should interview the other two.

Anna Coombs lived in the top half of a run-down house in Wandsworth. She had a living room, the end of which had been partitioned off to form a kitchenette, and a bedroom with a shower cabinet in the corner, described audaciously by the West Indian landlord as an en suite bathroom.

'Good day,' said Kate cheerfully. 'I'm from the police.'

'I've given up the game, if that's what it's about,' said Anna Coombs listlessly. She was drawn, clearly tired and looked as though she drank more than was good for her.

'Tomming, were you? No, it's not about that,' said Kate as she followed the girl into the sitting room and looked round. The room was in a state of chaos; the air redolent with the smell of stale cigarette smoke. A couple of tired armchairs flanked a Formica-topped coffee table with chipped gold-trim edges, and the carpet was threadbare in places. The fireplace was full of dog-ends and empty cigarette packets. A small, laminated dining table stood against a wall, its leaves extended, and was piled high with magazines. And both the dining chairs were covered with items of clothing.

'What then?'

'The murder of Michael Leighton.' Kate decided that shock tactics were likely to be the only way to get a spark of reaction from this woman.

'Best thing that ever happened,' said Anna Coombs.

'I take it you didn't like him.' Without waiting for an invitation, Kate sat down in one of the armchairs.

'I hated his guts, as a matter of fact.'

'We're trying to discover who killed him,' said Kate.

'Could have been any one of the girls, I should think,' said Anna, but didn't really sound as though she meant it.

'Why d'you say that?'

'Because he was a cruel bastard, that's why.' Anna looked across the room, a vacant expression on her face. 'I was lucky to escape. It was only moving here, so that he couldn't find me, that I was able to get away.'

'Tell me about it?'

'I was on the game, like I said.' Anna picked up a cigarette packet, found it was empty and tossed it into the fireplace with the rest. 'You haven't got any cigarettes, have you?' she asked.

'Sorry, no,' said Kate. 'I don't smoke.'

'I was working Shepherd Market then.'

'When?'

'Nearly two years ago. And Leighton picked me up one

night. It was pouring with rain and I hadn't had a john all night. I thought he was just another trick . . .' Anna glanced up at the Australian detective, knowing instinctively that she would understand the jargon of the prostitute's trade. 'Anyway, he offered me a grand for the whole night.' For the first time the girl smiled. 'He was quite an old guy and I reckoned he'd be good for one and I could kip for the rest of the time. Not that it mattered. Believe me, love,' she said, 'I'd've done everything he asked for that grand.'

'And did he? Ask for everything?'

'No, not then. He took me to a hotel, down Victoria somewhere, in this big car he was driving.' Anna Coombs sighed. 'And we screwed for most of the night. I was surprised, I can tell you. Like I said, he was no chicken, but he kept coming back for more.'

'When did you see him again?' asked Kate.

'When he bailed out the next morning, he asked if I'd be interested in making some movies. Well, I knew what he was on about, straightaway—'

'So what did you say?'

'I said I'd think about it. One thing you learn on the game, love, is to trust no bastard. It's all very well, him saying about making movies. I knew they'd be skin flicks, but that might have been a load of fanny . . .' Anna broke off and smiled. 'No, what I really mean is that you get all sorts of offers. But I've heard of girls getting taken in like that, being offered loads of money to become exotic dancers in the Middle East, and the next thing they know is they're in some Egyptian brothel spending all day and all night staring at the ceiling for about two quid a week. You've got to be careful, see?'

'But you accepted his offer?'

'Well, he seemed like a real gent. Well, at first anyway. He said I was to think about it and he give me this card with the address of the studio on it.'

'The one near Waterloo?'

'Oh, you know about that, do you?'

Kate nodded. 'Yes, we raided it a few days ago.'

'Oh!' said Anna and looked surprised. 'Anyway, I took a stroll down there and I met this Harry Pritchard. Tall, good-looking guy with a pony-tail. Well, he seemed straight enough. Showed me round and gave me a cup of coffee and told me what went on. He never pulled no punches, neither. He said he knew I was on the game – seems Leighton had told him to expect me – and said that it would still be screwing, but without the risk.' She laughed scornfully. 'That was rich, I can tell you.'

Kate was impatient to get to the nub of the story and didn't want to interrupt the girl's flow, but decided to nudge her gently in the right direction. 'So what went wrong?'

'Well, the first few times I did it with Harry while some other guy operated the camera.'

'Who was he? Any idea?'

'No, I never heard his name, and he never showed up again. Least, not when I was there.'

'What was he like? How old, for instance?'

Anna shrugged. 'I don't know. About thirty, I s'pose. Blond-haired guy. Quite dishy in a way. Anyway, then Leighton turned up and I had to do it with him, but worse than that was some guy called Ray. That's what he told us to call him anyhow. He was creepy and I never fancied it with him.' She gave a hopeless sigh. 'But the money was good and I wasn't out in all weathers and I never had no pimp to pay, neither.'

'What happened about your pimp?'

'That worried me a bit. When Leighton first asked me to work for him, I said what about Chester and he said he'd be taken care of. Well, I didn't know what he meant by that, and I didn't want to know, neither.'

'Chester was your pimp, was he?'

'Yeah, a West Indian guy.'

'What was his other name?'

Anna looked nervous. Pimps were dangerous people to cross. 'What d'you want to know that for?' she asked.

'Just in case we find him with his throat cut,' said Kate. 'After all, you did say that Leighton would take care of him.'

But still Anna Coombs was hesitant. 'Well, I don't know,' she said. 'I mean, he could—'

'I could ask around Shepherd Market?' said Kate. 'See if anyone can remember who Anna Coombs's pimp was.'

'Chester Smart,' said Anna promptly.

'So why exactly did you part company with Michael Leighton?'

'He wanted to chain me up and make a film of me getting whipped,' said Anna. 'One of the other girls had got involved in it, poor little bitch, and she told me about it. You wouldn't believe what that bastard did to her. It was awful. She could only face it when she was high on drugs. Well, I'm not into that stuff, so I split.'

'What did Leighton say about that?'

'I didn't wait to find out. I was living in Streatham at the time and I just went home, grabbed my gear and took off. That's how I finished up here.' She waved a limp hand around the room.

'But you were seen at the studio only a few days ago. Why did you go back?'

'When I heard that Leighton was dead, I went to see Harry and asked him if there was any work. He's okay, is Harry, and he said yes.' Anna looked directly at Kate. 'I couldn't go back to Chester. I'll get cut for sure if he ever finds me. And I had to have the money, you see. The welfare doesn't pay enough. Not when you've got a kid.'

'This other girl, the one who was on drugs and got whipped. Who was she?'

'A kid called Beverley. I don't know her other name.'

FIFTEEN

'WHERE THE HELL DO WE start, Charles?' asked Detective Superintendent Craven-Foster. He and Charles Morgan, the DI who had accompanied him, were sitting at a table outside a café facing the fishing port in Paphos. With them was a detective constable from the local police station, a young man called George Christofides. Each had a glass of raki in front of him, a local drink that tasted of aniseed, not unlike ouzo.

As a courtesy, the two British policemen had called at the Paphos police headquarters earlier in the day. The superintendent had offered any assistance he could, but expressed some doubts about whether they would have any luck in discovering the identity of the mysterious stranger called Jock. He did however, make a valuable contribution to their enquiries: he loaned them Christofides, who spoke fluent English, to act as their interpreter.

'We could start with the fishermen, I suppose,' said Morgan. 'See if anyone tried to hire a boat.' He turned to Christofides. 'What d'you think, George? It's your patch.'

Christofides looked around, as though fearful of being overheard. 'Perhaps it's like it in your police force, sir,' he said, lowering his voice, 'but here in Cyprus we have enough problems, what with the Turks in the north and everything, that we don't really have time to solve other people's crimes for them. I think, maybe, our officers didn't try too hard. I'd be surprised if they made many enquiries. So yes, let's try the fishermen. They hear it all and if there's anything to learn, you may learn it from them.'

They started in earnest the following morning. It was tiring, foot-slogging work, but it was marginally easier than using a car, given the acute traffic congestion. Abandoning their lightweight suits in favour of short-sleeved shirts and slacks, the two British detectives, sweltering in a temperature that reached the high eighties, began their enquiries in Kato Paphos. The harbour was packed with tiny fishing boats of all shapes and sizes, among them the occasional expensive yacht. Gnarled boatmen, their faces the colour of walnuts, constantly harangued visitors to take a trip round the bay. The sun beat down mercilessly on a calm blue sea overlooked by the ruins of Paphos Fort. And the seagulls screeched constantly.

Avoiding the occasional pelicans, who seemed to regard the coastline as their own personal domain, the policemen trudged from one boat-owner to another, and from one fisherman to the next, always asking the same questions, and always getting the same negative replies. They spoke to any British soldier or airman they found in the harbour-side cafés, but ignored the tourists, most of whom were in Paphos on package holidays and were staying in one of the garish, modern hotels that lined the seafront.

At the end of the second day, Craven-Foster and Morgan were on the point of giving up, but after a meal at their hotel – they had declined the offer of accommodation at the Akrotiri base – they decided to give it one more day. Buying George Christofides one last drink, they arranged to meet him again the following morning.

And it was the following morning that Detective Constable George Christofides came up with the goods.

DS Robert Hurley eventually found the house in Pinner to which the estate agent in Crystal Palace had said that Lee Watson had moved.

'I remember the name,' said the woman who answered the door. 'But she was only here for a couple of weeks. I only do bed and breakfast, you see. It's not really suitable for long-term letting.'

'D'you happen to know where she went when she left here, Mrs . . . ?'

'Mrs Molloy,' said the woman. 'What's it about?'

'I'm a police officer and—'

'In some sort of trouble, is she?' asked Mrs Molloy, her interest immediately aroused.

'Oh no, nothing like that,' said Hurley hurriedly. 'It's just that we need to trace her. To return some stolen property. Result of a burglary.' He told the lie easily.

'That's nice,' said Mrs Molloy. 'She'll be pleased. We've had our fair share of burglaries, all of us round here, but the police never seem to catch anyone. Still, I suppose you've got your work cut out these days, what with all this terrorism and drugs and that.'

'We certainly manage to keep busy,' said Hurley, hoping that the woman would not invite him in for tea. Right now, his fancy was for a pint of lager. 'So you've no idea where she might have gone, then?'

'No, I'm ever so sorry. She paid her bill and that was that. If I kept a record of everyone who stayed with me for B and B, I'd need a book three inches thick.' Mrs Molloy smiled at the prospect, but suddenly peered over Hurley's shoulder at a woman emerging from the house opposite. 'Now I wonder where that madam is off to, all dolled up,' she said. She tossed her head and glanced back at Hurley. 'I wouldn't mind betting her husband would be interested in knowing where she gets to every Tuesday afternoon. Playing fast and loose, if you ask me.'

'So you've no idea where Mrs Watson might have gone to then, Mrs Molloy?' asked Hurley wearily.

'Do what?' asked Mrs Molloy vaguely, as she dragged her attention back to the detective. 'Oh, yes, Mrs Watson.' She gave the question some further thought. 'Now you come to mention it, I seem to remember that she said something about going to Brighton. Yes, I'm sure it was her. Can you remember what she looked like?'

'No,' said Hurley. 'I'm afraid I've never seen her.'

'What was this Mrs Watson's first name?'

'Lee,' said Hurley. 'Mrs Lee Watson.'

'Yes, I remember her now,' said Mrs Molloy. 'Lee Watson. Yes, she did say something about going to Brighton.'

'I don't suppose she mentioned whereabouts in Brighton, did she?' asked Hurley hopefully. 'Didn't say anything about staying with relatives or anything like that?'

'No, I'm sorry. It was nearly a year ago, you see.'

'Well, thank you for your help, Mrs Molloy,' said Hurley. 'And for your time.'

'Hope you find her,' said Mrs Molloy as she closed her front door.

'So do I,' said Hurley to himself.

Kirsty Newman lived in Gipsy Hill, in south-east London, in one of the maze of streets that lay to the north of Westow Hill.

Compared with Anna Coombs's flat in Wandsworth, Kirsty Newman's was quite palatial.

'Nice pad you've got here,' said Kate Ebdon when, reluctantly, the Newman girl had admitted her.

'You come to admire the decor, love?' asked Kirsty, 'or did you want something?' She was clearly unhappy at the arrival of the Australian woman detective.

But Kate knew how to deal with hostile prostitutes. 'Yeah, I want something,' she said. 'Tell me about Michael Leighton.'

'What d'you want to know?' Although she didn't really have the legs for it, Kirsty Newman was wearing a tight, black mini-skirt, and a close-fitting red, satin blouse that dipped very low at the front. Kate could see that she was not wearing a bra.

'How long did you work for him?'

'Who said I did?'

'Me,' said Kate. 'Our observation team saw you leaving the studio at the back of Waterloo where you took part in making skin flicks.'

'Now just hold on—'

'And we later seized a quantity of videos on which you,

Kirsty mate, are to be seen performing some of the most fantastic sexual gymnastics I've ever seen.'

'Know all about sexual gymnastics, do you? Be a bit different from the sort I do, I imagine.' Kirsty leaned back in her chair, an insolent smirk on her face. The implication was clear: that because Kate was a policewoman she was also a lesbian.

'Cheap little whores like you make me tired,' said Kate without raising her voice. 'And if you'd like a trip down to Gipsy Hill nick where, for a start, we'd have you searched, you just say the word. But if you don't, you'll wipe that sneer off your tarted-up face and answer a few questions.'

'You can't talk to me like that,' said Kirsty, sitting up slightly.

'I just did,' said Kate. 'So what's it to be?'

'I've got nothing to hide,' said Kirsty defensively.

'Look, sweetie,' said Kate, 'I don't give a bloody toss about you screwing for the viewing public, but I'm interested in murder and I'm interested in drugs. So, if you want to play it the hard way, that suits me. Got it?'

Kirsty Newman clearly did get it. 'I don't know anything about murder or drugs,' she said, a little too quickly.

'Let me spell it out for you then. Michael Leighton, who was screwing you on what we call Exhibits Numbers Seventeen, Thirty-four and Seventy-five' – Kate reeled off the first three numbers that came into her head – 'was found shot to death aboard his yacht, along with two of your fellow actresses.' She laid sarcastic emphasis on the last word. 'And we know that they'd all taken drugs. And we also know that Leighton had offered drugs to most of the girls who turned tricks for him. Were you one of them? Yes or no?'

'I never took any.' Quite suddenly, Kirsty began crying.

'You can knock that off, too,' said Kate sharply. 'Doesn't cut any ice with me. So, who offered you drugs and what was it?'

Dry-eyed as quickly as she had been crying, Kirsty shot

Kate a hostile glance. 'Marijuana was all he offered me,' she said softly.

'What about cocaine? Flash coke about, did he?'

'Not to me.'

'What about Beverley?'

'Beverley?'

'Look, Newman, don't sod me about. I don't have the time for it. Yes, Beverley. According to another witness' – the police rarely identified one witness to another – 'she was well under Leighton's thumb, apart from other parts of his anatomy. He fed her cocaine and he chained her up and he whipped her. But only because the part called for it, as most nude actresses say,' she added caustically.

'He did me too,' said Kirsty softly.

'And you stood for that?' Kate was amazed at what some women would do for money.

'Had to. I was tied up,' said Kirsty with just the trace of a smile.

'Why the hell did you stay with him then?'

'Because he threatened that he would hand me over to the police if I didn't. He said that he'd got a copper on his payroll and he only had to say the word and that would be that. He said he'd make sure I never worked again.'

Kate didn't believe that for a moment, but she had to pursue it. She knew that if she didn't ask the question, Fox would want to know why she hadn't. 'Did he say who this copper was?'

'Course he didn't.'

'How did you meet this Leighton bloke?' asked Kate.

'Booked me one night. I was doing house calls then . . .' Kirsty Newman paused. 'Are you going to do me for this?' she asked.

'Christ no,' said Kate. 'I've got more important things to worry about than stupid tarts hawking their mutton. So what happened?'

'I'd been putting my telephone number in phone boxes. You know the sort of thing. And I got a call from him one night. Asked me to meet him at a hotel down Victoria somewhere.'

'And you had sex?'

'No. He stripped me off and looked me over. Then he asked me if I wanted to make some blue movies. The money was good so I said yes.'

'And that's where it began?'

'Yeah. I went to this studio, the one you mentioned near Waterloo Station. We'd do a session about twice a week. Did it with Leighton and Harry Pritchard. Well, you've seen the films, so you said. Oh, and there was some nasty little bastard called Ray who used to turn up every so often. That would have been funny if it hadn't been so sick.'

'Why did Leighton pick you?' asked Kate. 'Did he say? I mean, there must have been dozens of girls he could have chosen from.'

'Haven't a clue,' said Kirsty, but she sounded insincere.

'You must have big boobs then. I'm told he was a boobs man.'

'See for yourself,' said Kirsty angrily, and ripped her blouse open.

Detective Constable George Christofides was smiling broadly when he met Craven-Foster and Morgan in the foyer of their hotel the following morning.

'You're looking pleased with yourself, George,' said Craven-Foster.

'I have found your man for you, sir,' said Christofides, still beaming.

'You have?' With a look of astonishment on his face, the detective superintendent sat down in one of the wickerwork chairs and ordered coffee. 'Tell me about it.'

'After I left you last night, sir,' said the Cypriot policeman, 'I had an idea. I thought to myself that if this man Jock was a typical ex-soldier, he would have had to find himself a woman. So I made some enquiries in the red-light quarter of Paphos.'

'And?' Craven-Foster leaned forward.

'And that is your man, sir.' Christofides laid a credit card on the table. 'He is called John Tanner.'

'Where in hell's name did you get that from, George?' asked Morgan, picking up the credit card and examining it.

'From a prostitute called Andrea Nemitsas.'

'What was she doing with it?' asked Craven-Foster.

'She stole it, sir.' Christofides grinned. 'I asked lots of questions around the quarter. And when the police start questioning prostitutes, they get worried. If they know anything, they tell you, just to get rid of you. One or two of the women had had sex with this man Jock. Apparently he told them that was his name. One of the girls told me that he had also been with Andrea Nemitsas, but when I spoke to her she was not happy to tell me anything about him. She does a lot of business with the British. She speaks good English, you see.'

'So how did you get it out of her?' asked Morgan, moving slightly to allow the waiter to set down the tray of coffee.

Christofides shrugged, as though the answer was obvious. 'I searched her room, sir, and I found the credit card.'

Craven-Foster threw back his head and laughed. 'Well, George,' he said, 'I've got to hand it to you. That was bloody brilliant. What's going to happen to her?'

'That's up to you, sir. I could have arrested her, but I thought that I'd ask you first. If she's arrested, then we have to try to get in touch with this John Tanner, and it might not be good to alert him. Not before you've arrested him, eh?' Christofides grinned again and took a sip of his coffee.

'Well, if you ever want a job in the Metropolitan Police, George,' said Craven-Foster, 'I'll put in a good word for you.'

'I might,' said Christofides. 'My uncle has a restaurant in . . .' He paused. 'Yes, in Harlesden. You must go there. He'd be pleased to see you. Tell him I sent you.'

'Well, if there was a copper on Leighton's payroll, I'll have the bastard,' said Fox when he had listened to Kate Ebdon's account of her interview with Kirsty Newman. 'But I'm not having bloody CIB tramping about all over my enquiry.' Fox was unimpressed with the way the Yard's Complaints Investigation Bureau dealt with matters concerning corrupt policemen. Fox would hand him over, if in fact he existed, when, and only when, it suited him. He glanced up at the woman DC. 'Thanks, Kate,' he said. 'You did a good job.'

Kate was just closing the door behind her when she paused and stuck her head back round it. 'By the way, guv'nor,' she said, 'Kirsty Newman did have big boobs.'

'Get out,' said Fox.

Even though it was not yet midday in Paphos, several prostitutes were already loitering in the mean, narrow street where Andrea Nemitsas conducted her business. Children played in the hot sunshine and several mangy dogs, when they weren't fighting each other, made forays into the unsavoury food shops with which the street was lined, to be chased away by irate shopkeepers wielding brooms.

In common with whores the world over, the Paphos street-women had an innate ability to recognise the police, and the appearance of Christofides, Craven-Foster and Morgan set in motion a bush telegraph that alerted all the women to their presence within minutes.

'This is the place, sir,' said Christofides, turning into a passageway at the side of a coffee shop and leading the way up a flight of stone steps. At the top, he banged loudly on a door. 'Andrea, are you there? It's the police.'

Moments later, the door opened an inch or two and the frightened face of a young girl peered round it. Seeing that it was Christofides, she opened the door wider. 'What d'you want?'

'These gentlemen are from Scotland Yard. They want to talk to you.' Christofides pushed his way past the girl. A double bed dominated the room and an ancient wardrobe stood in one corner. Alongside it was a wash-stand with a bowl and a large jug. A small table and two old chairs completed the sparse furnishings. There was a small rug on the otherwise bare boards that, in one place, were wide enough apart to be able to see the shop below, from which came a constant aroma of coffee.

Andrea Nemitsas was about eighteen and typically Greek in appearance, with dark skin and black, shiny hair that reached her shoulders. Dressed ready for work, she was wearing tight-fitting shorts of some shiny blue material, a red satin blouse that strained over her large breasts and left her midriff bare, and a pair of shoes with high, spindly heels.

'I am very sorry, sir.' Andrea addressed Craven-Foster, the oldest of the three policemen, in the hope that he could exercise some clemency in her favour. 'I did not mean to steal it. I found it on the floor after the man had gone.'

Craven-Foster was not in the least interested in what was, at best, a minor theft. 'I want you to tell me about the man,' he said. 'We are not bothered about the credit card.' Christofides had agreed to forget the matter in the interests of getting the girl to talk more freely. Apart from which, it would give him a lever when he wanted information from the girl about other crimes.

'He came here three times.' With a sweep of her hand, Andrea indicated the double bed.

'How long did he stay?' asked Craven-Foster.

'Not long. He was . . .' Andrea paused, searching for the right word. 'He was very urgent.' She raised a quizzical eyebrow and a brief frown crossed her face.

Craven-Foster smiled. 'Yes,' he said, 'I think I know what you mean. Did he talk about anything? About hiring a boat? Or about a yacht that might be here in Paphos? Did he say, for instance, that he was here on holiday?'

Andrea shook her head. 'No, sir. He was very silent. He just wanted sex and when he had finished with me he left.' She shrugged as though disappointed that she could not help the British policeman any further.

'Tell me what he looked like.'

Andrea described the man as fully as she could recall. According to her, he was six feet tall and very muscular

– she particularly remembered his thighs – and had very even, white teeth. His hair was brown and short, like a soldier's. 'And he had a birthmark here,' she said, and turning slightly, placed a finger in the centre of her left buttock.

SIXTEEN

'YOU RECKON THIS JOHN TANNER is our man Jock then, do you?' asked Fox, fingering the stolen credit card that Craven-Foster and Morgan had brought back from Cyprus.

'As sure as we can be, sir. The prostitute's name was Andrea Nemitsas and we went to see her with young George Christofides. Good copper, that lad. He'd obviously frightened the life out of her and she was only too willing to co-operate. We got a good description of Tanner and she particularly remembers a birthmark on his left buttock.' Craven-Foster grinned. 'So we went to see the two squaddies who you had brought over here, Corporal Higgins and Private Farmer, and they confirmed parts of the description that Andrea Nemitsas had given us.'

'Not the birthmark, I trust,' said Fox mildly.

Craven-Foster smiled. 'No, sir, not the birthmark.'

'Any idea where he was staying? Or for how long?' asked Fox.

Craven-Foster shook his head. 'No, sir. As you know, the two soldiers spoke to him on the twentieth of June and the murders took place on the thirtieth, so it's reasonable to assume that he was there for the whole of the time between those two dates.'

'If he's our man.'

'Exactly, sir. If he's our man,' said Craven-Foster. 'George Christofides suggested that he probably stayed at one of the cheaper hotels in Ktima, or even took a room somewhere, but there are so many of them that it was impossible to check, not in the time available anyway. The local superintendent agreed to let George make some enquiries and he'll let us know if he turns up anything.'

'Right then.' Fox handed the credit card back to Craven-Foster. 'Get someone to find out where this character lives, John, and we shall talk to him. In a kindly fashion.'

Detective Sergeant Robert Hurley's first call was at the Central Police Station in Brighton where he told Detective Sergeant Weaver of the Sussex Police about his search for Lee Watson. Weaver was sitting at his desk in the CID office, his tie slackened off and his shirt-sleeves rolled up in an attempt to combat the sweltering heat.

'Well, good luck, is all I can say to that, mate,' said Weaver. 'There are over a hundred and fifty thousand people living in the Brighton area, plus the tourists, daft bastards.' He sighed. 'Why anyone wants to come here for a holiday beats me. Personally, I prefer Portugal.' He stood up. 'Best place to start is the front office. We can do a search of the "Stop" Books, see if she's been turned over for anything. We'll try the Charge and Persons at Station Books, too.' He paused. 'Got a driving licence, you said?'

'Yes,' said Hurley. 'But the address is shown as Crystal Palace. We know that she moved from there to Pinner in Middlesex about a year ago. And we also know that she only stayed in Pinner for a fortnight. She told the woman she lodged with that she was coming here.'

'We'll do the Fixed Penalty Notice Register as well then, just to see if she got a parking ticket.' Weaver grinned. 'Most people coming to Brighton get one,' he added. 'And just for good measure, we'll do the Process Register too.'

And that is how, four hours later, DS Hurley got lucky. Mrs Lee Watson had been stopped for speeding on Marine Parade two weeks previously and had been reported for that, and for failing to notify the DVLA at Swansea of her change of address.

It was a big stroke of luck, too. Mrs Watson wasn't living in Brighton at all. The address that the traffic police had recorded for her was in Epsom. In the Metropolitan Police District.

'Got it,' said the chief security officer of the credit-card company, an ex-policeman called Peter Telford, as he turned from the VDU. 'John Tanner reported the loss of his card by phone from Cyprus. I don't know why the girl put this on, but there's a note saying that he seemed in a bit of a stew about it, apparently. Anyway, she told him not to worry and that he wouldn't be charged for its misuse now that we knew about it.' He scribbled a few lines on a sheet of paper. 'And that's his address,' he added, handing it to DI Morgan. 'Incidentally, he said that he didn't want a replacement card and sent a cheque a few days later to clear his account. As far as we're concerned, he's no longer a client.'

'Thanks a lot,' said Morgan. 'Didn't think it'd be that easy. Wore out a lot of shoe leather tramping around Cyprus, I can tell you.'

Telford grinned. 'Glad I'm out of it,' he said. 'Thirty years in the job is enough for anyone.' He glanced back at the VDU. 'Want the name of his bank, Charles?' he asked. 'Might come in useful.' He took back the piece of paper from Morgan and wrote down the additional details. 'Dick Campbell's their security director now. Used to be a DAC.'

'Thanks,' said Morgan. 'Incidentally, is there any record of his having used his credit card in Cyprus?'

Telford turned back to the VDU and brought up Tanner's record of transactions. 'Nothing,' he said, and turning to face Morgan once again, added, 'but it can take ages for vouchers to come through, particularly from somewhere like Cyprus. If they do, we'll send him another bill.'

Morgan grinned. 'I'm not worried about your money,' he said, 'but I'd be interested to know if anything turns up.'

'If it does, I'll give you a bell,' said Telford.

When he received the four hundred cassettes that Fox had

seized from the studio at Waterloo, Detective Inspector Bradley of the Obscene Publications Squad had seated himself in front of a video-player and wearily began the onerous task of making evidential notes for the Crown Prosecution Service. Needless to say, it took him some considerable time and, contrary to popular belief, the task did not stimulate him. Or any other policeman whose thankless job it happened to be. But it wasn't only the obscenity aspect that interested Bradley; he was conversant with the main points of the enquiry into the triple murder and knew what his commander was looking for.

Now, some eight days later, DI Bradley telephoned Fox. 'I've got one on the screen that I think you ought to see, sir,' he said. 'It's the one you mentioned, of a couple of girls being beaten. Have you got a minute to come down?'

'Too bloody right,' said Fox. Stopping only to collect Kate Ebdon, who knew more of the participants in this ugly business than anyone else on the team, he pushed open the door of the viewing room. 'What have you got?' he asked.

'A bit nasty this one, sir,' said Bradley, swinging round in his chair. 'And a dead cert for prosecution.'

'Run it through,' said Fox, pulling a chair over and sitting down beside the DI.

'I'll fast-forward it to the bits I think are of interest, sir,' said Bradley and pointed the remote control at the set.

The first frame at which Bradley stopped showed a naked girl chained by her wrists to a cross-bar above her head. 'That's the Waterloo studio,' said Fox, leaning forward. 'And that's probably Beverley Watson,' he added as the camera moved to the girl's face. Then Michael Leighton came into camera-shot wielding a whip with which he began unmercifully to beat the girl. Her screams were very real.

Bradley fast-forwarded the video again and stopped to reveal another girl being subjected to similar treatment. This time it was Pritchard dealing out the punishment, but after a short while, his place was taken by Raymond Webb, leering sadistically. The camera obligingly zoomed in on the girl's tear-stained and terrified face.

'That's Kirsty Newman, sir,' said Kate.

A few frames later, Kirsty Newman appeared again, this time shackled to the bed that dominated the centre of the studio, and was then raped, in turn, by Pritchard and Webb. And finally, by Michael Leighton. Despite her bonds, there was no doubt that she was resisting violently. Either that or she was a damned good actress; but Fox chose to think that she was not that good.

'I shall derive a great deal of pleasure from nicking those bastards,' he said angrily.

There was no way that Fox was going to miss the arrests of Webb and Pritchard. He had known that they would come eventually, but he had wanted something substantial with which to charge them. And now he'd got it. But, unfortunately, he could not be in two places at once and it was essential that both men were arrested at the same time. Fox opted for Raymond Webb and sent DI Evans to arrest Pritchard.

It was still hot, though less humid because of the pouring rain when, at six-thirty the next morning, Fox, golfing umbrella raised, hurried up the path of Raymond Webb's house in Richmond followed by Kate Ebdon. Six other detectives remained in their cars outside, the windscreen wipers moving lazily to and fro. The job of these extra detectives would be to search the house after Webb had been arrested.

Fox approached the front door and pressed the bell-push. Somewhere inside the house a set of chimes played a mellifluous tune. Fox wrinkled his nose and muttered something about lack of taste.

The door was opened by a woman in a quilted housecoat. 'Oh!' she said. 'I thought you were the postman.' She looked disdainfully at Fox, in the act of shaking his large, colourful umbrella, and at Kate in jeans and a tee-shirt that was wet across the shoulders. 'What d'you want?'

'Are you Mrs Webb?' asked Fox.

'Yes, I am.'

'Police,' said Fox tersely and, in no mood for niceties, pushed past Webb's wife.

'What d'you want?' demanded Mrs Webb again, her voice rising to an indignant screech. 'You can't just push in here like that. Raymond!' She shouted in the direction of the staircase.

Raymond Webb, wearing a dressing gown, appeared at the top of the flight of stairs. 'What's the matter?' he called, but seeing Fox in the hall, hurried down. 'What's the meaning of this?' he demanded angrily. 'I . . . I . . . I've had just about enough of this . . . this harassment.' He was clearly outraged by the arrival of the police and was stuttering badly.

'And I've only just started,' said Fox nastily. 'Raymond Webb, I am arresting you for being concerned in the making of obscene films.' He paused, and as Webb was about to say something, added, 'And for causing grievous bodily harm to Kirsty Newman with intent to cause grievous bodily harm. And finally, and most importantly, that you did, on divers occasions, rape the said Miss Newman.' He was being deliberately and unnecessarily formal, but he wanted to impress Webb with the seriousness of the charges. 'Anything you say will be given in evidence.' And with that, he handcuffed Webb.

'What on earth are you talking about?' screamed Mrs Webb and started to attack Fox with her fists.

Kate Ebdon seized the woman's right arm and forced it up her back in an old-fashioned and crippling hammer-lock and bar before pushing her against a wall from which a long-case barometer stared down. 'Shut your racket, missus,' she said quietly, her Australian accent grating on Mrs Webb's suburban ear, 'and behave yourself, or you'll get nicked too.'

Mrs Webb, still restrained by Kate's grip, now turned her wrath on her husband. 'Raymond, do something.' And then she frowned as the realisation of her husband's arrest dawned on her. 'What have you been up to?'

'Nothing, dear,' said Webb. 'It's all a mistake.'

'I'll get on to our solicitor then, straightaway,' said Webb's wife, 'if you've no objection,' she added sarcastically, turning her head to address Kate.

'No, don't do that. Not yet,' said Webb. 'I told you. It's a mistake. I'll sort it out.'

'In that case, I shall complain about it.' Mrs Webb was calmer now and Kate released her. 'It's not a police state, not yet, and you can't just come in here and do this.' She gestured at the abject figure of her handcuffed husband, standing in his dressing gown and slippers, his hair tousled. 'You're surely not going to take him out like that, are you?' she demanded. 'My God, Raymond, what d'you suppose the neighbours will think?' She appeared to be far more concerned about her reputation in the genteel area of Richmond where they lived than about the fate of her spouse.

Fox glanced at Kate. 'Take her into another room,' he said.

Kate steered Mrs Webb into the sitting room, leaving the woman's husband to face Fox in the hall. 'What the hell's this about rape and . . . What was it you said?' asked Webb.

'Causing grievous bodily harm,' said Fox mildly.

'But this is nonsense,' said Webb.

'It might be nonsense to you, but I doubt if Miss Newman saw it that way.'

'Where's your proof? You're not going to take the word of a whore, are you?'

'Even whores have rights,' said Fox, thoroughly enjoying Webb's discomfiture, 'but to put you out of your misery, the whole thing's on a video which is now in police possession.'

Suddenly, Webb slumped on to the bottom step of the staircase, sitting with his head bowed and his manacled hands hanging limply between his knees. 'I didn't know they were filming that,' he said in a whisper. 'He told me that the cameras had been switched off.'

'Who told you?' asked Fox.

'Mike. Mike Leighton.'

Fox laughed. 'I should have thought that you, of all people, would have known not to trust *him*,' he said.

Evans had noticed, on his previous visits with Fox, that Pritchard lived in the back room of his studio in Soho, and at the same time as Fox was arriving at Webb's house, the DI rang the bell, regretting that there was no shelter from the torrential rain.

After a while, Pritchard's voice responded. 'Who is it?' he asked.

'Police,' said Evans.

'I don't receive visitors at this time of the morning.' The distortion of the intercom failed to disguise the sarcasm in Pritchard's voice. 'Come back later.'

'Please yourself.' Evans spoke mildly into the box on the wall. 'You can either open the door or we'll break it down.' He was a man not easily aroused, but he too had seen the video of Pritchard and Webb abusing the two girls. One of the DCs with Evans grinned, and hefted his sledge-hammer nearer the door. But he was to be disappointed. There was a buzzing noise as Pritchard released the lock and Evans pushed the door open.

Pritchard was standing at the top of the stairs as Evans and three other detectives ascended. 'What the bloody hell's the meaning of this?' he asked truculently. He was wearing only a pair of jeans, and his hair, normally gathered into a pony-tail, was loose around his ears.

'I have a warrant for your arrest,' said Evans as he reached the first floor, and he recited the same three charges that Fox was at that moment putting to Webb in faraway Richmond.

'What's happening, Harry?' A sleepy blonde, with just a sheet wrapped around her, appeared from behind Pritchard.

'Nothing for you to worry about, sweetheart,' said Pritchard. 'Go back to bed.'

'And who are you, miss?' asked Evans.

'Cindy,' said the girl.

'Cindy who?'

'Cindy Evans.'

DI Evans glared malevolently at the DC beside him who had had the temerity to snigger. 'And what are you doing here?' he asked the girl.

'What does it look like?' said Cindy with a cheeky smile and promptly returned to the back room.

'What's this all about?' asked Pritchard.

'I've just told you,' said Evans. 'Now, you can either get dressed, or you can come as you are. It's up to you.'

SEVENTEEN

FOX AND EVANS, AND THEIR respective teams, were not the only officers out in the early hours of that morning. At six o'clock, Detective Superintendent John Craven-Foster was also out and about. And getting wet. But he was in Catford where those residents of a quiet street not far from Hither Green Cemetery who happened to look out of their windows, were surprised to discover their road full of silent but aggressive policemen in blue berets and overalls, and carrying guns.

The house that these policemen now surrounded was where John Tanner lived, according to the information that DI Morgan had obtained from the credit-card company. Stealthily a number of armed officers made their way round to the back of the house, seeking what sparse cover there was in the shadows of garden fences and one tree.

During the briefing the previous afternoon, there had been a prolonged discussion between Craven-Foster and the chief inspector of the Yard's Firearms Branch, known internally as SO19, about the tactics to be employed. One option was to break into Tanner's house and chance being confronted by a ruthless criminal; the alternative was that they should use a loudhailer and call on him to surrender, thereby risking the possibility of an extended siege and real danger to anyone else in the house whom he might take hostage. It was what the police tend to call 'a no-win situation'. After a certain amount of desultory debate, it was agreed that police should attempt to gain entry through a window and rely on the fact that Tanner would probably be in bed. And, with luck, asleep.

With two other armed policemen covering him, a third eased open the downstairs front-room window, fortunately unlocked, and slid over the sill, instantly aware of an overpowering stench of boiled cabbage. Rapidly, other officers followed and quietly searched the ground-floor rooms. Then, just as silently, they ascended the staircase, once pausing as a board squeaked alarmingly.

Working on the principle that people usually slept in the front bedroom, the officers looked into the other two bedrooms first. And into the bathroom. Satisfied that those rooms were empty, an officer violently kicked open the door of the master bedroom and he and several others rushed in and surrounded the bed, training their guns on it.

The crash of the door being kicked open had awoken the two occupants of the room and they sat up in alarm. Both clearly in their sixties, the man was bald-headed and the woman had her grey hair in curlers.

'Armed police,' one of the officers shouted. Given that they were in uniform and openly carrying firearms, it seemed an unnecessary observation. But it was in the rule-book, so he said it.

'What d'you want?' The man seemed strangely unconcerned that his bedroom was full of armed policemen at twenty minutes past six on a Thursday morning.

'Where's John Tanner?' demanded Craven-Foster who had brought up the rear of the raiding party.

'He don't live here any more,' said the man.

'Where is he then?'

'Search me, guv'nor,' said the man, yawning. 'He left here about three weeks ago.'

'Is he a relative of yours?' asked the infuriated Craven-Foster.

'Nah, mate. He just had a room here. Dunno where he's gone. He never said. Just said as how we was to tear up any post what come for him.'

* * *

The forlorn figure of Raymond Webb sat on a hard-backed chair in the interview room at Richmond Police Station. A nearby table bore a pile of video-cassettes and several packets of white powder, all of which had been found secreted in the loft of Webb's house by Fox's search team.

Having gone through the rigmarole of starting the tape recorder and telling it the who, why, where and when of the interview, Fox turned to face the prisoner and cautioned him, yet again. 'And I have to remind you that you are entitled to the services of a solicitor,' he said. He had already explained this aspect of the law to Webb prior to removing him from his house, and now he did so again. Although he might have had grounds for denying Webb access to legal advice, Fox was not prepared to risk it. He wanted to be absolutely certain that the charges he intended to bring would not be thrown out because of some procedural omission. And apart from anything else, it didn't matter much what Webb said, or if he said nothing at all. Fox was quite satisfied that he had sufficient evidence upon which to convict Webb, but the man might, even at this stage, be able to throw some light on the murder of his erstwhile partner Leighton.

'I don't want a solicitor,' said Webb glumly. Even now, he hoped to talk his way out of what he firmly believed to be a misunderstanding, and the last person he wanted told of these unsavoury accusations was the family solicitor. And the prospect of discussing it all with someone whom Fox had described as a duty solicitor, appalled him even more.

'Very well.' Fox turned over a sheet of paper on the table in front of him. 'Six packets of white powder were found in the loft of your house.' He looked up and indicated the packets on the other table. 'That substance will be taken to the laboratory for testing in due course and I have no doubt that it will prove to be cocaine. In which case, you will also be charged with its possession. D'you wish to say anything about that, Webb?'

'It is cocaine,' said Webb miserably. 'But it's not mine.'

'How fascinating,' said Fox, and waited.

'It was Mike Leighton's. He asked me to keep it for him.'

'How very convenient.' Fox, at his disbelieving best, inclined his head.

'It was when he was going off on his holiday—'

'When he was murdered, you mean?'

'Yes. He said that he didn't want to leave it around and asked me to store it somewhere safe.'

'Have you any idea where he obtained it from?'

Webb decided that there was no point in defending his late partner any longer, and to tell the police what he knew might just help him to escape from his present predicament. 'He got it abroad somewhere. He didn't say where but he certainly had plenty of the stuff whenever he came back from a trip in his yacht.'

'How much did he bring in?'

Webb shrugged. 'I don't know, but certainly enough to keep him in luxury. I think he must have been trading in drugs in a fairly big way because his fruit machine business was going downhill rapidly, I can tell you that.'

'He supplied others then?' Fox raised an eyebrow.

'Yes.'

'Who?'

Webb lifted his head, a cynical smile on his face. 'You don't imagine that he'd have told me that, do you?' he asked. 'But I do know that he had an arrangement with a black bloke in the West End. Mike would supply him with cocaine and the black bloke would provide him with women to take part in his blue movies.'

'Name?' demanded Fox.

'He never mentioned his name,' said Webb.

'I see.' Fox only half believed that and, in any event, he would still charge Webb with possession, if not with supplying. 'Let's turn now to the videos.'

'What about them?' Webb looked uncomfortable.

'One of them shows, quite graphically, you and Pritchard seriously assaulting Miss Kirsty Newman with a whip. A later part of the same video shows each of you, and Leighton, raping her.' Fox had deliberately not posed a question. He had sufficient evidence upon which to base charges, and he knew that he was not entitled to interrogate the prisoner further. Not about the assault and the rape anyway. But if Webb cared to offer some explanation, or make some excuse, then Fox was quite prepared to listen to it.

'She was acting,' said Webb. 'She agreed to all that.'

'It is a facet of English law,' said Fox portentously, 'that no one may give consent for an assault upon his or her own person.'

'But, Christ, we've made dozens of films with that sort of stuff in them. There was a very good market for it. And the girls got paid well. They'd pretend to be resisting, but it was all play-acting. They did it quite willingly.'

Fox shrugged. 'Doesn't alter the law on the subject,' he said casually, 'and that'll be the first thing the judge explains to the jury.' He took out a cigarette and lit it, smiling at Webb's startled reaction at his reference to a judge and jury.

'It was nothing to do with me,' said the anguished Webb. 'It was all Mike's idea.'

'And he's not here to deny it,' said Fox mildly.

'But it's true. Mike set the whole thing up. He found a market for these films and Harry Pritchard and I just went along with it for a bit of fun. In fact, so did Mike. Not that he made much money out of it, not even enough to cover the overheads. Pritchard got more out of it than Mike did.' For a moment, Webb looked wistful. 'Well, would you turn down the opportunity of having sex with all those girls?' He stared at Fox as though trying to will him to agree.

'Is that all you have to say?' asked Fox, although having seen Webb's hatchet-faced wife, he almost understood the man's distorted view.

'I tell you, the girls were willing.' Webb was beginning to sound desperate now. 'Why else did they keep coming back?'

'Did Leighton give them drugs?' asked Fox.

Webb looked down at the table. 'Yes,' he mumbled.

'You'll have to speak up,' said Fox sharply.

Webb raised his head. 'Yes, he did.'

'Why?'

'As a reward, I suppose. A lot of the girls were on it.'

'Or to make them less inhibited? Make them perform better?'

'I don't think so.'

'Not the view of some of the women we've interviewed,' said Fox mildly.

'It was nothing to do with me. It was all Mike Leighton.' Still Webb was trying to avoid the consequences of his own actions. 'He only started all this blue film business to provide himself with a ready supply of women. He used to get a terrific kick out of watching the videos of him and a group of girls having sex. He only did it for his own gratification.'

'And yours, I gather.'

Webb didn't reply to that, but hung his head again.

'Strange that you should say there was no profit in it,' Fox continued, 'because he wasn't sending them to Karel van Hooft in Mons as an act of charity.'

'I don't know anything about that.'

'But you sent a consignment to van Hooft after Leighton's death, Webb, so don't tell me you know nothing about it.' Fox had learned the name of the recipient of the tapes from the Brussels gendarmerie. 'Incidentally, Mr van Hooft was very cross about that last consignment.' He didn't know that for certain, but it was a guess that was unlikely to be contradicted. 'You see, all the tapes were blank.' For the benefit of the tape recorder, Fox announced that the interview was now terminated and switched off the machine. Then he looked at Webb again. 'I wouldn't be at all surprised if van Hooft came over here to do some sorting out.'

Webb looked up sharply, a trace of fear crossing his face. 'What?' he gasped.

Fox grinned. 'Don't worry, old sport,' he said. 'He won't be able to get at you where you're going for the next few years. Not unless he's got friends in Parkhurst.'

'I think I need to see my solicitor after all,' said Webb, his face ashen. He was perspiring freely now.

'First sensible thing you've said so far,' said Fox as he stood up.

Following Webb's arrest, Kate Ebdon had gone straight from Richmond Police Station to Kirsty Newman's flat in Gipsy Hill. What with the pouring rain and the traffic, it took her all of two and a half hours to get there.

'Oh, it's you again.' Kirsty Newman was attired in an unflattering dressing gown and had clearly been awoken by Kate's ringing of the doorbell.

'Yeah, it's me again. I want to talk to you.'

'Better come in then. I'll put some coffee on.' Kirsty waited until Kate had settled herself in the sitting room and then walked through into the kitchen. 'What d'you want now?' she shouted.

'I'll tell you when you've made the coffee,' replied Kate and started to read a two-day-old copy of the *Daily Mirror.*

'Have you found out who murdered Leighton then?' asked Kirsty, coming back into the room a few minutes later. She set the coffee down and began pouring it.

'No, not yet.'

'What d'you want then?'

'Thanks.' Kate took the proffered cup of coffee from the other woman. 'We've turned up a video showing you being whipped by Webb and Pritchard, and then being raped by them. And Leighton.'

'So what?' Kirsty sat down opposite the woman detective. 'I told you that had happened.'

'You didn't say anything about being raped.'

'Get real, love,' said Kirsty. 'What d'you think skin flicks are all about if it's not about women getting screwed? Just because it looks as though we're being raped doesn't mean that we are.'

'Looked pretty real to me.'

'Oh, you know all about that, do you? Been raped often, have you?'

'They wouldn't live to tell the tale,' said Kate mildly, and for a moment Kirsty looked at her, knowing that what she had said was undoubtedly true. 'We arrested Webb and Pritchard earlier this morning,' Kate went on, 'and my guv'nor's charging them with GBH on you and with raping you.'

Kirsty Newman put her cup down with more force than usual and some of the coffee slopped over into the saucer. 'You've done what?' she said, unable to conceal her surprise.

'You heard me.' Kate took a sip of coffee. 'And we want a statement from you detailing all that was done to you. And we'll want you to go to court.'

'You must be bloody joking,' said Kirsty, clearly alarmed at the prospect of becoming involved in any proceedings.

'We can always subpoena you,' said Kate quietly.

'Well, you bloody do that, but you can't make me say anything. I'll just stand there and stay shtum. Even if they do send me down for contempt of court.'

'You seem very conversant with legal procedure,' said Kate, knowing full well that what Kirsty had just said was absolutely true.

'You get to learn the wrinkles when you're on the game,' said Kirsty in matter-of-fact tones. 'But there's no way I'm saying a bloody word. Christ, d'you realise what you're asking? If I turn up at court and start telling the tale, I'll never work again. It's the whores' code, love,' she added. 'Take what's handed out and keep your mouth shut. Or get out. And I can't afford to get out.'

'But you said the other day that you're not on the game any more.'

Kirsty gave a cynical laugh. 'There's no difference. There are plenty of girls who'd take part in porn movies if they got the chance, but those who give evidence against the blokes who make them don't work again. And you can forget being a call-girl too. The sort of clientele I was dealing with have got a lot to lose, and word would soon get out that I was a mouth. Best I could hope for after that would be King's Cross, and frankly I don't fancy the idea of earning my living being screwed every ten minutes by a drunken Mick up against the railings. Forget it, love. I don't want to know.'

Dick Campbell, one-time Deputy Assistant Commissioner Specialist Operations, and now security director of the bank which held Tanner's account, stood up, walked round his desk and shook hands with Detective Superintendent Craven-Foster. 'John, good to see you,' he said.

'Good to see you, too, guv'nor,' said Craven- Foster. 'You seem to be doing all right,' he added, casting a glance around Campbell's large oak-panelled office.

'Can't grumble.' Campbell waved a deprecatory hand. 'And you can forget the "guv'nor" bit,' he said. 'I'm not in the job any longer, thank God. What can I do for you?'

Craven-Foster explained the problem of John Tanner's disappearance from his Catford address and went on to tell Campbell why police were anxious to interview him.

'A customer's account is confidential, John,' said Campbell gravely. 'And I'm afraid there is no way in which I can divulge any information about it or about him.' He grinned at Craven-Foster's sudden frown. 'What d'you want to know?' he asked.

'His present address,' said Craven-Foster.

'You'll have to give me a day or so,' said Campbell. 'I'll have to make an excuse to examine the account, like we think he's fiddling the bank, but I'll get back to you as soon as I can.' He stood up and shook hands. 'Give that old rogue Tommy Fox my best, will you?' he said. 'He's a commander now, I hear.'

'Yes. In charge of SO1 Branch. And me.'

Campbell laughed. 'Well, don't let him get you down. He's got some strange working practices, but he's a bloody good detective.'

'So he keeps telling me,' said Craven-Foster.

EIGHTEEN

COMPARED WITH WEBB, PRITCHARD WAS coolly confident. Before being taken from his Soho studio, he had pulled his hair back into its usual pony-tail and donned a white, cotton tee-shirt that was deliberately tight enough to display his bulging biceps.

Having placed his prisoner in a cell at West End Central Police Station, where he now lounged truculently, DI Denzil Evans telephoned Fox at Richmond to report that Pritchard was in custody. 'D'you want to interview him, sir?' he asked.

'No thanks, Denzil,' said Fox. 'I might be tempted to hit him. We don't need anything from him to prove the offences, so just charge him. Do the business with the Crown Prosecution Service and go for an eight-day lay down at Marlborough Street tomorrow. Usual objections to bail. Interference with witnesses. You know the form. Then, if we need to talk to him about anything else, we'll know where he is.'

'Yes, sir.' Evans sighed; nothing changed.

Minutes later, Pritchard was brought into the custody suite and formally charged with raping Kirsty Newman, causing her grievous bodily harm with intent, and publishing obscene matter, namely video-recordings. For the first time since his arrival at the police station, he appeared to lose some of his confidence. 'This is all bloody rubbish,' he said. 'She agreed to it.'

The custody sergeant impassively wrote down this response, and then glanced up in case the prisoner should say anything else.

'But aren't you going to question me about this, with my

brief here?' Pritchard was irritated that the police appeared not to want to interrogate him about what they kept referring to as 'the alleged offences', and clearly thought that the arrival of his solicitor would be followed, shortly afterwards, by his own departure from the police station when the whole silly nonsense was cleared up.

'We don't need to,' said Evans dismissively. 'We've got all the evidence we need to take you to court. You can have a solicitor if you want one, but there's nothing else to be said.' And with that, he glanced at thc custody sergeant. 'He's all yours, skip.'

'Right, sir.' The custody sergeant beckoned to the constable who was doing duty as gaoler. 'Put him down, lad,' he said. 'Number Three.'

'It looks as though we've drawn a blank as far as Tanner's concerned, sir,' said Craven-Foster. 'I've had a call from Dick Campbell at the bank and the address they hold for him is the one we turned over in Catford.'

'Well, surely to God he must go into the bank from time to time,' said Fox.

'Apparently not, sir. Seems that a lot of people don't go anywhere near their bank these days. He can pay in cash at any branch and he can draw money from a cash machine.'

'Seems that I shall have to go and speak to Dick Campbell,' said Fox.

Craven-Foster looked doubtful. 'He did remind me that bank accounts are confidential, sir. I know he was half joking, but I think it meant don't push too hard.'

Fox waved a hand vaguely in the air. 'I'm the soul of discretion, John,' he said.

Later that afternoon, Fox was ushered into Campbell's office.

'Tommy, you old devil. How are you?'

Fox looked gloomy. 'I'd be a lot happier if I could crack this triple murder, Dick,' he said.

Campbell grinned. 'Well at least you've made commander.

Congratulations. I hear you inherited my secretary Brenda, too. She's a good girl.'

'She's all right now I've taught her how to make coffee,' said Fox, sinking down into a chair opposite Campbell's desk and mopping his brow. 'At least your air-conditioning's working better than ours at the Yard,' he added.

'Well, what can I do for you, Tommy?' asked Campbell. 'As if I didn't know.' He stood up and poured a couple of whiskies.

'I'm pretty convinced that Tanner's our man, Dick,' said Fox, 'but until we can lay hands on him, we shan't know for certain. But he looks like one bad bastard.'

'John Craven-Foster told you that we only have the old address for him, I suppose?' asked Campbell, sipping his Scotch.

Fox nodded. 'Yes, he did, but I don't really want to wait until he deigns to tell you where he's moved to. Could be months before he thinks of that, but my guess is that he won't. I'm betting that the loss of his credit card in Cyprus put the frighteners on him. You see, he had to ring the company and tell them it had been nicked. And he had to tell them he'd lost it in Cyprus just in case it was used the very next day. That Cypriot whore did us a favour. She unwittingly forced Tanner into admitting that he was in Cyprus at the crucial time.'

Campbell laughed. 'Dangerous things, credit cards,' he said.

'So are prostitutes,' said Fox drily.

'However, all is not lost, Tommy.' Campbell leaned forward and picked up a computer printout. 'It seems that in nine cases out of ten, Tanner uses the same cash machine to draw money. And he does so about once a week. And it's the maximum amount allowable, too.'

'I suppose you didn't happen to notice where this cash machine was, Dick,' said Fox airily.

'As a matter of fact, I did,' said Campbell. 'It's in Victoria. And, as an old copper, I would guess that it's miles away from where he lives.'

'Bloody wonderful,' said Fox as he contemplated the difficulties of keeping observation on a cash machine in central London. 'Why couldn't it have been somewhere like a remote Sussex village?'

'Because we don't have any cash machines in remote Sussex villages,' said Campbell. 'And even the machine that he uses in Victoria isn't one of ours, the cunning bastard.'

'If he's drawing a lot of money every week, perhaps he's trying to empty his account rather than tell you of his change of address,' said Fox.

'He'll have to do a lot of drawing then,' said Campbell.

'Got a lot of money then, has he?' asked Fox, gazing out of the window with a disinterested expression on his face.

Campbell handed Fox a scrap of paper. 'Do me a favour, Tommy. Drop that in the waste-paper basket, will you?'

Fox glanced briefly at the slip of paper before screwing it up and throwing it away. Later, Campbell retrieved it and put it through the shredder.

'I can't say I'm surprised,' said Fox when he had listened to Kate Ebdon's account of her latest interview with Kirsty Newman. 'She sounds like one very frightened woman.'

'She point-blank refuses to give evidence against either Webb or Pritchard, sir.'

'Take her down to Gipsy Hill nick, Kate,' Fox had said, 'and show her the video. She probably hasn't seen it and it might just persuade her that her performance was too realistic to be acting. The video's pretty telling evidence on its own and it might be enough, but I'd rather have her testimony to support the charges.'

Now, seated in a room at the police station, Kate switched on the video-player. Kirsty Newman had been extremely reluctant to accompany the detective, and it was only after a great deal of persuasion on Kate's part that she had agreed to view the film.

The Newman girl, dressed in black leggings and a shapeless white thigh-length tee-shirt, gripped the arms of her chair as that part of the video showing her being whipped came on to the screen. Tight-lipped and white of face, she forced herself to watch, but when the scene of her own rape came on, she turned her head away and dissolved into hysterical tears.

Kate turned off the machine. 'You're not going to tell me that was play-acting, Kirsty, are you?' she asked in tones more kindly than any she had used to the young prostitute previously.

Kirsty Newman looked at Kate, a hunted expression on her face. 'Of course it wasn't,' she said softly, 'but there's no way I'm giving evidence. It's all right for you, but you don't know what these people are like.'

'We'll protect you, Kirsty,' said Kate.

Kirsty laughed cynically. Young though she was, she was wise in the ways of those who ran the vice trade. 'For how long? Until the trial's over? Then what? They've a lot of friends, these people, and they'll wait. I don't want my face slashed and that's what'll happen. I've known girls on the game who've opened their mouths in the past and those who've lived have lived to regret it.' She stood up. 'No way,' she said defiantly. 'Forget it.'

Despondent, Kate Ebdon had just returned to the Yard when the news came through from Wandsworth. She took the message flimsy from the DC who had taken the call and glanced at it. 'Oh Christ!' she said, 'that's all we needed.' She stood up. 'I'll tell the guv'nor,' she added.

Tapping lightly on Fox's office door, Kate went in without waiting. 'Bad news, sir,' she said, proffering the message flimsy.

'What is it?' Carefully, Fox laid his spoon in the saucer and glanced up.

'Anna Coombs has been murdered, sir. Message just come in from Wandsworth.'

'And then there were four,' said Fox phlegmatically and took the message form from Kate.

Detective Superintendent Patrick Ringham of the area major

investigation pool was a competent detective and he was not best pleased at the arrival of the commander of SO1 Branch at the scene of his latest murder. But he was sufficient of a realist to know that it was inevitable. Anna Coombs's name, in common with all those who had come to notice during Fox's investigation into the triple murder off Cyprus, had been fed into the Police National Computer in case they should come to notice. But even Fox had not expected Anna Coombs to come to notice as dramatically as she had done.

'What's the SP, Pat?' asked Fox, wrinkling his nose at the sour smell which pervaded the prostitute's last home. He and Ringham were standing in the centre of Anna Coombs's seedy sitting room, while around them scenes-of-crime officers worked steadily at their task of gathering scientific evidence.

'The landlord is a West Indian fellow called William Wilberforce. He says that he had been out to get some cigarettes and when he came back, he heard Anna Coombs's baby crying. Apparently it went on for some time, so he came up to see if there was anything wrong. He says that the door was unlocked and after knocking, he came in. He found the Coombs girl lying on the floor, dead.'

Fox nodded. 'Who's the pathologist, Pat?'

'John Harris,' said Ringham. 'His initial opinion is that she was strangled manually. There were no signs of a break-in and the indication is that the killer was known to the victim.' He shrugged. 'But if she habitually left the door unlocked, perhaps it was just an opportunist killer. There's a lot of them about.'

Fox indicated Kate Ebdon whom he had brought with him to Wandsworth. 'Kate reckoned that the Coombs girl was in fear from her former pimp, a West Indian called Chester Smart,' he said. 'Might be worth having a chat with him.'

'I'll have him pulled in, sir,' said Ringham.

Fox grinned. 'No,' he said enthusiastically, 'you can leave that to me. He might have other information regarding my Cyprus job.'

'I'm not too happy about Wilberforce, sir,' said Ringham. 'The landlord.'

'Oh? Why's that?'

'I don't think he's telling the truth, guv. I think he may have been here all the time. He was as nervous as hell when I was talking to him.'

'Not surprising,' said Fox. 'Probably the first time he's found a dead body.'

'As soon as I've got time, I'll get back to him,' said Ringham.

'Want me to have a word with him?'

'By all means,' said Ringham flatly. He knew that once Tommy Fox had taken it into his head to interrogate a witness, even in someone else's enquiry, nothing would stop him interfering.

'Where is he?'

'Downstairs in his room.'

Fox, with Kate Ebdon trailing after him, went downstairs and tapped on the landlord's door. 'You'll be Mr William Wilberforce, no doubt?' he asked jovially when the West Indian opened the door.

'Yes, sir, that is I,' said Wilberforce.

'Splendid,' said Fox. 'Thomas Fox . . . of Scotland Yard.'

'A great honour to meet you, sir,' said Wilberforce, opening the door wide. 'Please step into my humble dwelling.'

'How kind,' murmured Fox and entered the small sitting room, similar in size and shape to the one above it where Anna Coombs's body had been found. 'Now, my detective superintendent tells me that you went down the road for some cigarettes.'

'Absolutely correct, sir,' said Wilberforce, avoiding Fox's gaze.

'Perhaps you'd tell me what happened after that.'

'When I came back, sir, I heard Anna's baby crying. She was a good little girl and I didn't hear her very often, but she kept on. Thinking that something was amiss, I went up and knocked on the door, but there was no answer. I tried the door and it was open. So I went in.'

Wilberforce's eyes rolled. 'And there was poor Anna on the floor, sir.'

'And she was dead,' said Fox.

'Very, sir. I have not seen anyone more dead.'

'Oh? You've seen other people dead, have you?' asked Fox.

'Only on the TV, sir,' said Wilberforce. 'But you can tell, even from that. Her tongue was sticking out and her eyes were open. And there was blood coming from her nose.'

'So what did you do then?'

'I called the police, sir, nine-nine-nine, and they came very promptly.'

'Well, I'm pleased to hear that,' said Fox. 'Now then, where is it that you get your cigarettes?'

'Only down the road, sir. The shop on the corner of the street.'

'So how long were you out of the house?'

Wilberforce looked thoughtful. 'Perhaps half an hour, sir.'

Fox raised an eyebrow. 'Half an hour to go to the corner shop and buy some cigarettes?'

Wilberforce shrugged and tipped his head to one side. 'It is a Pakistani gentleman who keeps the shop, sir, and he's a very chatty person. It is sometimes difficult to get away.'

'And this morning was one of his chatty days, was it?'

Wilberforce smiled nervously. 'Every day is one of those days, sir.'

'What did you talk about today?' Fox sounded uninterested and looked at a picture of the Queen that occupied a place of honour over Wilberforce's fireplace.

'Oh, this and that. The weather, and the test match. Extremely keen about cricket is Mr Patel. Not that his lot are very good at it.' Wilberforce smiled and shook his head. 'They will never beat the West Indies,' he added.

'Perhaps so,' said Fox, who didn't know the first thing about cricket. 'So if I go down the road and talk to Mr Patel, he'll remember this conversation, will he?'

For the first time since the interview began, Wilberforce

looked disconcerted. 'Perhaps not, sir. He was very busy this morning. There were many customers.'

'But he still had time to have a conversation with you about cricket that must have lasted, what . . . ?' Fox looked thoughtful, pretending to calculate the time it would take to walk to the corner and back and deducting that figure from the half hour that Wilberforce said he had been away. 'Shall we say twenty minutes, William, old fruit?'

'Ah!' said Wilberforce and relapsed into silence.

'Shall we start again, William?' said Fox, sitting down in one of the landlord's armchairs and crossing his legs. He took out his cigarette case and offered it to Wilberforce who took one and immediately produced his lighter. 'Allow me, sir,' he said, applying the flame to the end of Fox's cigarette.

'Well?' Fox smiled. 'You were here all the time, weren't you, William?'

Wilberforce looked quite frightened. 'Sir, I promise you that I had nothing to do with this terrible crime.'

'I didn't think for a moment you had, William,' said Fox comfortingly, 'but I would rather like to know who did.'

'I think this man is very dangerous, sir.'

'I don't think there's much doubt about that,' said Fox, 'and the sooner we lock him up, the safer it will be for everyone, you included.' He glanced at the picture of the Queen. 'I'm sure Her Majesty would expect a loyal subject to assist the police, William, don't you?'

Wilberforce shot the picture a reverent glance. 'I suppose so, sir,' he said, but clearly was still reticent.

'It would be a great inconvenience for me to have to start prosecuting people who told me lies.' Fox gazed around the room, a distracted expression on his face.

Wilberforce sighed heavily and sat down. 'I am very sorry, sir, but I was frightened, you see . . .'

Fox nodded understandingly. 'And what happened?'

'I heard the outer door bang. It's left open during the day, but it's locked at night.'

'Very wise,' said Fox.

'I heard someone going upstairs and then I heard some argument. A man's voice. Then I heard this bang on the floor and someone running downstairs again. So I opened my door just that much . . .' Wilberforce held finger and thumb a fraction apart and contrived to look conspiratorial. 'And I saw this black man going past and out of the front door.'

'There you are, William, that didn't hurt at all, did it?' Fox turned to Kate. 'Take a full statement from our friend here,' he said, 'with as complete a description as possible.' And facing Wilberforce once more, he asked, 'Would you know this man again?'

'I think so, sir,' said Wilberforce cautiously. He knew very well that he could identify the man he had seen running down the stairs; it was the advisability of doing so that worried him.

NINETEEN

DETECTIVE SERGEANT ROBERT HURLEY WAS feeling very pleased with himself. 'I've tracked down Lee Watson, sir,' he said. 'Lives in Epsom. Everything tallies. She's on the electoral roll and on the council tax register. And I've made a couple of sightings, so I now know what she looks like.'

'Good work, Bob,' said Fox, 'but she'll have to wait.' Interviewing Bernie Watson's first wife had suddenly been pushed way down his list of priorities. 'We've got a murder at Wandsworth and we're mounting a hunt for John Tanner.' He looked thoughtful. 'You're not busy at the moment, are you, Bob?'

Hurley was not quick enough to come up with an excuse. 'Well, no, sir . . .'

'Good. You can join Mr Evans's surveillance team, keeping watch on a cash machine in Victoria for this Tanner fellow. At least it's not far to walk.' Fox beamed at the DS. 'Just down the road in fact.'

It had been Denzil Evans's inevitable misfortune to be selected by Fox to oversee the observation on the cash machine. Apart from the descriptions obtained from Andrea Nemitsas, the Cypriot prostitute, and the two soldiers who claimed to have had a conversation with 'Jock', the police had no real idea what Tanner looked like. A search of Passport Office records had proved inconclusive; although several men called John Tanner had been issued with passports over the preceding ten years, the chance of identifying anyone from his passport photograph is somewhat remote, and the police placed no great reliability on this source of information.

Once the observation on the cash machine had begun, the police discovered that it was used almost continuously during working hours, and they realised just how many men fitted the description they had of the man believed to be Tanner. Evans had deputed twenty officers to maintain the surveillance and they were now deployed in positions where they could watch people using the machine without, they hoped, being too obvious. But, if as seemed likely, Tanner was a professional 'hit man', he was probably also an expert in counter-surveillance techniques, and that promised to make the watchers' task even more difficult.

Added to that was Fox's injunction that Tanner was not to be challenged, but was to be 'housed' so that police could discover where he lived. If he was arrested near the cash machine and denied any involvement in the Cyprus murders, they would be hard pressed to make a case on the evidence they had available to them so far. And if he was as cunning as Fox shrewdly assumed he was, Tanner would be carrying no evidence of identity other than the cash-card which, rather than admit to murder, he would probably quite cheerfully claim to have stolen. And to have forced the identification number out of the loser. Unbelievable though such a story might be, it would be very difficult to disprove. The only chance of linking Tanner with the murders was to find out where he lived and hope that there was some evidence there. But even that possibility was recognised as being slim.

Having undertaken to lay hands on Chester Smart, the late Anna Coombs's pimp and possibly her murderer, Fox now found that he was running short of men. But he did not anticipate that the operation to arrest Smart would be a protracted one. A pimp was disinclined to leave his charges for too long in case another predator moved in on his territory.

As the commander of SO8 Branch as well as SO1, Fox had no qualms about imposing on Detective Superintendent

Gavin Brace, his successor as operational head of the Flying Squad, to provide the additional men he needed.

'Morning, Gavin.' Fox breezed into Brace's office. 'How's Fiona?'

'She's fine, thank you, sir.' Brace looked askance at Fox who rarely enquired after the health of his subordinates' wives. 'You want something, don't you, sir?' he asked with a grin.

Fox smiled. 'I need to borrow a team from you, Gavin.' He dropped into one of Brace's chairs and offered him a cigarette. Then he explained about the urgent need to arrest Chester Smart whose address was unknown to police.

Brace nodded. As a one-time detective chief inspector at West End Central Police Station, he knew that a Soho pimp like Smart would almost certainly be found in the area sooner or later. Probably sooner. 'You've still got Evans and Ebdon, sir,' he said, plaintively fighting a rearguard action.

'I know, I know,' said Fox cheerfully. 'But this damned enquiry is more complex than I thought it would be.'

Brace sighed. Fox was his commander after all, and there was no way he could refuse an order, particularly when the apprehension of a suspected murderer was involved. 'Any team in particular, sir?'

'No, Gavin. You know what you've got running. I'll leave it to you,' said Fox.

Brace glanced down at the list that was rendered to him daily, and which showed the dispositions and availability of the Flying Squad. 'I can spare Jack Gilroy and his team, at a pinch, sir.'

'Excellent,' said Fox. 'I just don't have the men on SO1, what with this obo we're keeping on this damned cash machine for Tanner. But as far as Smart's concerned, I reckon one night, possibly two, and we'll have him.'

'I think Jack Gilroy will enjoy that, sir,' said Brace, yielding to the inevitable.

It was on the morning of the second day of the observation that the attention of Evans's team was drawn to a man approaching the cash machine. Drawn by the suspect's own furtiveness. Dressed in jeans and a tee-shirt, the six-feet-tall man was some way away when the watching police first noticed him, glancing about as he walked towards the bank. Casually – too casually – he strolled past the machine, but ten or twelve yards further on, he turned and retraced his steps. Searching the area once more with his eyes, he thrust a card hurriedly into the machine and pressed a number of the buttons. Quickly pocketing his money, he strode swiftly away towards Parliament Square.

The air was suddenly alive as radio transmissions kept each of the observers informed of what was happening. Disregarding the strange looks they were getting from members of the public, fascinated by grown men and women talking up their sleeves, the police conjectured on the likelihood of the man being Tanner.

Eventually, Evans made a decision. 'Right, give it a run,' he said, 'but if he gets at all sussy, break it off. There's always another day.'

The first trio of detectives, well-practised in the art of following, fanned out into the standard ABC pattern of foot-surveillance: one officer ahead, the other two behind, constantly changing places so that if the suspect glanced behind him – and few people did – it would not be obvious to their quarry that he was of interest.

But Tanner – if it was him – was careful, and that reinforced the views of the police that, at last, they had got the right man. And, as Evans said, if it wasn't Tanner then his behaviour made it almost certain that he was guilty of something.

Despite the suspect's extreme caution, the police managed to keep him under observation without apparently alerting him to their presence. He reached the top of Victoria Street and paused opposite Westminster Abbey, looking around. Seemingly satisfied that he was not being watched, he nevertheless ambled slowly along the west side of Parliament Square in front of the old Middlesex Guildhall, clearly aware that such behaviour would increase the difficulties of anyone who happened to be following him.

'This bastard knows a thing or two about surveillance,' said a detective into his sleeve.

Reaching the north-west corner of the square, the suspect waited until the traffic lights turned to green and suddenly darted across the road towards the Treasury, risking his life as he weaved in and out of vehicles that had just started to move off. But it was to no avail; several of Evans's team, anticipating such a ploy, were already on the other side of the road. Pausing only to buy a newspaper, the man adopted the same routine when he reached Parliament Street at the top end of Whitehall but, again, some of the detectives were already on the opposite pavement waiting for him. Pushing his way irritably between parties of dawdling tourists, the man finally reached Westminster Underground Station and ran down the steps, two at a time.

As the target bought a ticket to Waterloo, the officer who was immediately behind him banged some money down and asked for Temple in an attempt to allay any suspicion that the man might have that he was being pursued.

A woman detective constable received news of their quarry's destination by radio and, pushing her police pass into the automatic barrier, followed the suspect down to the platform.

Evans, having heard all of this over the air, and knowing that his target would inevitably be delayed by having to change at Embankment Station, raced across Westminster Bridge by car, taking three other officers with him. It was a calculated risk but, by good fortune, Evans succeeded in getting those officers in place on the concourse at Waterloo Station by the time the suspect stepped off the escalator, followed by other members of the team, and made his way over the foot-bridge to the other main-line station at Waterloo East.

'He's bought a ticket for St John's,' said an anonymous voice over the air.

Working on the principle that if there isn't a crowd make

your own, seven or eight officers, each giving the impression that they were unknown to each other, crowded on to the platform. The man they were following appeared to suspect nothing, presumably believing that, even if he had been observed drawing cash, he was now far enough away not to have to worry any more.

At St John's Station, in south-east London, the man alighted without a backward glance, strolled out into the hot July sun and waited patiently until he was able to cross Lewisham Way at the point where it met Loampit Hill. He turned left and then, almost immediately, right into Sandrock Road. Ten minutes later, he entered a house in one of the maze of streets bounded by Shell Road and the railway line that ran between St John's and Ladywell.

'Got the bastard,' said Evans.

'If he's our man,' said DS Hurley and received a sour look from the DI.

The army authorities in Cyprus responded with alacrity when Fox asked for the services of the soldiers who had first spoken to the man 'Jock' and, within hours, the two men were, once again, in Fox's office.

'Hallo, sir,' said Corporal Wayne Higgins. 'Never expected to be back here so soon. Have you caught him then?'

'That rather depends on what you tell us,' said Fox. And he told the two soldiers that his plan encompassed their sitting in an observation van in Lewisham from about half-past five the following morning. Initially, it all sounded rather exciting, and certainly a change from their mundane military duties. But it didn't take long for them to discover what most policemen had already discovered: that there's no fun, no romance and no drama in it.

Ever since the mid-eighteenth century, Shepherd Market, two hundred yards north of Piccadilly in London's Mayfair and within spitting distance of the finest hotels, has been the haunt of prostitutes. From time to time, efforts had been made to suppress their trade; the Sexual Offences Act and the Street Offences Act had made a slight dent in the 1950s and 1960s, but overall they had had about as much success as Canute's attempts to turn the tide. Consequently, the area is still used by young women offering their bodies for sex, but now in uneasy juxtaposition with young homosexual men doing the same.

Quite a few members of Detective Inspector Jack Gilroy's team of Flying Squad officers had served in the West End before becoming detectives, and they were familiar with the curious relationship that existed between policemen and prostitutes. In the old days, the girls would be arrested in rotation – once a fortnight usually – and taken to the police station where they would be charged and bailed to appear at court next morning. There they would plead guilty, pay a nominal fine, and carry on working. It was all very civilised.

On the first evening of the combined SO1 and Flying Squad operation to find Chester Smart, Detective Sergeant Percy Fletcher loped through Shepherd Market. He was well-versed in the ways of the area and had served for several years as a CID officer at West End Central Police Station.

'Hallo, love,' called one girl, more brazen than the rest. 'Long time, no see. Looking for a freebie?' she asked and grinned lasciviously. She knew Fletcher – and knew him to be Old Bill – but, for all that, she knew that she was unlikely to be arrested by a plain-clothes officer. At least, not for tomming; that wouldn't be playing the game.

Fletcher grinned back and stopped. 'You always were a cheeky bitch, Paula,' he said, lowering his voice, and glancing at the girl's short skirt. 'You'll catch your death in that pelmet.'

''Bout all I will catch tonight, Mr Fletcher,' said the girl softly. 'Trade's bloody awful. Load of wimps about these days, all frightened of catching Aids.'

Fletcher put his head closer to Paula's, giving the impression to the other women that he was arranging a mutually agreeable price. 'I'm looking for Chester Smart,' he whispered. 'Any idea where I might find him?'

A sudden look of alarm crossed Paula's face. 'What d'you want that bastard for?' she asked in equally low tones.

Fletcher weighed up whether to tell the girl and, realising that if he told her the truth he was more likely to get her help, said, 'We're going to nick him.'

'Time someone did,' said the girl quietly. 'He's not my minder, but he keeps an eye on Marlene over there.' She nodded towards a redhead lounging in a doorway, her lipstick like a neon sign even at that distance. 'But she won't tell you nothing. She's terrified of him. Anyway, what d'you want him for?'

'We want to talk to him about the murder of Anna Coombs,' said Fletcher, his head still close to Paula's, 'but keep that to yourself.'

''Struth!' said Paula. 'We heard about her, poor little tart.' There was little affecting their trade that West End prostitutes didn't get to hear about; it was all a matter of self-protection. 'He usually comes round first off about eleven, to collect,' she said. 'Know what he looks like?'

'Only that he's black,' said Fletcher.

'As black as your hat,' said Paula. 'And he's got a chiv scar down his left cheek. Usually dressed in black trousers and one of them white jackets flecked with black. Know what I mean? He sometimes wears a big black hat an' all, like a . . . What do they call 'em, fedoras?' She paused, worried that she had said too much. 'But I never told you nothing, Mr Fletcher.'

Fletcher grinned. 'Make it look good then, Paula,' he said.

'I'm not into that sort of malarkey, you filthy sod,' shouted Paula suddenly and slapped Fletcher's face.

'Bloody tramp,' Fletcher shouted in response and hurried out of Shepherd Market to the catcalls of the other prostitutes.

TWENTY

FOR FAR TOO LONG, CHESTER Smart had had things his own way. As far as he was concerned, he had convinced himself that he was above the law. That it couldn't, or wouldn't, touch him. And he had become over confident. Consequently when he had alighted from his Mercedes and strolled along Curzon Street, he had failed to notice a number of men hanging about in the shadows. Or rather, he had failed to register their presence. Not that furtively loitering men were anything unusual, particularly at that time of night, when they were frequently to be seen in the area summoning enough courage to engage the services of a prostitute, female or male. But if Smart had noticed these men, he would also have noticed that they were different from the usual punter, for they each had a steely glint in their eyes, even though they gave an impression of being uninterested in the passing scene. Or in Chester Smart.

Looking rather like the sort of happy-go-lucky black man often seen in American television crime programmes, Smart lolloped along the street. But it was a pose, and one that belied his true character. There was nothing happy-go-lucky about this man. He was sinister and ruthless and would not hesitate to use violence if it served his own ends. And he had frequently used it in the past.

Smart turned into Hertford Street, still ambling and occasionally smiling at passers-by. Turning left and walking a few yards further, he finally came into Shepherd Market itself.

It is well known that policemen can be nasty when the

mood takes them, and this is particularly true of Flying Squad officers. The moment that Smart had been sighted leaving his car, arrogantly parked on a double yellow line, DC Bellenger had called up the vehicle removal squad that DI Jack Gilroy had arranged to have standing by, on overtime of course. This implementation of traffic law would, in his view, serve a dual purpose in addition to the parking fine which would go some way towards paying for the crew's overtime. It would undoubtedly hinder Smart's escape if foolishly he decided to do what policemen call 'a runner' – in other words, to attempt to escape – and secondly, it would save documenting the vehicle as prisoner's property once Smart had been arrested.

The moment that the late Anna Coombs's pimp had turned the corner into Hertford Street, the tow-away squad moved in, and long before Smart had reached Shepherd Market, his Mercedes was on its way to the car pound at Hyde Park. Courtesy of the Commissioner of the Metropolitan Police.

Paula had not been quite accurate when she had described Chester Smart's hat as a fedora. It was, in fact, a wide-brimmed felt. But it *was* black. And he raised it extravagantly in a mocking parody of courtesy when he entered Shepherd Market. 'Why, hallo, ladies,' he cried, and smiled around at the girls. Receiving no response, he walked across to the prostitute called Marlene and took a wad of notes from her handbag. He gazed at them for a moment, then peeled one off and stuffed it into the girl's cleavage. 'You're not doing too well tonight, my child,' he said in low menacing tones. 'You'll just have to try harder, or uncle will get cross with you.' He turned to another girl, little more than eighteen, and took money from her too, pushing a note between her breasts before retracing his steps. He glanced at Paula, seemingly engaged in conversation with a 'trick', smiled, and made his gangling way out again, intent on visiting the rest of his stable who had pitches in and around Grosvenor Square.

The 'trick' was DS Percy Fletcher who had returned just before eleven in the hope of finding the pimp. Fortunately,

Paula was there too; she could as easily have been with a client.

'That's him, Mr Fletcher,' said Paula quietly, as Fletcher stood back.

'Bless you, Paula,' whispered Fletcher. 'I owe you one.'

'Huh!' said Paula. 'That'll be the day.' And then in a loud voice, 'I told you before, the answer's no.'

Not wishing to compromise his informant, Fletcher waited until he was out of earshot of the other girls to transmit a terse message over his personal radio.

The chase was on.

Smart was not happy walking about London at night – he considered it a dangerous place – and, intent on driving to Grosvenor Square, he made his way back to Curzon Street only to find that his Mercedes was no longer where he had left it. Momentarily nonplussed by this liberty that someone had obviously taken, he stopped and stared around, as though such a hostile and threatening stance would immediately cause whoever had taken his precious car to restore it.

And that's when the Flying Squad pounced.

However, even the most finely-honed plans have a tendency to go wildly awry at times. Usually when they are least expected to.

'Chester Smart!' DC Bellenger was perhaps a little too far away when he shouted.

Smart, his antennae immediately detecting danger, did not wait to see who wanted him or why. He guessed, accurately as it happened, and promptly took off in the direction of Park Lane.

Alerted to this unexpected and disastrous turn of events, DI Gilroy's team of eight, reinforced by another eight SO1 officers, began chasing Smart.

Smart ran across the road, narrowly avoiding being run down by a Ford Scorpio, and, turning into Park Street, crossed again and pounded towards Grosvenor Square, scattering pedestrians in his path. At one point he cleared an overturned waste-bin with an athletic bound, and an elderly

American tourist clutched his wife, forcing her against a wall, and muttered something about Chicago.

Unfortunately, Flying Squad officers have a great liking for beer and this tends to be something of an impediment when they are called upon to display physical attributes above and beyond their idea of the call of duty. But they persisted, never letting Smart out of their sight. One of their more enterprising number, DC Sean Tarling, hailed a taxi and directed the driver to 'follow that man'.

Having been convinced that he was not taking part in the making of a film without being paid the recognised Equity fee, the cab driver entered into the spirit of the affair. 'Is that him over there, guv'nor?' he enquired.

'Yeah, that's him,' said Tarling, still fighting to regain his breath.

'Want me to run the bugger down, guv?'

'No, for Christ's sake don't do that. We need to talk to him.'

'Don't look like he wants to talk to you, guv.'

At that moment, Smart saw the slow-moving cab and sensing that he was still in danger, turned into Upper Grosvenor Street. It was a clever move. And it was a one-way street. The wrong way. The cabbie was prepared to chance it, but the volume of traffic coming towards him precluded any chance of his forcing his way after the fleeing Smart.

Tarling leaped from the cab and paused. 'How much?' he asked.

'Forget it, guv,' said the cabbie. 'You'll lose him.'

'Thanks,' said Tarling and, pausing only to avoid a black Ford Scorpio, raced after the errant pimp.

Reaching the point where South Audley Street joins Grosvenor Square, Smart, now well into his stride, hurtled along the front of the American Embassy with Tarling and several others in hot pursuit.

A uniformed constable of the Diplomatic Protection Group gazed on impassively as the black man swept past him, followed at intervals by a number of heavies who looked remarkably out of breath. 'You entering him for the Derby?'

he shouted, recognising Tarling as one of his own as he thundered by.

Tarling had got his second wind now. 'Get stuffed, you fat prat,' he shouted back and grinned at the constable's sudden change of expression. But Tarling knew that an officer on such a sensitive post was not allowed to abandon it, whatever the provocation.

Smart had now skirted two sides of the square and was into Brook Street before the pursuing police had even reached the first corner.

And it was then that the pimp came unstuck.

As he passed a darkened doorway, an exquisitely-shod foot extended itself into his path. Smart tripped, his arms and legs whirling and thrashing the air in his attempt to retain his balance, but his momentum was, ironically, the cause of his downfall. Literally. He crashed to the ground and slithered for nearly three yards before stopping, winded and completely spent.

Interested passers-by now saw a well-dressed man emerge from the doorway and kneel on the inert figure of Chester Smart, and heard this picture of sartorial elegance say, 'You're nicked, my son.' Fox stood up, a closed cut-throat razor in his left hand, and looked despairingly at the handcuffed figure on the ground. 'I presume, dear boy,' he said, 'that you carry this just in case you are overcome with the desperate need to have a shave. Although I must say,' he continued, stooping to twist his prisoner's head round and inspect the wispy beard on the point of the man's chin, 'that you don't seem to have done a very good job.'

DC Tarling was the next officer to arrive on the scene and slumped against the black Ford Scorpio now stationary in the kerb. 'Blimey, guv'nor,' he said, 'how did you get here?'

'Happened to be passing,' said Fox airily, seeing no profit in dispelling the mystique with which his actions were usually surrounded. In fact, one of his informants had told him that Smart also controlled some of the women who plied their trade in Grosvenor Square, and he had deduced that the pimp was likely to finish up there if the Flying Squad failed to catch him earlier.

A number of other breathless Flying Squad officers arrived and two of them seized the figure of Chester Smart and dragged him into an upright position. 'What's the charge, guv?' asked one of them.

'For a start, assault on police,' said Fox. 'He kicked my foot.'

The van looked old and dilapidated, but the engine was in top-class condition. The two police officers and the two soldiers who had occupied it from half-past five that morning, had to wait nearly five hours before anything happened.

'Hallo, looks like a bit of movement.' The senior of the two detectives, a sergeant, watched closely through one of the narrow slits in the side of the nondescript observation van. 'Here, Wayne,' he said, 'what d'you think?'

Corporal Wayne Higgins peered out through the other slit at the figure now emerging from the house which had been under constant observation since their arrival. 'That's him,' he said. 'Here, Taff, have a look.'

Private Farmer now applied an eye to one of the slits. 'That's him,' he said. 'That's Jock.'

'Do we follow him, skip?' asked the other detective.

'No, we don't. The guv'nor just wanted him ID'd, and we've done that. Now we can go and have some breakfast, once we've made a call.'

At about the time that Corporal Wayne Higgins and Private 'Taff' Farmer were confirming that John Tanner was, in fact, the 'Jock' they had spoken to in Cyprus, Fox was sitting down opposite Chester Smart in West End Central Police Station.

After a night in the cells, and an examination by the divisional surgeon who had confirmed that, remarkably, the pimp had been uninjured by his fall, Smart had regained his former truculence. He lolled about in his chair, his legs stretched out and his long arms hanging loosely.

'I am Commander Fox . . . of Scotland Yard.'

'Congratulations, man,' said Smart, apparently unmoved by this announcement.

'Where d'you live?' asked Fox.

'I don't live nowhere, man,' said Smart. 'I'm what you call a night person. I just flit from place to place.' He moved slightly. 'But I want to know what I've been arrested for. You can't just go about arresting innocent citizens, holders of British passports an' that.'

'Anna Coombs, a prostitute, once worked for you,' said Fox without preamble.

If Smart was surprised by this, he didn't show it. 'I ain't never heard of the lady,' he said.

Fox smiled and lit a cigarette. 'You'll have to do better than that, Chester, old fruit,' he said. 'You see, I have firm information that she was one of your girls. And that she worked Shepherd Market and that you lived partly or wholly on her immoral earnings.'

Smart shrugged an extravagant shrug. 'So what? Lots of people go about telling lies about me.' He waved away a cloud of Fox's cigarette smoke. 'That's very bad for your health, man,' he said.

'Michael Leighton,' said Fox and gazed at the prisoner.

'Martin Luther King,' said Smart.

'What's that supposed to mean?' asked Fox.

'Nothing in particular. I just thought you was playing some sort of word association game.' Smart grinned insolently.

'Where were you the day before yesterday, at about ten o'clock in the morning, Chester?'

Smart looked at the ceiling. 'Difficult to say without recourse to my diary,' he said. 'And that is in my car what someone feloniously stole from me last night while you was running about arresting innocent folk like me.' But Smart's car had been searched thoroughly and, to no one's surprise, had yielded neither his diary nor anything else of evidential value.

'Why did you run away when you were challenged by

police?' asked Fox. He had already examined the statement made by DC Bellenger.

Smart opened his eyes wide. 'Is that who they were?' he said. 'Well, bless my soul. To tell you the truth, Mr Policeman, I heard this man shout at me and I took one look at him and I thought to myself, here's a robber, I thought. London is such a dangerous place and thinking that I was about to be mugged, like so many other innocent folk, I decided to run away.' He shook his head slowly. 'Now, if he had told me he was a policeman, I would have stopped immediately. Naturally.'

'Naturally,' murmured Fox. Although Bellenger had admitted failing to tell Smart that he was a police officer, Fox knew damned well that it would not have made a scrap of difference even if he had uttered those immortal words.

'Now, if there's nothing further, I'll be going on my way,' said Smart, grinning all over his face.

'Certainly,' said Fox, and for one moment DI Evans, who had been seated beside Fox throughout the interview, thought that he meant it. 'I'm quite happy to admit you to police bail.'

'Well, that's it, then,' said Smart, shuffling his feet.

'Once we've verified your address,' said Fox and stood up, beaming down at the prisoner.

'I'm afraid that I'm going to need Jack Gilroy's team for another twenty-four hours, Gavin,' said Fox. 'This bastard Smart refuses to come across with his address. We've done a registration check on his car, which is still in Hyde Park pound, but it's a duff address, needless to say.'

'What's the plan then, guv'nor?' asked Brace.

'I want every ponce in the West End squeezed until the pips come out,' said Fox. 'Or more specifically, until one of them surrenders Chester Smart's address. And any other information that happens to surface.'

Brace shook his head wearily; he knew when he was beaten. 'Very good, sir,' he said.

'Bless you, Gavin,' said Fox and glanced at his watch.

'And now,' he added, 'I must go and see the Commander Operations at Central. I need a few "feet" to help out.'

Brace suddenly felt an uncharacteristic and heartfelt sympathy for the Uniform Branch commander whose office was high above Whitehall.

TWENTY-ONE

FOX WAS SITTING IN HIS office, stirring fretfully at his coffee. But it was not the coffee that was causing his impatience; Brenda, under Fox's tutelage, was probably now the best coffee-maker at Scotland Yard. No, Fox was impatient with the slowness of his enquiry. And with the intransigence of Peter Frobisher, the Assistant Commissioner, Specialist Operations.

Webb and Pritchard were locked up, remanded in custody and awaiting the deliberations of the Crown Prosecution Service. Chester Smart was also locked up. But, although strongly suspected of murdering Anna Coombs, he had only, so far, been charged with carrying an offensive weapon and living on the immoral earnings of prostitution, the last probably being too tenuous to secure a conviction. And John Tanner had been 'housed' to an address in Lewisham where, this very morning, Detective Superintendent John Craven-Foster was mounting an operation to arrest him.

Despite all this, the Assistant Commissioner had insisted that Fox attend the monthly Crime Summary and Assessment Meeting, a pet event in Frobisher's calendar.

Unlike Chester Smart, John Tanner had not become over confident; he had just become careless. Having convinced himself that no one knew where he lived, he saw no reason to exercise caution when he was moving around the Lewisham area. And that suited the police fine.

At eleven o'clock precisely, Tanner emerged from his house and glanced up and down the street. But he failed to see anything suspicious about the observation van, a different van from the one used by the two soldiers the previous day, which was parked at the end of his road. Elsewhere in the vicinity, obscured from direct view and sweating in their bullet-proof body armour, a team of armed police from the Yard's tactical firearms unit waited, together with numerous other police officers, ready to close in on Tanner the moment they got the signal from Craven-Foster. Having discussed strategy at some length, it had been decided by the police that it would be counter-productive to storm the house where Tanner lived. Suspecting him to be 'armed and dangerous', as the police say, such an operation would create unnecessary risks and, on the basis of previous experience, might well result in failure. Consequently, the decision had been made to take him in the open.

'He's on the move, guv,' said a detective's voice over the personal radio network, unable to disguise his satisfaction that, after so many hours of inactivity, something was happening.

The upright figure of Tanner, attired in jeans and a blue shirt, strolled casually down the road towards Hilly Fields, unaware that at least ten pairs of eyes were watching his every movement.

Minutes later, as he was walking along Brookbank Road, the police swept into action. One moment the street was empty, the next it seemed to be filled with vehicles and the sound of screaming tyres. Four detectives leaped from cars that had scarcely stopped and grabbed Tanner, forcing him to the ground. As he twisted his head, he saw that he was surrounded by a ring of very aggressive policemen, all of whom were levelling firearms of a varying nature at his head.

'What the bloody hell—?'

'John Tanner, I'm arresting you on suspicion of murder,' said Craven-Foster formally. Craven-Foster was a very formal sort of detective. 'Anything you say—'

'You've got the wrong bloke, mate,' said Tanner. The words came out in a series of grunts because he was still pinned firmly to the ground.

* * *

Fox read the message that the secretary had brought into the conference room and then glanced at the Assistant Commissioner who was seated beneath the forbidding portrait of Sir Richard Mayne, one of the first two commissioners of the Metropolitan Police.

'I'm afraid something very important's just cropped up, sir,' said Fox, 'if you'll excuse me.' And without waiting either for Frobisher's permission or his inevitable protests that there was nothing more important than this meeting, he rose, nodded briefly to the other Specialist Operations senior officers and left the room.

Returning to his office, Fox promptly issued two orders. The first was that Tanner should be brought from where he was being held at Lewisham to Belgravia Police Station, and secondly, that Tanner's house was to be searched with all due despatch. Then he strolled up to the Commanders' Mess for lunch.

Fox leaned back in his chair, crossed his legs and folded his hands in his lap. For some time he gazed at the relaxed man sitting opposite him. Although Tanner was wearing jeans and a shirt, he was immaculate. The jeans were pressed and the shirt clean and freshly-ironed, its sleeves carefully rolled to mid-forearm. He was clean-shaven, and his black leather shoes had obviously been polished every day, including today. There was an indisputable air of the soldier about him.

'Jock,' said Fox.

Tanner smiled but said nothing.

'Also known as John Tanner, yes?'

'If you say so,' said Tanner.

'What were you doing in Cyprus?'

'Who says I was in Cyprus?' Tanner did not seem at all dismayed that Fox knew that much about his recent movements and even smiled at the irony of a police car passing the police station at that very moment, its siren wailing.

'We know for a fact that you were there between the

twentieth and the twenty-ninth of June,' said Fox. 'On the twentieth, you were seen talking to two British soldiers' – Fox was careful not to compromise Higgins and Farmer – 'and on the twenty-ninth, you spent some time with a prostitute in the red-light quarter of Paphos.'

Tanner smiled again. 'So?' he said. 'Is that a crime?'

'Were you there?'

Tanner shrugged. 'You've just told me I was, old son,' he said. 'And you blokes never make mistakes, do you? I mean all these miscarriages of justice that I've read about in the newspapers recently is all fiction, isn't it?'

'Why were you there?' demanded Fox.

'I don't have to tell you,' said Tanner, 'but just to put you out of your misery, I was on holiday. That all right, is it? I mean, I'm not fiddling the social security and I'm not drawing the dole, so if I feel like going on holiday, that's okay, isn't it?'

'So you were on holiday?' persisted Fox.

'Yeah.'

'Were you stationed there when you were a soldier?'

'Who says I was a soldier?'

'I do,' said Fox irritably. He was growing weary of this cat-and-mouse game, but he knew that he was facing a real professional. A check with the Ministry of Defence had revealed that although there were one or two John Tanners currently serving with Scottish regiments, the last one to be discharged had left some fifteen years previously. And he had been a Scotsman from Perth. But apart from that, this John Tanner was too young to have been out of the army for fifteen years anyway.

'Yeah, I was stationed there. So what?'

'But under another name,' said Fox.

'Maybe.' And then Tanner also grew tired of the questioning. 'D'you want to tell me why I'm here? That guy said something about murder' – he gestured at Craven-Foster – 'but I told him at the time that he'd got the wrong man.'

'I have reason to believe that on or about the thirtieth of June this year you murdered Michael Leighton, Patricia

Tilley and Karen Nash on a yacht some fifty miles off the Cyprus coast,' said Fox.

Tanner threw back his head and laughed. 'Ye Gods,' he said, 'you've certainly got an imagination, mate, I'll say that for you.' He leaned forward. 'Well, if you think that you're going to force a confession out of me,' he continued quietly, 'you've got another think coming. I've got nothing to say, and that's the way it's staying. And, by the way, I've changed my mind. I want a solicitor.'

Detective Inspector Evans had been put in charge of the team that was searching the house which Tanner had rented, fully furnished, some weeks previously.

The detectives, aided by scenes-of-crime officers, followed a set plan. Starting at the front door, they moved meticulously through the house, step by step, until they reached the loft. The outhouses were searched thoroughly, the dustbins were emptied and their contents examined, and the insides of the chimneys, apparently unused for some time, were carefully inspected.

The police found nothing that would assist their case. No guns, no correspondence, no personal belongings. Apart from a few items of clothing and the usual toiletries, it was as if Tanner had never been there.

Fox was not satisfied, and that meant that Evans was not satisfied. They started again, this time prepared to rip up floor-boards, slit open mattresses and, if necessary, to start dismantling the house itself.

Fox's onslaught on the pimps of the West End was fierce and concentrated. He had spoken to the Commander Operations of the Central Area and explained what he was seeking. The result was that as many uniformed police as could be mustered flooded the area, backed up by the territorial support group.

The pimps disappeared as if by magic, thinking that they were the subject of police interest. Some of the prostitutes, recognising the futility of trying to pick up 'tricks' with so many policemen about, went home. But a defiant few still hung about, wondering why there was such an intense police presence and wondering too, how long it was going to continue. But they didn't have long to wait to find out.

Detective Inspector Jack Gilroy and his team of officers moved into the area and began to question the women. It was always the same question.

'Know Chester Smart, do you, darling?' asked DC Bellenger of a sultry blonde in shorts and a blouse that was open to her navel, and who was leaning nonchalantly against a wall, her black-nylon-clad legs apart.

'Never heard of him, love,' answered the blonde. She would not have admitted it even if she had known. 'Why?'

'We want to know where he lives,' said Bellenger. And the added request, that if the girl should happen to hear, she should get in touch with the Flying Squad, did little to placate her or the other girls. Or their minders when this disturbing news reached them. Which it did, very quickly.

By the time the operation had finished – at just after midnight – there was not a single pimp who did not know what the police wanted. And the threat, that they would be back tomorrow night, and every night until they found out, did nothing to hearten the pimps or the prostitutes whose trade had stopped as suddenly as a train hitting the buffers.

It was at half-past eleven the following morning that Evans, whose team had been at work for most of the night, answered a knock at Tanner's front door.

'Mr Tanner, is it?' A bespectacled man stood on the doorstep, clutching a clipboard.

'No,' said Evans. 'I'm a police officer.'

'Oh,' said the man, 'has there been an accident?'

'Not yet,' said Evans, upon whom, in recent months, some of Fox's humour had rubbed off. 'Who are you?'

'Mr Williams. I'm from Lewisham Council.'

'And?' said Evans.

'It's about the lock-up, you see,' said the man from the council, staring down at his clipboard. 'We've had notification from a Mr . . .' He searched for the name on his list. 'Ah, here we are, a Mr Miller, that Mr Tanner has rented a garage from him.' He paused. 'That's a coincidence, isn't it?'

'What is?' asked Evans.

'Both names of tradesmen, Miller and Tanner.'

'Hilarious,' said Evans, 'but what about Messrs Miller and Tanner?'

'Mr Miller has told us that he wishes to stop paying council tax on the garage because now that Mr Tanner has rented it, he, that is Mr Miller, thought it only fair that Mr Tanner should pay the council tax.' Williams glanced up at Evans. 'It's a bit complicated, I know, but—'

'Come in, Mr Williams, come in,' said Evans warmly, and reached out to take hold of the man's arm lest he should escape.

Fox's operation to discover Chester Smart's address was repeated for a second night and created for the vice trade its own little recession. This time, prostitutes were arrested in droves and a few men, prepared to pay for sexual gratification, found that they too had suddenly interested the police by their actions.

It was enough. At ten o'clock the following morning, an anonymous telephone call to the Flying Squad office gave the police what they wanted. As far as the vice trade was concerned, Chester Smart had suddenly become a pariah.

Fox was delighted, both with the success of his operation to flush out Chester Smart's address and with the news from Lewisham that Tanner had rented a lock-up garage.

Tanner was taken from Belgravia under strong escort and arrived at the lock-up garage – where he met his solicitor – at about the same time as Fox and Mr Miller who, against his better nature, had been imposed upon to assist the police.

'Is this the man to whom you rented this garage, Mr Miller?' asked Fox.

'Yes, that's him,' said Miller. 'Good morning, Mr Tanner.'

'Who's he?' asked Tanner. 'Another of your stooges is he? Because I've never seen him before in my life.'

Tanner's solicitor laid a hand on his client's arm and told him to be quiet.

Fox ignored this automatic response and turned to DS Hurley. 'Take a statement from Mr Miller and then run him home, Bob.' Then, addressing Evans, he asked, 'Did you find any keys in the house, Denzil?'

'I'm afraid not, sir.'

'Oh well,' said Fox, 'it looks as though we're going to have to break in.' He turned to Tanner. 'Unless you want to give me the key . . .'

'Don't know anything about any keys and I don't know anything about this garage either,' said Tanner. 'And as for this, well, it's a diabolical liberty.' And he held up his handcuffed wrists. Again, Tanner's solicitor told him not to say anything.

'Swann.'

'Yes, sir,' said Fox's driver, wearing his usual mournful expression.

'Can you open that with the minimum of damage?' Fox waved at the lock-up.

'Piece of cake, guv,' said Swann. 'Simplest thing in the world, these up-and-overs.' Within seconds, he had opened the garage door and stood back triumphantly. 'Told you, guv,' he said. 'Nothing to it.'

'Bloody prima donna,' muttered Fox and stepped into the garage.

TWENTY-TWO

APART FROM A BARE TABLE, the garage appeared at first sight to be empty. But then Fox glanced up at the rafters. Across two of them was a wooden box some four feet long and a foot high by a foot wide. Each of the box's corners was protected by a metal plate, and it was padlocked.

'What's in that?' asked Fox, gazing at Tanner.

'Dunno,' said Tanner. 'Never seen it before. Must belong to that geezer who reckoned he knew me, but who I've never seen before.'

'I do strongly advise you to say nothing, Mr Tanner,' said the ex-soldier's solicitor.

'Oh, put a bloody sock in it, will you,' said Tanner.

A couple of Fox's team of detectives moved the table and stood on it so that they could reach the box. 'Christ, it's bloody heavy, guv'nor,' said one of them as they manoeuvred it down from the rafters and on to the table.

For a moment or two, Fox gazed at the heavy chest. 'Well,' he said to Tanner, 'are you going to give me the key? Or do we break it open?'

Tanner shrugged. 'My brief's told me not to speak to you,' he said.

'Very well.' Fox gestured to a detective who went out of the garage, to return moments later with a case-opener. Placing the tip of the jemmy under the hasp, he levered off the staple and the padlock. Another officer opened the lid.

'Bless my soul,' said Fox, peering into the box. 'What do we have here?' Inside was a rifle, carefully wrapped in oilcloth, resting on a bed of upholsterer's foam, and several boxes of 7.62 millimetre ammunition. There was also a Browning automatic hand-gun and a commando knife.

'Want me to unwrap it, guv?' asked a detective.

'Don't you dare touch it,' said Fox, 'not until Fingerprint Branch have examined it.' He turned to Evans. 'Do the usual, Denzil,' he said. 'Exhibits labels, statements. All that.'

'Yes, sir, I do know about that,' said Evans wearily. He wondered whether Fox realised that his DI was on the verge of being made a detective chief inspector.

'Good.' Fox rubbed his hands together. 'You can take the good soldier Tanner back to Belgravia,' he said, and watched as Tanner was led back to the police van that had brought him to Lewisham. He turned and offered Tanner's solicitor a cigarette. 'Don't look so glum,' he said. 'There are always other clients.'

The solicitor nodded towards the departing police van. 'Between you and me, Mr Fox,' he said, 'I should think his best chance is to plead guilty and throw himself on the mercy of the court.'

'May I quote you on that?' asked Fox as he thumbed his lighter.

'Quote me on what?' asked the solicitor and grinned.

The woman who answered the door of Chester Smart's detached house in Clapham was white. She was wearing a white skin-tight one-piece suit made of stretch polyester, and red ankle boots. When she saw Fox, Evans and Kate Ebdon standing on her doorstep, instead of Chester Smart whose return she was clearly expecting, her face assumed an expression that combined both surprise and disappointment.

'Who are you?' The woman spoke with an Ulster accent.

'Thomas Fox . . . of Scotland Yard, and I have a warrant to search these premises.'

'What the hell for?' demanded the woman.

'Drugs, among other things,' said Fox. 'And who are you?'

At first, it seemed that the woman was not going to answer

the question, and Kate Ebdon moved closer to her. 'The officer asked who you were,' she said, her Australian accent lending her voice a slight menace.

'Katharine Delaney.'

'*Mrs* Delaney, is it?' asked Kate.

'If you like. I divorced that bastard years ago.'

Fox pushed past the woman who was obviously reluctant to admit him and the others, and peered around the hallway of the large house before walking into the front room. It was apparent that Chester Smart had spent a great deal of money on the decor and furnishings, but the result was bizarre and gaudy, and definitely did not accord with Fox's idea of good taste. From the odour that pervaded the whole house, it was clear that both Smart and Mrs Delaney were partial to curry.

Kate Ebdon, as usual, made for the address and telephone books which she found in a drawer of the sideboard. 'This is interesting, sir,' she said to Fox. 'Smart has Michael Leighton's office telephone number in this book.'

Apart from that, the search, which had needed to be nowhere near as thorough as the one at Tanner's house, produced a quantity of drugs, including cocaine.

'This yours?' Fox asked Katharine Delaney.

'It's for personal use.'

'What, a kilo? You must get through a hell of a lot.'

'What's this really about?' asked the woman. 'You didn't just drop in to look for drugs, did you? You could have picked any of the houses in this street.'

'It's about Chester Smart having been arrested on suspicion of murdering Anna Coombs,' said Fox.

'The bastard,' said Katharine Delaney suddenly. 'He told me he'd finished with her.'

'I think he probably did,' said Fox drily. 'By manual strangulation. Perhaps you'd better tell me more.'

Katharine Delaney sat down quite suddenly on a *chaise-longue.* She was probably about thirty-five, but looked older, and her auburn hair was dragged back from her face into a wild bunch at the back of her head. Fox thought it looked like out-of-control wire wool. 'I told him that unless he finished with her, I was out of here,' she said.

Fox didn't believe that the Delaney woman would have given up the good life she obviously enjoyed that easily. 'You mean he was having an affair with her?'

'What else would I mean?' If anything the woman's Ulster accent had become more pronounced.

Fox didn't believe that either. 'What exactly is your relationship with Chester Smart?' he asked.

Katharine Delaney shot the detective a disbelieving glance. 'A sexual one, of course,' she said brazenly. 'What the hell sort of other relationship does a man have with a woman?'

'You do know, I suppose, that Chester Smart controlled a number of prostitutes.'

'Of course I do. I was one of them when he first picked me up.'

'Really?' Fox wondered why Smart, having a coterie of far more attractive women than the one now seated opposite him, should have chosen her. 'Where was he on the twentieth of July, Mrs Delaney?'

'How the hell should I know?' said Katharine Delaney truculently. 'I never know where he is half the time.'

Fox decided that he was not going to get any helpful information from this woman and stood up. 'Arrest her for possession,' he said to Kate Ebdon.

'The drugs were Chester's,' said the Delaney woman suddenly. 'He used to get them from Leighton. Chester supplied him with women for some damned skin-flicks business he was running.'

'A likely story,' said Fox and nodded to Kate Ebdon.

Even though Chester Smart had already been charged with carrying an offensive weapon and living on immoral earnings, Fox had successfully obtained a magistrate's order to extend the pimp's detention in police custody. But nothing had been said to him regarding the murder of Anna Coombs apart from a question as to his whereabouts at the relevant time, a question he had avoided answering. He had been kept in custody because he had refused to tell police where he lived, but they now knew his address and time would be running out very soon. Unless they could charge him with murder. The finding of Michael Leighton's telephone number at Smart's house was an interesting discovery, but Fox was absolutely certain that Smart was not responsible for the three Cyprus murders. At least, not directly.

'We've arrested Katharine Delaney,' said Fox.

That did not seem to worry Smart who continued to sprawl in his chair in the interview room at West End Central Police Station. 'What d'you want me to do about it?' he asked.

'For possession of a quantity of a controlled substance, almost certainly cocaine.'

Smart grinned. 'I told her that would get her into big trouble one day,' he said. The fact that police had discovered where he lived evinced no surprise, and it was clear that he did not intend to take any responsibility for the drugs found at his house.

'We also found the telephone number of Michael Leighton in a book in your house,' said Fox.

'One of her fancy men, probably,' said Smart.

'She denies knowing him,' said Fox. 'And she said the book was yours. And the drugs.'

'Well, she would say that, wouldn't she.'

'Leighton was one of three people murdered off the Cyprus coast on the thirtieth of June. The other two were Patricia Tilley and Karen Nash.'

'Why you telling me all this, man? I never killed them and I never been to Cyprus in my life. In fact, I don't even know where it is.'

Fox sighed. It was obvious that he could sit and talk to Smart forever and would get nowhere. 'I propose to put you on an identification parade, Chester,' he said.

'What for?'

'We have a witness who claims to be able to identify the man who murdered Anna Coombs on the twentieth of July.'

Smart laughed. 'I hope he's got life insurance,' he said.

* * *

When Sam Marland, a senior fingerprint officer at the Yard, had finished with the rifle found in the garage at Lewisham, he handed it over to Hugh Donovan, the chief ballistics officer.

Now they were both in Fox's office.

'Good news?' asked Fox hopefully.

'Yes, indeed,' said Marland. 'Tanner's fingermarks are all over the weapon. Enough points to win the football pools.' He grinned and laid a copy of his formal report on Fox's desk.

'Excellent, oh, excellent,' said Fox and glanced at Donovan. 'Hugh?'

'The weapon is a Finnish M62 assault rifle, Tommy,' said Donovan.

'Not an AK 47 then.'

Donovan shrugged. 'Easy to confuse the two when you've only got spent rounds,' he said. 'Each is of 7.62 millimetre calibre and each has a four-groove right-hand rifling. And incidentally, each has a magazine holding 30 rounds.'

'Wonderful,' said Fox. 'Now you've done the commercial, is it *the* weapon?'

Donovan grinned. 'Yes,' he said. 'There's no doubt.'

'John Tanner, you are charged in that you did murder Michael Leighton, against the peace. You are not obliged to say anything, but anything you do say will be taken down and may be given in evidence.'

'My client has no reply to make to the charge,' said Tanner's solicitor.

The custody sergeant recited the sonorous prose twice more, substituting the names of Patricia Tilley and Karen Nash. And twice more, Tanner's solicitor said that his client had nothing to say.

'I shall make formal application for legal aid—' began the solicitor unnecessarily.

Tanner suddenly turned on him. 'You've done bugger-all so far, sunshine,' he said, 'so you can piss off. You're fired.'

As Tanner was taken back to the cells, his erstwhile solicitor shrugged and shook hands with Fox. 'Some you win, some you lose,' he said. 'Ungrateful bastard.'

'It's the stress, you know,' said Fox. 'But you'd have lost this one for sure.'

'A battle's not lost until the final shot's been fired,' said the solicitor pointlessly.

'Unfortunate analogy,' murmured Fox.

Probably breaking half a dozen of the rules imposed upon him by the Police and Criminal Evidence Act, Fox visited Tanner in his cell shortly after he had been charged. 'Who did you do this job for?' he asked.

Tanner was sprawled on his cot and didn't look up. 'Don't know what you mean,' he said.

'Look, you didn't know Leighton, or either of the women. So you must have had a reason to kill them.'

'I didn't,' said Tanner. 'I keep telling you, you've got the wrong man.'

'So you're going to have this on your own are you?'

'Guess that's the way of it,' said Tanner.

Under the rules imposed upon criminal investigation by Her Majesty's Government, presumably in an attempt to reduce the prison population, a villain may cheat all he likes, but the police may not. Consequently, a uniformed inspector oversaw the identification parade held to determine if the man whom William Wilberforce had seen leaving Anna Coombs's flat was Chester Smart. If Fox, or any of his team, had been involved, defence counsel would have suggested that they may have influenced the witness in some way.

Wilberforce entered the room nervously, as well he might; he had very firm views about identifying wrongdoers. In his experience, they tended to seek revenge. The uniformed inspector explained the procedure, having previously allowed Smart to stand anywhere he chose, and then invited the witness to walk along the line.

Summoning up unknown reserves of courage, the small

black man slowly examined each of the men on the parade. And then, unhesitatingly, he placed a hand on Chester Smart's chest. 'This is the man I saw, sir,' he said to the inspector.

'You're absolutely sure?' queried the inspector.

'Absolutely, sir,' said Wilberforce. 'There is no doubt.'

'Well, that's good enough for me,' said Fox when he was told that Smart had been identified, 'but whether it's good enough for that weary bunch of lawyers called the Crown Prosecution Service is another matter altogether.' He glanced at Evans. 'Where's Webb locked up, Denzil?' he asked.

'Brixton, sir.'

'Splendid,' said Fox, 'I think we'll pay him a visit.'

When Raymond Webb shuffled into the interview room at Brixton Prison, he appeared to have aged ten years. Although he was still allowed to wear his own clothes, he was now stooped and had developed a pallor that resulted from being kept in solitary confinement for his own protection. Sex-offenders, even on remand, were not very popular with the other inmates.

Fox sat down opposite the accountant. 'Last time we spoke, Webb, you told me that Leighton supplied a black man with drugs in exchange for the women he used for his pornographic videos.'

'What about it?' asked Webb.

'A man called Chester Smart has been arrested and will very likely be charged with the murder of Anna Coombs.' Fox sat back and waited to see what effect that crumb of information would have on Webb.

'Should that interest me?' asked Webb listlessly.

'Perhaps not,' said Fox, 'but it interests me. And don't tell me you know nothing about it. Leighton's telephone number – your office number – was found in Smart's house shortly after we arrested him.'

Webb sighed deeply. 'Smart was the one who used to supply Leighton with girls,' he said. 'Whenever Leighton wanted some new talent for his videos, he'd get in touch with Smart. He said once that it was an ideal set-up.'

But that was at odds with what Fox had heard from other witnesses. 'At least two of the girls we've spoken to claim that they were picked up in the West End by Leighton himself,' he said.

Webb sneered. 'Rubbish,' he said. 'Mike would never go out picking up whores. He was a bastard when he'd got them captive, but going out and picking them up. No way. I told you, it was an arrangement with Smart.'

'Why should these girls spin me a fanny about being recruited by Leighton then?'

'I should have thought that was obvious,' said Webb. 'They were terrified of Smart. If they'd shopped him to you, he'd have dealt with them. And they knew it.' He lapsed into silence for a moment or two. 'I suppose he found out that Anna had been talking to you and that's why he killed her.'

'If he killed her,' said Fox mildly, ever-mindful of the maxim that a man was innocent until proved guilty. Nonetheless, he was very satisfied with that gratuitous piece of information.

'I'm told you supplied women for Michael Leighton's porn movies,' said Fox.

'Is that a fact?' said Smart.

'And he supplied you with drugs in exchange.'

Smart laughed insolently. 'No way, man,' he said.

'Do you know a John Tanner, sometimes known as Jock?'

'Never heard of him,' said Smart.

And for once, Fox believed him.

TWENTY-THREE

DETECTIVE SERGEANT ROBERT HURLEY HESITATED before tapping on Fox's office door. He knew that the commander had had a lot on his mind and it was just possible that he had forgotten. Hurley knocked.

'What is it, Bob?'

'Lee Watson, sir. You remember that I tracked her down to an address in Epsom, and you said that you wanted to see her.'

'So I did, Bob.' Fox still recalled the slight note of reproof in Jane's reply when he had told her that Bernie Watson's first wife was unaware of the death of her daughter Beverley. He glanced at the clock. 'Ready?'

'Ready, sir?'

'Yes,' said Fox, standing up. 'No time like the present.'

'Oh, right, sir.' In fact, it was far from right. It was almost six o'clock and Bob Hurley's plans, to take his wife out, had just crashed. But then, as he frequently told her, she shouldn't have married a detective.

'D'you know how to get to Epsom, Swann?' asked Fox, once he and Hurley were being driven down Victoria Street in the commander's Scorpio.

'Of course I do, guv,' said Swann. 'It's a racecourse, isn't it?' Swann prided himself on knowing how to get to every racecourse in the country. And usually Fox was with him.

The large house to which Mrs Lee Watson had been traced was on the edge of Epsom Downs, not far from Tattenham Corner. Fox imagined that the divorce settlement must have cost Bernie Watson an arm and a leg. But these days he could afford it.

By the time Fox and Hurley arrived, it was almost eight o'clock in the evening; a pleasant summer's evening sullied only by the almost constant noise of aircraft, Epsom being on the flight-paths of both Heathrow and Gatwick Airports.

'Are you Mrs Lee Watson?' asked Fox. The woman who answered the door was of medium height and, he noticed immediately, had the figure of a girl half her age. He knew that she was in her mid-fifties.

'I am. And you are . . . ?'

'Thomas Fox . . . of Scotland Yard, and this is Detective Sergeant Robert Hurley.' With a flourish, Fox produced his warrant card for the woman's inspection.

'You'd better come in then,' said Lee Watson, 'although I can't imagine what you want with me.' She led them through into a room at the rear of the house, her exquisite perfume wafting after her. The room was tastefully furnished and the open French windows revealed a magnificent view of the downs.

'Wonderful,' murmured Fox. 'Truly wonderful.'

'It is rather nice, isn't it? Do sit down.' Lee Watson glanced at a clock on the mantelshelf. 'I'm just about to have a drink,' she said. 'Will you join me? Or do you have a thing about not drinking on duty?'

Fox waved a hand loosely in the air. 'I think we can stretch a point,' he said. 'Whisky, if I may.'

'Blended, or malt?' Lee Watson stood by the drinks table, a hand hovering over the collection of bottles that stood on it, her large blue eyes staring at him through big, round spectacles. Her dress was low-cut, and around her neck she wore several thin gold chains, the lower ends of the loops disappearing between her breasts.

'Oh, malt. Thank you.' Even someone as experienced in the field of human nature as Fox could not work out why Bernie Watson had exchanged this refined woman for the trollop with whom he seemed set to spend the rest of his life.

Lee Watson waved the bottle of twelve-year-old Cardhu gently in Hurley's direction and, receiving a nod of assent, poured two measures of the malt into tumblers. For herself, she prepared a gin and tonic and then sat down opposite the two detectives. 'Cheers!' she said. 'Now, tell me why you're here.'

'We had a job finding you, you know,' said Fox. 'The woman with whom you stayed in Pinner, said you'd moved to Brighton.'

'She was far too nosey for her own good, that Mrs Molloy,' said Lee Watson and smiled. 'Yes, that's what I told her, but it was only for the day.' She frowned. 'And those dreadful Sussex policemen did me for speeding.'

Fox took a sip of his whisky and set the glass down on the occasional table that Lee Watson had placed conveniently beside his chair. 'I'm afraid that I have some rather bad news for you, Mrs Watson . . .'

'Oh?' For a moment the smile slipped from Lee Watson's face. 'You're not talking about Bernie, are you? He was my first husband, you know.'

'Yes, I knew that. No, I'm talking about your daughter Beverley.'

A puzzled expression crossed Lee Watson's face. 'But she's dead. She died last August,' she said, 'just after I'd moved here. Probably as well, I did. I couldn't have stayed in that house in Crystal Palace.'

'But when I broke the news to your ex-husband, a couple of weeks ago, he seemed to think that you didn't know.' Fox sounded surprised.

'Broke the news? He must be going soft in the head,' said Lee Watson. 'He was with me at the funeral. It was the last time we spoke.' There was a constantly breathless surprise in the way she talked, and it was no sudden affectation; she kept it up all the time. 'Did he tell you he didn't know then?'

'I must have misunderstood him,' said Fox, knowing full well that he had done no such thing.

'Well, I'm sorry that you've had a wasted journey, er,

Inspector? You'd better have another drink just to make up for it.'

'Thank you,' said Fox, draining his glass. He let the error about his rank pass. He hadn't told her what it was and, in the circumstances, it was better that she didn't know. The advent of a commander calling to tell her of the death of a daughter she already knew was dead, might just cause her to wonder if there was more to it all. And Fox was now certain that there was.

Lee Watson dispensed more drinks and sat down again. 'I love policemen,' she said.

'Oh, really?' said Fox, somewhat taken aback by this sudden admission. 'Surprising really, in the circumstances.'

Lee Watson paused for only a second, and then she laughed. 'Because of Bernie, you mean? Oh, I know he was a crook, but he was good fun. When we were young, we went to every night-club in the West End, and we danced and danced. Oh, how we danced. Then when Beverley arrived' – she gave Fox a sly grin – 'a little unexpectedly I may say, Bernie was absolutely delighted, and he ruined us both. Of course, it wasn't so much fun when he was inside, but he always made up for it when he came out.' There was a faraway look in her eyes as she recalled the good times she had enjoyed with her ex-husband. And even Fox found difficulty in accepting that she had once been married to the south London villain he knew so well. He certainly couldn't visualise her in the sort of south London drinking clubs that had been frequented by Bernie Watson and his like in their youth. 'Of course, it got lonely when he was away, but at least I had Bev to bring up in those days. And . . .' She paused and smiled again, but obviously thought better of making what Fox imagined would be a compromising admission. 'Well, let's just say it was lonely and leave it at that.'

'When did you last see Bernie, Mrs Watson?' asked Fox.

'At the funeral, last August. I told you.'

'I wonder if I could ask you a favour?' Fox sipped at his whisky.

'Anything, my dear,' said Lee Watson, a twinkle in her eye.

'I would rather like to see Bernie myself to sort out this slip-up. So if you do happen to speak to—'

'There's no danger of that,' said Lee Watson sharply. 'Have you seen that creature he's got himself tied up with now? Well, I ask you. I don't know what he sees in her, but he's besotted. And she's just a gold-digger. When I think of all I put up with over the years, what with Bernie in prison. And then that fat madam comes along and that's it. No, Inspector, there's no danger of me speaking to Bernie Watson. Ever again.'

Fox acted with swiftness the moment that he and Hurley left Lee Watson. Getting through to DI Evans at the Yard on his mobile telephone, he instructed him to get a search warrant for Bernie Watson's house and to be ready to execute it early the next day.

It was nine o'clock the following morning when Fox and Evans arrived at Welling. Fox had not brought a strong team with him; he wasn't expecting any trouble from a professional like Bernie Watson.

'Well, well, if it ain't Mr Fox.' Watson, attired in a gaudy silk dressing gown, was his usual expansive self when he opened his front door. 'I must say you're an early bird. Come in, come in. We're just having breakfast. I daresay you'd like a cup of coffee.' He walked away from the front door and shouted for his wife. 'Gerry, it's that nice Mr Fox. See if you can rustle up two more cups of coffee, will you?'

'This isn't a social call, Bernie,' said Fox when the three of them were in Watson's tasteless sitting room.

'It's not? What's the problem then?'

'I saw Lee last night, your first wife.'

A slight frown crossed Watson's face. 'What did you see her for?' he asked.

'To tell her about the death of your daughter, Bernie.' Fox gazed steadily at Watson.

'That was very nice of you, I'm sure,' said Watson nervously.

The gross figure of Geraldine Watson appeared in the doorway carrying a tray of coffee. She was dressed in a track-suit made of some furry pink material that, unfortunately, was tight-fitting. And it was difficult to tell whether she had combed her hair or whether she regarded its wild appearance as the latest fashion. Her long finger-nails looked like great crimson claws. 'Good morning, Admiral,' she said, her face breaking into her idea of a fetching smile.

'I keep telling you, Gerry dear, Mr Fox isn't in the Navy. He's a commander in the police.'

'Do what, dear?' said Geraldine, a vacant expression on her face.

'Oh, never mind,' said Watson impatiently. 'Just pour the coffee, there's a good girl.'

Fox managed to keep a straight face at Watson's description of his wife as a girl. 'Lee Watson said that you knew about Beverley's death and that you'd attended her funeral,' said Fox.

'Really?' Watson was seemingly mystified by this statement.

'But you told me that the last time you'd spoken to Lee was some two years ago when Beverley first disappeared. And you gave a very good impression of being shocked when I told you about your daughter's death.'

'It must have slipped my mind,' said Watson lamely.

'I've got a search warrant for these premises, Bernie,' said Fox, ignoring the cup of coffee which Geraldine had placed on a table near his chair.

'You have? Whatever for?' Watson contrived to look genuinely surprised, even though, over the years, his properties had been the subject of more search warrants than, to coin his own phrase, most people had had hot dinners.

'But I don't have to execute it, Bernie, not if you're co-operative.'

Watson's mouth opened and closed. 'I'm not sure I understand what you mean, Mr Fox,' he said.

'You know what I'm looking for, Bernie, don't you? I'm looking for the video tape of your daughter Beverley being whipped and raped.' Fox paused. 'As a matter of interest, I've arrested John Tanner for the murders of Michael Leighton, Patricia Tilley and Karen Nash.'

That announcement clearly came as a terrible shock to Watson. Suddenly the image of the jovial villain vanished as his face creased into an expression of rage and his fists began to open and close threateningly. But his fury was not with Fox; only rarely was the anger of real criminals directed at the police officers who apprehended them. 'That bastard's grassed, hasn't he, Mr Fox?'

Fox sighed. 'You're not obliged to say anything, Bernie, but anything you—'

'Yeah, yeah. It's all right, Mr Fox, I know the form.' Watson laughed cynically. 'I bloody ought to after all these years. And Tanner was supposed to be a professional an' all.' He glanced at Geraldine who seemed puzzled by what was going on, although in fairness, she was hard of hearing. 'Gerry, love, pop up to the bedroom, will you? You'll find a couple of video tapes in a cardboard box on the top shelf of my wardrobe, behind the bag with the camcorder in it.'

'Do what, dear?' Geraldine smiled at her husband.

'Oh, never mind, I'll get the bloody things myself.' Watson stood up and walked wearily from the room.

'He's not been sending more of those dirty sex films abroad, has he?' asked Geraldine, gazing at Evans. 'I told him he'd get into trouble with the police if he kept doing that. He's a businessman now, is Bernie. I told him there was no need for that, but he said it was just a bit of fun. But I told him.'

Silently, Watson re-entered the room and handed Fox two video cassettes. 'They're the ones, Mr Fox,' he said as he sat down. For some seconds he stared gloomily at the empty York stone fireplace before looking up. 'I couldn't let that bastard Leighton get away with what he done to my Bev, could I, Mr Fox?' he said. 'I mean, it ain't natural, is it? He fed her drugs, poor little bitch, and then he got her involved in his skin flicks. I told her to leave it out, but she was always a headstrong girl. She could have had anything she wanted. I'm not short of the odd bob or two, so I don't know what she done it for. The thrill of it, I suppose. But the whipping and the raping, just for his bloody amusement. Well, I tell you, Mr Fox, that wasn't on. See, you can't rely on the police to deal with . . .' He broke off, ironically fearful that he may have offended the detective sitting opposite him. 'No disrespect, Mr Fox, because it's not your fault, is it? It's the bleedin' government. They don't give a toss about law and order any more, do they? See, it was different when I was at it. Well, you know that, don't you? It was just between us and the Old Bill. We all knew where we was, and if we got nicked for something what we hadn't done, well, we knew that made up for all the things what we had done and had got away with. Know what I mean?' His face cracked into a sort of lopsided smile. 'But these days, when the newspapers and the bloody television interfere in things that ain't none of their business . . .' He shrugged and spread his hands. 'Well, what could I do? I couldn't let that go, could I?' He shook his head. 'Cost me twenty-five grand an' all,' he added. 'But it was worth it. He had to be sorted, Mr Fox, did that bloody Leighton. I tell you, when I saw that video' – he gestured at the cassettes on the table – 'I just saw bloody red.'

Fox stood up. 'You're nicked, Bernie,' he said. 'Want to get dressed?'

'Yeah, thanks, Mr Fox.' Watson stood up and made his way upstairs to his bedroom.

'Want me to go with him, guv?' asked Evans.

Fox shook his head. 'No, Denzil, he won't do a runner. He's an honest villain, unlike the nasty bastard he had topped.' And Fox reflected on the difference between Watson and the odious collection of individuals, Webb and Pritchard mainly, who had surrounded the equally odious Leighton. 'There are times, Denzil,' he added, 'when I think what an unfair world this is.'

TWENTY-FOUR

FOX DIDN'T BOTHER TO SIT down when John Tanner was brought into one of the interview rooms at Brixton Prison. He just dropped three bound copies of a statement on the table. 'You're entitled by law to that,' he said.

'What is it?' Tanner glanced down at the neat pile of paper but made no attempt to pick it up.

'It's a statement made yesterday by Bernard Watson in which he admits having solicited you to murder Michael Leighton. And he further states that he paid you the sum of twenty-five thousand pounds to commit that murder. You're not obliged to say anything, but anything you do say may be given in evidence. And if you wish to make a statement in rebuttal of Watson's statement, you are, of course, free to do so.'

'The stupid bastard.' For the first time since his arrest, Tanner's face showed some emotion, some reaction to the trouble he was in. 'What the bloody hell did he do that for? Got religion or something, has he?' He sat down suddenly. 'I didn't want to kill the women,' he said. 'But they were there, and I couldn't leave any witnesses, could I? I tried setting fire to the bloody thing but obviously it didn't catch.'

Fox turned to leave the room but paused at the door. 'The one thing that's been puzzling me,' he said, 'is how you managed to get that M62 rifle out to Cyprus and back again, given the stringent controls at airports.'

Tanner grinned. 'And it's going to go on puzzling you, copper,' he said.

* * *

'I'm afraid, Mr Fox,' said the Crown Prosecution Service solicitor, 'that it has been decided not to proceed against Webb and Pritchard on either the count of rape or the count of causing grievous bodily harm with intent.'

'What?' Fox was clearly outraged by this decision.

'The problem is, you see,' the solicitor went on smoothly, 'the lack of corroboration.'

'But you've got the bloody video. What the hell else d'you want?'

'The factor that swayed the decision was the reluctance of . . .' The solicitor paused to extend an elegant forefinger and move the piece of paper that was in the centre of his desk. 'Ah, yes, the reluctance of this Miss Kirsty Newman to testify. The whole business of pornographic films is a very grey area these days. Society tends to be more tolerant and although the offences do exist in law, the fact that Miss Newman won't come to court does imply, I'm afraid, that she was a willing party to the treatment she received. She had, after all, been engaged in the making of pornographic films for some time, voluntarily. I suspect the jury would take the view that she was just a very good actress.'

'They're not going to get the chance to make that judgment, are they?' said Fox angrily. 'I just hope it never happens to your daughter.'

'I don't have any children, Mr Fox,' said the solicitor blithely.

'That doesn't surprise me,' said Fox and he swept out of the office, slamming the door.

Because of the Crown Prosecution Service decision, when Webb and Pritchard came to trial, they each faced only the one indictment of being concerned in the making of pornographic films. Webb, additionally, was indicted with possessing cocaine. Pritchard was sentenced to a term of eighteen months imprisonment and Webb received three years.

Tanner's counsel successfully petitioned for his client to be tried separately from Bernie Watson, but Tanner was still convicted and sentenced to life imprisonment with a recommendation that he serve at least twenty-five years. And Chester Smart was also sentenced to life for the murder of Anna Coombs whose only sin, in her pimp's eyes, had been to talk to the police. And even then, she hadn't said very much.

Katharine Delaney had been let off with a caution and the last the police heard of her was that she had taken up residence with another West Indian pimp.

The last trial was that of Bernie Watson. He cut a sad figure as he entered the dock in Number One Court at the Old Bailey. Gone was the ebullience, the fun, and the jokey, jovial villain. In his place stood an old man, bowed down at the thought of yet another long prison sentence.

But at least Bernie Watson had the benefit of a competent counsel. A young man, and not even a silk, he succeeded in introducing the video showing Beverley Watson being beaten and raped. The women on the jury were in tears at the end of the barrister's impassioned plea of justification for the actions of the reformed criminal whose crime, if such it was, had been to avenge the terrible death of his only daughter.

But it was to no avail. The judge, the Common Serjeant of London, told the jury to set aside their sympathy for Watson, and their antipathy towards Leighton, and decide the case on whether Watson had committed the offence with which he had been charged. And on the basis of that exhortation, the result was inevitable. Bernie Watson was found guilty of inciting John Tanner to murder Michael Leighton.

But the judge was not entirely without compassion, even after Watson's ignominious record was read out to the court. He sentenced him to a mere five years in prison, being pretty sure in his own mind that Watson would qualify for parole in twenty months' time.

But even a sentence as lenient as that did not appease Geraldine Watson who had been stunned by the long list of her husband's previous convictions. The last time Bernie Watson ever saw his second wife was when she leaned over the front of the public gallery, waving a ham-like fist at him. 'Bernie Watson, you bastard,' she screamed. 'I hope you bleedin' rot in hell. Who's going to pay the bills now, you tosser?'

At long last, Bernie Watson said what he'd been wanting to say for most of the past three years of his disastrous marriage to the gross Geraldine. 'Shut your bleedin' gate, you fat cow,' he shouted back.

'Remove that woman,' said the judge, raising his eyes to the public gallery and gazing mildly at the gesticulating, shouting figure of Geraldine Watson. Struggling, screaming and kicking, she was finally taken out, but not before several members of the posse of ushers and policemen who had responded to the judge's direction had sustained painful cuts and bruises.

Fox walked out through the two sets of double doors at the entrance to the court-room and into the lobby of the old part of the Central Criminal Court, relieved that at last the series of trials arising out of the triple murder in Cyprus was over.

'Mr Fox.'

Fox turned as the elegantly-dressed figure of Lee Watson came towards him. 'Mrs Watson, I didn't realise you were here,' he said.

'I've been in the public gallery throughout the trial.'

Fox nodded. 'Anything I can do for you?' he asked.

'I know it might be a bit difficult, Mr Fox,' said Lee Watson, 'but would it be possible for me to see him before they take him away?'

Fox smiled. 'I'll see what I can do, Mrs Watson,' he said.

Jane Sims was attired in jeans and a man's white shirt. 'Is it all over, Tommy?' she asked.

'Yes,' said Fox. 'We got a result. At long last. So how about dinner?'

'I thought you always had a party at the Yard when you'd finished a case.'

'Not any more,' said Fox. 'The Commissioner doesn't like

that sort of thing. And, for that matter, neither do I. There's nothing to celebrate in seeing people sent to prison.'

Jane smiled. 'You do have a heart after all, Tommy,' she said.

'Anyway,' continued Fox, ignoring the girl's good-natured taunt, 'I'd much rather take you out to some quiet restaurant.'

'I hoped you'd say that. I'll get changed,' said Jane and walked through to the bedroom. About five minutes later, she called out, 'There's a bottle of champagne in the fridge. I got it specially. Be a dear and bring it in, will you?'

She was standing in the centre of the room when Fox entered, the bottle of champagne in one hand and two glasses in the other. 'You haven't got far,' he said, glancing at the black satin robe she was wearing.

Slowly, Jane undid the sash. 'One of us had to take the initiative,' she said and slipped the robe from her shoulders, allowing it to fall to the floor.

But the saga of the skin flicks and all that emanated from their making, did not finish with the trials.

As Webb and Pritchard had already discovered, the inmates of Her Majesty's Prisons do not like sex offenders, and although they had not been tried for either the rape or the beating of Kirsty Newman, the prison telegraph had worked overtime and news of their activities was common knowledge.

The weak-willed Webb found that, at mealtimes, his food repeatedly missed his tray and ended up on the floor of the mess hall, to the intense annoyance of prison officers who always seemed to think, unfairly in his view, that it was he who was responsible. And his cell always stank of urine, mainly because the other prisoners thought it a bit of a laugh to empty their pots into it, and more often than not over its occupant.

And so it was that the treatment to which Webb was subjected by his fellow prisoners during the first few months of his incarceration, eventually became so intolerable that he hanged himself.

Pritchard, however, was a much tougher character and he didn't respond to threats, even punching his way out of a few confrontations. Nevertheless, the mattress in his cell somehow caught fire one night and he was suffocated. It was later found that the door had become inexplicably jammed.

At least, that was the verdict of the coroner's jury. But then they didn't know just how many friends Bernie Watson had got on the inside.